SECRET
HARMONIES

Also by Andrea Barrett

LUCID STARS

SECRET

HARMONIES

Andrea Barrett

**Delacorte
Press**

Published by
Delacorte Press
Bantam Doubleday Dell Publishing Group, Inc.
666 Fifth Avenue
New York, New York 10103

Portions of this novel first appeared, in different form, in the follow-ing periodicals: "Secret Harmonies" in *Northwest Review*; "Animal Sounds" in *Prairie Schooner* (under the title "Animal Magic"); "The Sky Is the Color It Used to Be" in *Mademoiselle*; and "The Apple Picker Hits the Road" in *Michigan Quarterly Review* (under the title "Here at the Starlight Motel").

Library of Congress Cataloging in Publication Data
Barrett, Andrea.
    Secret harmonies.

    I. Title.
PS3552.A7327S44   1989   813'.54   88-33572
ISBN 0-385-29771-8

Manufactured in the United States of America

Published simultaneously in Canada

October 1989

10 9 8 7 6 5 4 3 2 1

BG

With thanks to
Thomas Gavin
and
Nicholas Delbanco

CONTENTS

Prelude 1

Learning to Sing 5

Secret Harmonies 27

Animal Sounds 47

Distant Heartbeats 73

The Sky Is the Color It Used to Be 101

Dreams of Life.......................... 125

The Apple Picker Hits the Road 157

O My Charmer, Spare Me 181

Lives of the Composers 205

The Music of Ghosts 231

It seemed to him that he heard notes of fitful music leaping upwards a tone and downwards a diminished fourth, upwards a tone and downwards a major third, like triplebranching flames leaping fitfully, flame after flame, out of a midnight wood. It was an elfin prelude, endless and formless; and as it grew wilder and faster, the flames leaping out of time, he seemed to hear from under the boughs and grasses wild creatures racing, their feet pattering like rain upon the leaves.

—James Joyce,
A Portrait of the Artist as a Young Man

She stood there in a daze, conscious of herself only because of the beating of her pulse. She thought she could hear it escaping and merging with a deafening music filling the countryside. The ground beneath her feet was more yielding than water, and the furrows looked to her like immense dark waves breaking. All the memories and thoughts in her head rushed out in a single motion like the thousand bits of a firework display. . . . She was suffering only from love, and felt that her soul was draining away at the thought of it—like the mortally wounded, who in their agony feel their lives ebbing away through the bleeding wound.

—Gustave Flaubert,
Madame Bovary
(trans. by Mildred Marmur)

PRELUDE

THE children crossed into the heart of the swamp and huddled like tadpoles hiding from the great blue heron. It was fall; the children might have been mistaken for trees. Their hair shone gold, tawny, auburn, chestnut, pure red, deep brown as leaves, and their arms and legs were as thin and flexible as twigs. Like all the children who came into the swamp, these children were lost. Luke Wyatt and his younger brothers Roger, Chuck, and Jimmy were there, pale and blond and fearful and marked with the smell of the turkeys their parents raised. Peter Strazzabosco was there, along with his cousins from Whately and the Keefes and the Gambles and Penny Weiss. There were Kevin and Jane Glover, and Chloe McCarthy, and Sally Lambert standing next to Henry Cardoza. Jamie and Mike Rondine were there, and Nick Dwyer shadowed by the pines, and Eric Elzenga looking shyly over at Cybil Staudemeyer. Hank Dwyer, Nick's second cousin, held the hand of his youngest sister, Tonia, whose slanted eyes and low-set ears set her apart. In the center of the crowd stood Hank and Tonia's sister, Reba, her red hair shining like a sumac and her whole life's restlessness written on her face. Anyone might have read there all the things she'd do and be.

"The creek runs away from our farm," Reba Dwyer

said. "If we walk around the shore of the pond, we'll find where the creek comes in, and then we can follow it home."

Her own father had once found his way out in just this fashion, but Reba didn't know that; she'd spend much of the next fifteen years rediscovering things other people already knew. A cloud shot by, pink-fringed from the lowering sun. A hawk took off from a tree over Reba's head and flew, arrow-straight, in the direction of home. Reba had led the children here, on a leaf-gathering expedition —the youngest ones were supposed to collect all the different leaves they could and iron them between wax paper, for school. Each of them bore a bouquet of flame-colored leaves in one hand—gold aspen, birch, witch hazel, mulberry, basswood, beech, chestnut; orange-and-brown oak, hornbeam, serviceberry, chokecherry, ash; red sumac and dogwood and cherry, tupelo, maple, sweetgum. Some carried pinecones and various pods as well.

"We're going to be late for chores," Reba's brother, Hank, said nervously. Even then, his eyes were always fastened on Reba. "Dad's going to yell."

"He won't notice," Reba said. She was perfectly calm; she'd led this army here and she'd lead them home. She turned her back and headed for the pond's shore, knowing the others would follow her. They did, all but Tonia, who'd somehow detached herself from Hank. Tonia toddled off on her fat legs in the opposite direction, heading deeper into the swamp. She walked blind, her oversized head tipped back as she gazed into the brilliant colors of the canopy above. Her mouth was parted in a smile; her arms flapped gently at the wind. Something guided her between the stumps, around the mossy hillocks and holes. And she might have been lost forever, if Reba hadn't run back for her.

LEARNING
TO SING

REBA Dwyer always thought that she lost Luke Wyatt, or began to lose him, when she was in tenth grade and told him about her first meeting with Jessie Thayer.

This was in Rockledge, Massachusetts, in 1972—thirty miles up into the hills, past Leeds and Haydenville, past Maglione's Nursery, a string of scruffy bars Reba would come to know all too well, the VA Hospital where her mother worked, worn farms resembling her parents' place. Past broken fences, glacial erratics, old cars resting on cracked axles, tractor parts and tire treads, second-growth woods worth nothing cheek by jowl with weedy fields. A small clinic, the Elks' Hall, and Holy Redeemer Church on the outskirts; then a blue sign nailed to a telephone pole, reading "Rockledge—Named for Ledges of Rock." Past the church, the road emptied onto a small square set about with tired white houses. At one end were a few small stores: Wally's Hardware, Bob's Red & White Grocery, Elzenga Printing. This was Luke and Reba's world, all they knew, and Reba had every reason to think Luke could understand whatever she said. He was her best friend and the first boy she'd ever kissed.

"Shut your eyes," Luke had whispered.

All that afternoon they'd been sitting in the toolshed, playing gin and hiding from Reba's father. The air was hot and dusty and made them sneeze, and they shared Luke's torn handkerchief. Three days before, on Reba's twelfth birthday, they'd sliced each other's index fingers with Reba's pocketknife and mashed the wounds together, exchanging blood. Luke wasn't satisfied with that. He set down the cards and edged closer to Reba.

"Shut your eyes," he said. "Open your mouth."

Reba shut her eyes. "You drop a bug in here and I'll break your arm," she warned.

"Don't worry," Luke said, and then he leaned over and stuck his tongue in her mouth. Reba let him play there for a minute and then she bit his tongue lightly and spit it out.

"That's a sin," Luke said, with some satisfaction. "Swopping spit. It's a sin because our tongues touched. It's much stronger than that blood-brother bit."

"*Sin,*" Reba said mockingly, hissing the word until Luke had to laugh. A few hours later they washed up and biked over to Rockledge Methodist, where they sang together in Reba's father's choir. Each time Reba looked over at Luke, he rolled his eyes and let his wet tongue droop. When Reba giggled, her father stopped playing the organ and barked at her.

"Something funny?" Bowen said. "Want to share it with the rest of us?"

Reba made a face at her father and flapped her arms like wings, a gesture Luke picked up on right away. "Angels," he whispered behind her. "Ha."

And Reba smiled and hummed something to him. Years earlier, when Luke's father's car had burned up in front of the Dwyers' house and left only a pair of charred shoes on the backseat and a pool of red collecting near them, it was Luke and Reba who'd calmed the other children down and figured out what had happened. They were in grade school then, just children themselves. They'd all been upstairs, three Dwyers and four Wyatts, when the car horn shorted out and blared and sent them running to the window and then outside. The grown-ups were gathered by the burning car, swaying slightly with their drinks still in their hands. Reba's father, Bowen, was trying to look puzzled; Reba's younger sister, Tonia, had crinkled her sweet, Chinese-looking face in terror and dismay. When Luke's brother Roger leaned over the shoes and said, "Where's Dad?" Reba's father, drunk again, had looked at the shoes for a long time before saying, simply, "Here."

Luke had drawn a long breath, but then Reba had tapped him and gestured toward the porch light. Together, they'd spotted Luke's father slipping from the shadow of the spruce trees, a wicked grin still on his face. The fathers had known each other since they were boys. "Got you," Reba's father had laughed. He'd punched Luke's arm and said, "Got you—only kidding," but Luke and Reba refused to smile at him. They pieced together the story of how the open can of paint on the backseat, the tin of turpentine, and the old rags had conspired to ignite a car left in the hot sun while the grown-ups drank all day. "Spontaneous combustion," the mothers had said, glaring at the fathers. "Go back to bed."

Later, after the grown-ups had spent that whole summer referring to the seven of them—Reba, her brother, Hank, and her sister, Tonia; Luke and his three brothers— as "the angels" because of the way they'd looked that first minute, staring down from the upstairs window in their white bedclothes, Luke and Reba had their revenge.

When Halloween came that year, Reba and Luke had dressed like demons and shrouded the younger children in ghostly sheets. While their parents drank inside Reba's house, still, again, all seven children had gone to the backyard and raked the leaves into one huge pile. Luke told Reba and Reba set the younger ones to work, transforming the leaf pile into a huge leaf doughnut. They cleared the leaves from the center, making a damp space inside a leaf ring three feet high, and then they all squatted down inside the ring, six feet from the leaves on every side. Luke held on to Reba as he lit the leaves. They caught right away and flames leapt over their heads.

"Now!" Luke and Reba had shouted together, and then all seven of them had screamed as if the house were burning down. The grown-ups ran to the kitchen window, their mouths popped open—from the window, Reba knew that the ring looked like a solid pile with them burning in the middle. When the grown-ups hit the yard, Luke and Reba shouted, "Angels! Angels!" and flapped their arms like wings. The younger ones picked up on it right away. "Angels!" they cried, until the grown-ups got close enough to see them safe within the ring.

"Just kidding," Luke told Reba's father sweetly.

They'd been grounded for a month then, not for the first time or the last, but they left messages for each other in a hollow beneath a gray boulder that stood halfway between their farms. As protection, they used a musical code so simple anyone might have broken it; so bizarre that no one ever did.

"Sphinxes," Reba informed Luke the day they invented the code at school. "That's what you call letters encoded as notes. Like the way Bach stuck his name in some of his music—B, A, C, B-flat."

"That doesn't spell Bach," Luke had pointed out patiently.

"B-flat is written *H* in German," Reba said. "I know. I read it in a book."

"So let's use the code in the book," Luke said.

"Let's make our own," said Reba.

They wrote in notes on music paper Reba stole from her father, using a treble clef.

"This is great," Luke said, and when he wrote in code he always started with Reba's name because he liked the sound of it, which was something like a deranged door chime.

After the fire, after the secret code, after the blood and spit they'd swopped, Reba had figured Luke was bound to her forever. He had all the dirt on her family— he knew her Hungarian mother, Mag, who looked after the broken men at the VA Hospital and spent her time trying to fix small electrical appliances. He knew her crazy grandmother Lily and Lily's horde of cats; quiet Hank, who always lost everything; and Tonia, frozen forever at eight or ten although she was only a year younger than Reba. He'd seen Bowen so drunk that he stood by the road at midnight, trying to hitch rides with cars that never came. And Reba knew all about Luke. His parents raised turkeys where Reba's raised chickens, but their lives were otherwise more similar than either of them liked to admit.

The two of them ran away periodically and were always in trouble. They'd run to the Gorge; they'd run to the swamp. They'd spent the better part of a long night curled in the dog's box in Luke's basement with their blankets wrapped around them, head to toe and toe to head and sound asleep. They had forged each other's parents' names on report cards for so long that no one would have accepted an authentic signature. For years, they'd com-

11

pared chores and humiliations—Luke's chores, they agreed, were worse during the holiday butchering and maybe worse all the time, because turkeys make chickens look smart. In a rain, the turkeys would tilt their heads to the sky and drown.

"Look at that," Luke used to say to Reba, when they were in his father's barn. He'd point to some old turkey keeled over on his apple-fattened breast, and Reba would cover her eyes and they'd both chime *"Gross"* as loud as they could. The barn smelled of mildewed feathers and mites and manure turned to powder. Reba never ate turkey after she knew Luke; Luke never ate eggs after he saw the layers imprisoned in the Dwyers' sheet-metal sheds.

They had so much in common that Reba thought nothing of telling him how she met Jessie Thayer. She was fourteen then; Luke was a year older but hardly looked it. The two of them were sitting under the railroad bridge one afternoon, laying pennies out to be flattened and smoking stolen cigarettes. Reba said, "I met this girl today, when I snuck into the bathroom for a smoke."

"What girl?" Luke said. His hair was parted in the middle and pushed behind his ears, and the torn flannel shirt he was wearing had once been Hank's.

"Jessie Thayer. She was smoking too, and she jumped about a mile when I came in. I told her everything was cool."

Reba went on to tell Luke how she and Jessie had stepped into a stall, facing each other across the cracked toilet while they got acquainted. When the outer door had swung open again, they'd tossed their cigarettes into the toilet and pressed the stall door shut. Reba had squatted on the toilet so her feet wouldn't show; Jessie had crouched down so her head wouldn't stick up. Mrs. Tetwilliger had banged on the door and demanded to know who was in there. "Come out right now!" she'd said. "I know you're smoking."

Reba had made a face at Jessie—Mrs. Tetwilliger was the worst teacher in the whole school and Reba thought they were doomed. "Come on," Mrs. Tetwilliger said. "Out. We're going to the principal's."

But Jessie had saved them. She coughed and looked at Reba and then said, sweetly, "It's me—Jessie Thayer. I think I'm sick. I was in gym and I started bleeding so bad . . . see?" She'd opened the sanitary napkin box nailed to the wall and, to Reba's amazement, dug out a fiercely soiled pad and dangled it over the stall door. "Think I should go to the nurse?" she asked. Mrs. Tetwilliger had gasped and fled.

"She doesn't believe young ladies bleed," Reba told Luke. "Or if we do, that we'd admit it. It's like she thinks she bleeds rosewater and shits calico packets tied with satin bows."

Reba waited for Luke to laugh, but Luke was silent. It wasn't as if he hadn't seen blood before—he'd lived with turkey blood, chicken blood, the blood they'd sliced from their own fingers and mingled together, even the false blood of his father's false death. Reba thought this was more of the same, but apparently she was wrong. She forgot Luke didn't have sisters.

"Nice," Luke said finally, in a pained voice. "Real nice."

"Come on," Reba said. "It was funny."

Luke made a face and said, "That girl sounds like a real pig." And after that, whenever Reba mentioned Jessie's name to him he grew silent or squirrelly or skittered away, as if she'd done something wrong.

Reba kept seeing Jessie, wondering all the time if

Luke was right. She and Jessie had little in common, at least on the surface: Jessie was pretty and blond and wore fancy underwear, and her father, a real estate broker, had moved them from Whately into a tidy house above the smelly farms. Nothing like Reba's odd house, Reba's odd family. Reba never brought Jessie home; the first night she stayed over at Jessie's, Jessie's mother gave her hot chocolate in a cup kept separate from the rest, as if Reba had the plague. And still Reba would have moved there if she could. The Thayers had framed pictures on the walls and pillowcases that matched their sheets; Jessie's baby brother slept in a cherry crib and took the air in a fancy blue stroller. "The Crown Prince," Jessie called him, with the same contempt she exercised on her parents and her house. But Reba envied him. She could remember Mag carrying Tonia around in a cardboard box with a crib mattress inside and Tonia snuffling and snorting about on it like a guinea pig.

At dinner her first night there, Reba copied Jessie's ways with a knife and fork and then went off with her to a party at Larry Keefe's. Jessie's mother said, "You two be home by eleven, hear?" The girls said, "Yes, yes," and went to the party, where they made fun of everyone and wouldn't dance with the boys their own age. Back at Jessie's, Reba found that she and Jessie shared a talent for emphasizing the irrelevant.

"It was nice," Jessie said in response to her mother's questions.

"There was dancing," Reba said.

"His parents were home."

"They had meatballs."

Then they went off to bed. Jessie's room had twin beds decked out with yellow ruffles and dotted swiss, which Reba coveted and Jessie despised; Jessie wanted to paint the room black. As soon as the girls heard Jessie's parents snore, they drank the crème de menthe and Scotch and vodka they'd siphoned off into jelly jars and hidden beneath the ruffles. When they were done they tumbled out Jessie's window, crept down to Rockledge Gorge, and sang old songs until the stone walls rang. That's how Reba discovered that Jessie could sing.

"Why don't you come sing in choir?" Reba asked.

"Church sucks," Jessie said.

"I know, but you get to sing. The organ's great."

"I could try," Jessie said.

She did. They had practice on Thursday evenings and church on Sunday mornings, and Jessie seemed to welcome being out of her tidy house as much as Reba liked being in it. Jessie had a clear pure soprano, not great but good; Reba had her big true alto even then. They both had perfect pitch and harmonized easily by ear.

The first Thursday they sang together, Reba closed one ear with her finger and made up the bottom part to "Jesus, Jesus, Rest Your Head" while Jessie sang the melody. The rest of the choir sat up and stared, and Reba's father craned his head around the organ, shaking it in disbelief. "Like angels!" he said. "Like freaking birds!"

But Luke came up to Jessie afterwards and said, "So you're the rag lady," jealous enough to die now that his lovely boy soprano had cracked. Jessie laughed at him, and that laugh changed Reba's life forever. Jessie said, "Rag lady, turkey king—comes to the same thing, doesn't it? Blood's blood." Luke blushed a terrible blush and walked away, and Reba knew she shouldn't have told Jessie about him. She ran after him and tried to apologize.

"She was just being funny," Reba said. "I only told her where you lived."

"Sure," Luke said bitterly. "Hang around her for a

couple of weeks and you think you can say anything. Just because the two of you can sing."

"Want to meet at the swamp tonight?" she asked. "It's snowing. It'll be nice."

"Fuck off," he said, and he walked away. Reba knew all she had to do to keep him was abandon Jessie, but her feet were rooted to the ground.

Luke quit choir that week and wouldn't look at Reba in school. He stopped leaving notes for her; stopped meeting her in the swamp. He started playing basketball and going out with girls. That spring he started seeing Sally Lambert, and when Reba stopped him in the halls to tease him, he never laughed.

Reba thought she didn't care; she was doing everything with Jessie by then and her whole life had turned secret. She and Jessie pored over Mrs. Thayer's dog-eared copies of *Valley of the Dolls* and *Peyton Place,* reading the good parts out loud to each other, and they raided Reba's gray bungalow as well. Reba's father had all sorts of old recordings, mostly operas, and Reba and Jessie used to sneak these out and play them late at night in Jessie's room. This was Jessie's idea—she was wild for Maria Callas (whose voice resembled hers not at all), and she loved Bowen's scratchy albums of her assorted arias. The "Suicidio" from Ponchielli's *La Gioconda,* Mathilde's "Sombre forêt" from *William Tell*—whatever was lush, romantic, wild. Neither she nor Reba knew any Italian, but they didn't care; they sang along with the records in a made-up gibberish of open vowels as they painted black lines around their eyes. *La Traviata* sent them into swoons— they loved Violetta's "Ah, fors' è lui" and her pathetic farewell to her past at the end of the last act. "Courtesans," they said, rolling the unfamiliar word around in their mouths and narrowing their painted eyes as they cursed their own dull lives.

They sang, they dreamed, and at church, Reba's father took Jessie under his wing. Crazy as he was then, Reba knew he could see what he had: his own daughter, who could sing an alto part without listing toward the melody, and Jessie, who could lead the sopranos to Mars. "Sing!" he'd scream at them, his feet flying on the organ pedals. "From the diaphragm!"

They sang. Thursday nights they were sometimes weak, never out of tune but not quite perfect either. Sunday mornings they sang like cardinals. No one understood the change, not even Reba's father. He couldn't know that on Sunday mornings Reba and Jessie got up before dawn, if they'd slept at all, leaned out Jessie's window to smoke bowls of the hash Jessie got from older boys in Whately, and finished off with coffee and cigarettes. That's what Reba remembered most later, the picture she'd always carry in her head—she and Jessie standing across from each other in the choir loft, wide-eyed and hollow-cheeked, letting the pure notes form in their throats like eggs. They floated to church and shouldn't have been able to sing at all, and yet their voices almost brought the church walls down. They stood against the wall that housed the organ pipes, and when Reba's father pedaled the bass notes, their bodies shook and they dreamed of hurricanes and changed lives. Jessie sang solos; Reba sang solos; they sang duets. Below them, their neighbors closed their eyes. Afterwards, the girls went back to Jessie's house and slept till afternoon. No one knew why they were so tired.

But then, no one seemed to know anything. No one but Reba and Jessie knew how they'd started with Sunday mornings and worked their way up to the big stuff, daring each other all the way; or how they tiptoed out on Saturday nights and drank and sang, then drank and got high, then went to parties at older boys' houses and to bars in town where they weren't carded because pretty girls were rare. Jessie was pretty and more than that; with her around, Reba never had any trouble. They made a bet to see who'd lose her cherry first, and Jessie won.

It was spring by then: Reba and Jessie were both fifteen and had known each other eight months. Late one Saturday night, they tumbled out of Jessie's window and met David and Dennis Strazzabosco, cousins Jessie knew from Whately. They piled into Dennis's car and drove, wove really, all of them chugging Colt 45's, to David's apartment. Reba's heart was pounding hard. Two in the morning—Reba wasn't sure what to expect but knew it was more than sitting around getting high. They played records and smoked hash and danced slow and close; when the boys turned the lights out, David and Jessie crawled into David's bed and left Dennis and Reba on the floor, nested in a heap of soiled quilts. Someone made little mewing noises that made Reba nervous.

The boys drove Reba and Jessie home before the sun came up; inside, Jessie told Reba she'd done it. "He said I was good," she told Reba proudly. "He said I was a natural." Reba stared at her jealously: Jessie sat cross-legged and smiling, her blond hair smooth, her face unmarked by the night while Reba's own hair stuck up all over. "So?" Jessie said. "What about you? Did you like it?" Reba had to admit that she still didn't know. While they got high and got ready to go to church, Reba told Jessie how she'd chickened out at the last minute, when she'd felt Dennis's hairy leg prying her own legs apart. "He swore at me," Reba admitted. "Then he made me do him with my hand."

Jessie laughed and touched Reba on the arm. "We'll find you someone better next time," she promised. And then they went to church and sang a piece Reba would always remember, a Bach cantata in which the theme and countersubject crossed each other like a braid. Double counterpoint, Reba's father told them; Reba thought it was beautiful. Her life was divided into two, the only way she could manage to survive, and she could feel the parts tangling whenever she relaxed.

For the next two years Jessie kept her word, finding Reba someone better over and over again. Because Jessie didn't like to go off alone, when they went out she picked the best from the men who swarmed around her and dangled the second best in front of Reba like bait. Or at least that was how it seemed to Reba, who sniffed and sampled until she gave in one night to a twenty-year-old summer student from the university. He didn't last long; after him, Reba found the others easy. Ralph, Tony, Henry, Frank, Jack, Matt—she forgot some names. She forgot some nights. She never saw anyone more than twice. She and Jessie swopped men the way she and Luke had swopped spit, and she spent her sophomore and junior years glued to Jessie's side. They bought long earrings together and stole eye makeup from Woolworth's. Around them their classmates got older, went steady, got pregnant, dropped out; a boy Reba had once known cut his thumb off in a die-press. Reba felt the people she'd grown up with slipping away from her, sinking down behind a pale mist. Luke married Sally Lambert, graduated, and vanished, all without ever saying good-bye. Reba heard that Sally was pregnant. And when Reba's teachers told her she looked tired, she said she was helping out with the chickens a lot, although the truth was that she did her chores so poorly, her father picked on Hank instead.

It was a mystery to Reba how they never got caught, pregnant, hurt, but they never did. They were smart in certain ways—they went out with men from other towns and never used their last names, never gave out phone numbers. They appeared; they disappeared; they did what they wanted. When boys from their own school asked them out they said they couldn't, they had to sing, and they sang so well on Sunday mornings that everyone believed them. Reba thought they'd go on this way until they graduated and fled, which they had always planned to do together.

What Reba didn't count on was the man with the long white hands. Jessie had a thing for hands, and one night, in a Hatfield bar, a man with hands like carved marble came up and bought Jessie a drink without even looking at Reba. Jessie flushed and turned her back on Reba, as if they hadn't come in together. She and the man danced one long dance together and then drove away in a yellow van without saying good-bye. Reba hitched home alone and slept in her parents' house; when morning came she went to church by herself. She and Jessie didn't get high and they sang like mice.

"What happened last night?" she asked Jessie later.

Jessie shrugged, said, "Nothing," and turned away.

When they sang again the next week, Jessie frowned and plugged her ear; Reba was singing louder than Jessie and Jessie lost the melody. A few weeks later, Jessie quit choir and stopped asking Reba over to her house. She wouldn't tell Reba anything about the man except that he was married. Sometimes she'd ask if she could tell her parents she was staying over at Reba's house; Reba always said, "Sure," but got no satisfaction from that. On Saturday nights she went out alone, but she didn't know what to do once she was out. Without Jessie she lost her nerve; without Jessie, men let her be. She went home alone at midnight or one, confusing her parents. Her father found new music with solos in her range; she sang a lot because she had nothing better to do. In the sheds, to the chickens; down at the Gorge, to the stone walls; at night, driving home alone. She hardly saw Jessie their whole senior year.

At night, she found herself dreaming of Luke and the way they used to be, and when she did it seemed like she'd lost something years ago and hadn't missed it until now. She didn't call Luke, but he must have heard her anyway, because they ran into each other the week before Reba's high school graduation. Reba had taken her brother's car to the Empty Bucket, where she and Jessie used to go; she found Luke inside, drinking schnapps and beer by himself.

"Well," Luke said when Reba walked in, as if the conversation they'd let drop had ended only yesterday. "No Jessie?"

"Jessie's busy these days," Reba said, scanning Luke's face. Somewhere, sometime, he'd grown a pale beard that suited him and made him look older.

Luke didn't ask her to sit but she sat anyway. "Poor baby," he said nastily. "No one to play with?" Reba realized he was drunk. "How come you don't keep in touch?" he continued. "Think you're too good? Jessie and Reba, Reba and Jessie, never see one without the other—you two queer or what?"

"Queer as ducks," Reba said. "You could have picked up the phone yourself, you know. That what being married does?"

"Was," Luke said glumly. "Was married. Sally thought

she was pregnant but she wasn't, and after we figured that out she split. She ran off with Dale Gorman."

"Jesus," Reba said. "That's tough." Luke shrugged and she told him how she'd landed a scholarship for the music school in Springfield and how her father, almost in spite of himself, had helped. "The old lady's bullshit," she told Luke. "Hank's out of the house already, and the old man's just getting weirder, and once I go it'll just be Mag and Lily left to take care of Tonia and all those chickens. But I don't care—I've got to get out of here."

"Don't we all," Luke said. "Wanna get drunk?"

She did. She didn't tell Luke what she and Jessie had been doing, but she told him about her family and about the farm, and she decided it felt wonderful to tell anyone anything. "I missed you," she said, and when she did she knew it was true. "You still sing?"

"Naah," Luke said. "My voice never came back."

He explained about Sally some, and Reba listened and then stood up and walked outside, suddenly aware that she was about to be sick. After she was, she stretched out on the asphalt parking lot and laid her head on the stone curb. Luke joined her a few minutes later.

"You okay?" he asked. He lay beside her like a carving on a tomb, his hands folded peacefully on his chest, his legs perfectly straight and still.

"Sure," she told him. "Just dizzy."

He moved his ankle until it touched hers and said, "I wish we'd stayed together."

Just for that minute, he looked so kind and sweet and straight that Reba wished they had too, wished all her time with Jessie hadn't happened. Luke kissed Reba and then he laughed when she reminded him about their first kiss, laughed again when she reminded him about the leaf fire.

They almost made love in the parking lot, but Luke was too drunk and so they tried singing instead.

"Just sing the melody," Reba told him. "I'll pick up the harmony." They sang "Heart Like a Wheel" but Luke was right—he couldn't sing anymore. When he tried to hum the notes for Reba's name in their own code, he transposed it down a third and it came out as ACGF instead. He had decent relative pitch, not perfect pitch like Reba, and without a piano or someone to guide him he always started on the wrong note.

"I guess you don't want to stay here," Luke said. "Now that Sally and Jessie are gone?"

"I can't," Reba told him. "I got this scholarship and all . . ."

"Yeah," he said. "Well, maybe I'll come visit you in Springfield sometime. You keep in touch, okay?"

"I will," she promised, but she never did. Too drunk to drive, she drove off anyway, and once she left Rockledge she didn't go back. No one visited her—Luke never came and Jessie never called, although she'd hinted that she would. Reba found herself more lonely than she would have believed.

When she moved into her dorm room in the fall of 1975, she saw right away that nothing she'd brought with her from Rockledge fit in, not her clothes, not her language, not her friends. She kept the cheap stereo Jessie had given her, and some records and some jeans, but she got rid of the dangly earrings and the flashy tops and almost everything else. She got a job—nights she waitressed at Nico's Pizza Palace; days she went to school with Springfield girls and took voice and piano, theory and French. Her teacher, Mrs. Barinov, fought to prune the brass and harshness from Reba's voice.

"Modulate!" she shrieked to Reba. "Make like bell, like bird!"

Reba tried to fit her voice to the other girls' the way she tried to fit in with them, but they were mostly from the suburbs and Reba made them nervous. She knew they'd grown up in clean white houses and sung in junior high musicals; they went to orthodontists and gynecologists and had their clothes dry-cleaned. They didn't know about turkeys and chickens and couldn't begin to accept the kind of life Reba and Jessie had lived. Reba tried to explain it to them but it didn't go well—it was like explaining Jessie to Luke all over again, only worse. A few weeks after she got to school, she told a story to a group of girls hanging around the lounge one night and trading tales. High school stories, nothing worse: getting drunk one night, getting high, making it for the first time after a prom. At one point Weezie Bergman smirked and said, "I got a diaphragm," as if this were some big deal. Weezie was sitting on a sofa with her court around her; Reba was sitting in an armchair nearby, not exactly unwelcome but not really part of things and wishing she were. "My mother made the appointment this summer," Weezie continued. "After she found out about Fred. She was pretty pissed about it, but she figured with me going away and all, she'd better do something."

The girls laughed knowingly, and Reba thought she felt something in the air that she could join. *I'll tell something I did,* she thought. A story like theirs, something common as worms. She looked around, leaned forward, and said, "We used Pepsi."

Weezie turned to her politely and said, "For what?"

"You know," Reba said. "Instead of a diaphragm."

"Give me a break," Merissa said.

About then, Reba realized she should stop, that

maybe this story wasn't so common after all. She could feel herself walking on marbles and still she plunged ahead. She said, "Didn't you ever? We'd open a bottle of warm Pepsi afterwards, then shake it and pop it up so it sprayed inside. The bubbles did the rest—the acid or something killed the sperm."

Alice, the one with the perfect teeth, said, "That's dis*gust*ing. Don't you people have doctors up there?"

Weezie made a face and whispered, *"Gross,"* and the other girls sniffed as if Reba had laid a fresh cowpat on the couch. Then they turned their backs and talked about school, never to speak to Reba again.

Right there is when Reba first realized she was in trouble. Not just for then but for years, decades, possibly forever—she could feel something spreading inside her like a virus, like a germ, something that would haunt her the rest of her life even if she never told anyone another tale. After that she got high whenever she sang and pretended she was singing with Jessie or Luke. On Sundays, when the other girls went home, Reba sang in churches all over Springfield and Chicopee. When she did, her voice poured down from the choir loft like a bolt of raw silk. She twined her hands in the folds of her faded blue skirt and opened her mouth, burning all the history she couldn't say —the fires and angels and turkeys and chickens, Jessie and Luke, Tonia in her cardboard box and the Crown Prince in his crib, the men and the dark bars—into each note. She pruned Mrs. Barinov from her voice and made like an oboe, pure want, and she watched as people looked up startled from below. She was singing, she was learning to sing, and as the last round tone left her throat she was wondering how anyone ever learned to live.

SECRET
HARMONIES

◆

IN the winter of 1976, the winter it snowed so much in Rockledge and the winter after Bowen's oldest daughter, Reba, took off, the chickens took the plague and died. The vets found no name for the chicken plague until after it did its work; it wasn't coccidiosis or mites or Newcastle disease, and it wasn't pullorum. It was something like fowl pox, only worse, some virus the chickens had lived with for decades that suddenly turned on them, causing their feathers to fall and their skins to crust, as if they were transforming themselves back into eggs. At the time, Bowen saw the plague as fate, something to do with overcrowding and inbreeding and stress, no doubt, but probably also rooted in the cloud that hung over his house that winter, which seemed to float like a curse from Magda, his wife.

He and Mag were alone that winter, rattling around their shabby bungalow like grit in a paper bag. Bowen could hardly keep track of where everyone else had gone. Reba had run off to music school in Springfield after he'd helped send her there; sometimes he could hardly believe this himself. Hank had stormed out of the house, cursing Bowen for a fool, and had moved into the Hillview on Main Street. And Tonia had gone to spend a few months in Chicopee with Mag's sister, Sonie, who, still determined that Tonia was only slow and not retarded, was sending Tonia to a progressive school and bombarding her with flash cards at home. This left Bowen and Mag alone together for the first time in twenty years. Within weeks, Mag stopped dying her coarse black hair and allowed a thick white stripe to march down the center of her head. She stopped making her famous strudel, her famous goulash; started serving meals from cans and wearing huge flowered housedresses. The chickens died day by day and Mag swore this was Bowen's fault, punishment for all he'd done over the years. On bad nights, Bowen feared she might be right. His habits had slipped as he spent more time in the basement with his projects and his vodka bottles, and he knew he wasn't the farmer his father had been.

Grind, grind, grind. He could hear the gears of his life shattering against each other, stressed metal giving way, parts pinging on an outer shell. That's what he was listening to the late February night when he sat with Mag in the sunporch he'd built when his children were small. They were discussing Mag's day at the VA Hospital, where Mag worked as a nurse's aide, and Bowen was trying not to wince at the confusion of wires on Mag's lap, a jumble that had once been their toaster oven. When Mag got up for a cigarette she dumped the wires on the floor and then sorted idly through the mail: bills, flyers, more bills, late notices, threats. Their basic mail those winter days. Mag opened a creased envelope addressed to Bowen; when she read it she sighed this sigh she'd had since the minute seventeen years ago when she'd first caught sight of Tonia's thick tongue and slanted eyes. Bowen looked up and Mag passed the letter to him. He read the smudged message aloud. "Dear———," it said. Above the line, someone had scratched his name.

SECRET HARMONIES

This letter has been sent to you for luck. The original is in France; it's been around the world nine times. The luck is now being sent to you, and you will get it within 10 days provided you send the letter back out. This is no joke.

Do not keep this letter! Send 20 copies of it to friends and associates who need luck. Send no money: fate has no price. See what happens. You'll be surprised even if you don't believe in luck. An Australian preacher received $50,000 after mailing this. Jack Carmichael lost his wife 2 weeks after getting this, because he failed to circulate it. After his wife died, he sent it out and won a lottery.

Remember—send no money! This charm will bring you luck if you share it:

> Hear the secret harmonies.
> Count birds, fish, ferns, and trees.
> Count stars, sand, grass, and snow;
> Divide by God. The answer shows
> All music comes from these.
> Hear the secret harmonies.

—Friar Thomas

The charm made Bowen laugh. He'd had no kind of a year at all, hadn't seen luck's face in so long he wasn't sure he'd recognize it if it kissed him. He'd met fate, not luck, fate that weighed on his shoulders like a bag of stones and had cost him everything. He'd been paying for years, ever since he'd returned to Rockledge from Italy after the war, his head still full of music and his eyes still scorched by the brilliant sun. Whitewashed buildings, white goats, dark girls in white dresses, white sand, white sky—he'd come back home to find everything the same and only himself changed. The farm he'd grown up on still the same, the same; Magda Savlov, whom he'd left behind, still living with her parents next to their tool-and-die shop and waiting for him; his crabbed father still cursing the rocky earth. Not for him, he'd sworn right away; he'd enrolled at the state university as soon as he could. An aggie school then, it was filled with veterans. He took animal husbandry and plant-and-soil science courses to be practical, but in between he slipped in all the music he could, building on the piano lessons he'd taken for years and secretly hoping he might do something with this. Nothing, was what that had come to—nothing at all. His father died and left him the farm, and after the "For Sale" sign he stuck in the lawn rotted and crumbled away, shot full of holes, he bowed to the future and married Mag, whose pretty face was already puckering. He ended up just as he'd been meant to, with a distant wife and an unprofitable chunk of ground slung around his neck, three children tying him down like guy wires. Every few years he stuck a new sign in the lawn; no one ever stopped or called. It made him dizzy, still, just to think of it, and here was this letter come to taunt him again.

As if to confirm his thoughts, Mag flicked the letter with her fingernail after Bowen read it, said, "What a fool!" and then laughed, not cruelly but in that way of sensible women who think luck is earned and not given or found.

"Who?" Bowen said.

"That Friar Thomas," Mag replied. "One of those men in a long brown dress who isn't allowed to talk to anyone."

She turned away, leaving Bowen to wonder how he'd ended up with a woman unable to understand why a man would want to go into the swamp alone and listen to birds and reeds. Pretty, she'd been once, and quiet in a way

Bowen had interpreted as understanding rather than uninterested. He'd tried to tell her how he used to wander the swamp, but she'd looked at him mystified: she thought he and his father liked hunting there because they liked killing animals. As far as Bowen could tell, Mag didn't hear snow or mud or rain except to think of the inconvenience; she didn't hear their dog bounce under the ice at night, *tok, tok, tok.* She heard children, cars, directions, news; when she finished the letter she threw it under the supper scraps as if that would shut it up.

Bowen rescued the letter after Mag left, scraped off the grease, and brought it downstairs to the basement, where it was dim and quiet and suited him fine. He had a small shop, a workbench, a couch with a broken leg, beneath which he hid his supplies, and an old record player good enough for his scratched albums. He poured himself a drink and then he read the letter a few more times and put it away. Not expecting luck: he couldn't say much for the harmonies in his life just then, not much at all. The women he directed in the Methodist Church choir sang as if they were dead and not yet angels; each time he fed his remaining chickens, their clamor deafened him. He'd missed more things than he could count, but somehow he heard that letter, which found its way into his pocket and then, that Monday, called him over to a Xerox machine at the post office. He made twenty copies without thinking: all his change. His pockets felt light for the first time in weeks. When he got home he stuck the copies in his sock drawer, never meaning to mail them. He would have sworn he didn't know twenty people he'd wish luck on, good or bad.

Mag did the laundry on Wednesday night. While she washed and dried and put things away, Bowen copied music for his Cub Scout meeting and put the final touches on the whistles he'd been making. Mag came slamming down the basement steps as he was tuning the last one, screeching "Bowen!" and waving the twenty copies at him as if they were a sheaf of girlie magazines. Her hair was sticking up and her face was doughy. Bowen couldn't remember when she'd gotten old.

"How can you be such a fool?" she said.

He had no answer—it seemed to him that she treated him like a child no matter what he did, and there he was at his workbench, making little kids' whistles. For the boys, that was all: something for the boys he'd taken on two years ago, when he'd begun to see that his family was lost. He laid his arm over the whistles casually, so Mag wouldn't have more to be mad at. And then he said, "I wasn't going to *mail* them."

"I wasn't going to *mail* them," Mag mocked. "That's great. Nothing better to do with your spare change?" She tossed the copies on the concrete floor and huffed away.

"I'll throw them out!" Bowen called after her.

But Mag didn't answer him, and he didn't throw them out. He gathered them up instead, thinking how much Mag hated to be confronted with his lack of common sense, how she always felt the whole world resting on her shoulders. They were delicate, still, beneath their fatty cushions, the birdbones of a woman meant for another life.

Bowen slept in the basement that night, listening to the snow pile up on the bulkhead and dreaming strange dreams. The snow was what sent him off: snow that buried his dead chickens and sent him inside, snow that had taken his youngest brother, Nick, five years ago, when he drove his pickup truck off the soft white road and into the Gorge. Snow last month at Bowen's niece's wedding, piling up on the Elks' Hall steps while he and his remaining brother,

George, their wives and children left behind, sat inside drunk as skunks. They'd listened to the band—a saggy drummer, a lanky pianist, a tall guy with a battered cornet, and a natty singer. In a corner they fenced memories of Nick away and talked without saying much. Pink-dressed girls with shining clips in their hair danced near the head table, popping their knees and clapping their hands. Two of these belonged to George, and Bowen hadn't been able to take his eyes from them. The band-leader held his microphone out to the girls halfway through something with a driving bluesy beat, and the girls swarmed about it in a tight circle, their heads bent low. Bowen couldn't catch the words; what he heard was the "Ooh, *ooh!*" that ended each syncopated line. They were George's girls, and they sang wonderfully, but not half so well as Nick once had, not nearly so well as Bowen's own Reba or Reba's friend Jessie Thayer. It hit Bowen then that no one left in his life could carry a tune; his life was full of noise but none of it was music. And later, after he and George had ended up outside, drunker than either one of them could believe and huddled together under one shared coat on a picnic table beneath the white pines, George had said, "God, I hate the snow," and Bowen had said, "I do too," realizing as he said it that this was true. The snow silenced everything.

In his dream, the plows and sand trucks roamed the hills behind him and George like ghost machines, sending out a hazy glow from their blank headlights. No noise, although their engines should have been roaring. No tracks; as the machines passed over the road stayed white. In a corner of the yard, below a branch releasing its pale load in a small avalanche, Bowen glimpsed Nick on a pair of skis, standing near their father. Their father balanced a bundle of cattails on his shoulder, and a shadow shaped like a golden retriever led the two spirits away: to France, Bowen dreamed. To Italy, heaven, hell. No one asked him to follow; the shadows left him behind.

He woke listening to the concrete walls make the small sounds louder, as if he were sleeping in an ear trumpet. When he slept again, he dreamed of his children in diapers and snowsuits, back in the days when he could still do something for them. The surrounding farms had swarmed with children then—the Wyatt boys, the Rondines and the Elzengas, George's girls, the Lambert tribe, all fluttering like a flock of birds around his own three. He dreamed of Tonia crouching on a chair, bent over a fat manila drawing pad with her thick tongue between her teeth. A green crayon, tan paper, her hand clutching the crayon like a hoe as she struggled to make her alphabet. One huge letter for each page, shaky and often backward; twice through the alphabet and the pad was full. He saw his timid Hank, fussing with his food and paling at the least sight of anything announcing its animal origins—a bit of tendon, exposed bone at the joint of a chicken leg, white blood vessels dotting a slice of liver. Always clinging to Reba, Hank was, always looking to her. And then there was Reba, her mouth open in a song or in a cry for help, he couldn't tell which. She was an open-mouthed sort of girl, always crying or laughing or singing or screaming, never one to hide much more than the essential facts of her life. Like where she was, what she was doing and with whom; like what she thought of him. He'd loved her best of all his children and didn't know what she thought of him—she didn't seem to understand that all his disciplining of her, all the hours he'd spent teaching her, were only meant to make her tough. *One* and *two* and *three,* he'd shouted, as she bent over the piano at the church. If you don't have the rhythm, you have nothing.

Her green eyes narrowed at him under that mop of red hair, her long hands struggling. And him fading, sagging, his hair gone so thin that he always needed to wear a hat.

He woke in the morning feeling sweaty and strange, and just to be done with it, he took all twenty copies of the letter and mailed them off to the VA Hospital. He marked them "Residents—J Wing," which was not the wing where Mag worked but another, smaller wing where the residents were retarded and where, in the old days, Bowen's father had been in the habit of sending geese and ducks after they'd been lucky in the swamp. This was Thursday, Bowen's day to lead choir practice. He went to church early so he wouldn't have to see Mag, but he found the church cold and the organ cantankerous. Mrs. Gamble whined, "Mr. Dwyer—do we have to do this piece? My part's too high." Amy Rondine said, "We should break early tonight—the roads are terrible," and little Mrs. Stedman cleared her throat and said, "You know, I seem to be getting bronchitis," as if bronchitis would excuse her astonishing sour notes.

Nothing new there, Bowen thought. No worse luck than usual. This was what he had left of the music he'd meant to study and keep—a handful of cracked voices that couldn't free the notes from the paper they were printed on. He nodded, pleaded, did what he could, thinking how, since Reba and Jessie had left, his choir had slipped back to where it started years ago. Simple hymns, simple harmonies. He dressed their singing in fancy organ work and thought of his choir as one thin voice overlaid on a complex arrangement. When he got home, Mag was in a better mood. They went to bed and shared a beer, and Bowen asked Mag how her day had gone.

"Strange," Mag said, and she told him how a patient she knew had tried to convince her his lips were flowers.

"Two lips!" he'd cried again and again, touching his fingers to his mouth. Tulips, she'd finally understood. "You think he really believes that?" she asked, on the verge of being troubled.

"No," Bowen told her, denying the flowers as he'd denied ghosts and visions and wild thoughts throughout their married life—part of his job, part of what she'd always assumed he was meant to do. That's what she wanted from him—to be told there were no boogeymen out there, no shadows in dark suits. No heartbreak lying just beyond the line of sight. He told her to go to sleep and she did, snoring as gently as a fish. Bowen lay beside her thinking how his mother used to snore like that. When the weather was nice, his father used to sleep outside so the snoring wouldn't wake him, and Bowen had been considering this himself. He couldn't sleep in the snow, but he decided that, come summer, he'd take his Cub Scouts on an overnight hike, bed them down under a starry sky on a pile of pine boughs. Two years he'd had them—three Wolf Cubs and three Bears—and they'd never done an overnight hike. In part because of the way Mag laughed at him: "All the other den leaders are mothers with a son in their den," she often reminded him. "Don't you think that's strange?" *Sure,* Bowen wanted to say to her. *Strange.* Strange the way his heart went strange when he saw a couple, any couple, walking down a village street with their arms around each other and their faces bent close, their whole lives lying sweet before them.

Bowen's Cub Scouts came for their den meeting Friday, tossing their coats on the basement stairs and screeching like squirrels. Brian, Bowen's ten-year-old den assistant, led the den call. Bowen led the pledge and then passed out the whistles he'd been working on for weeks, cutting half-inch copper tubing to length, hacksawing small square holes in each, plugging the tops with wooden dowels etched with small slits. The whistles worked like organ pipes, their pitch dependent on the tubing's length. He'd made fourteen tuned to different notes, so each boy and he could have two, and he'd drawn the songs on big sheets of brown paper, so he could show them how to read music. He pinned the sheets to his corkboard and arranged the boys in order of the scale: Brian first, with whistles in A and B, Mark with C and D, and so on.

"Now," he said, when he had them organized. "Each of you should have the lower note in your right hand and the higher in your left."

The boys tweeted, listened, shifted whistles around.

"We're going to play some songs," Bowen continued. "I'll point to the boy with the whistles we need, palm down for your right-hand whistle and palm up for your left. Got it?"

The boys nodded gravely. Bowen started them on "Clementine" and they got it, more or less, the first time through. He found the whistles lovely, much richer in the basement than he'd expected. When they were finished, he led them to the corkboard and showed them how the written notes corresponded to the tune. Then he wrote each boy's name in under the notes he was to play.

"Try it without me," he said.

They crowded in front of the paper and slowly piped the tune.

"Not bad," Bowen said. "Not bad at all." He felt the way he had when he'd first taught Reba to sing: purely and happily astonished, as if there were light outside his basement, and heat, and hope. The boys played a while longer and then they had to go home. Bowen gave the music to Brian and said, "Get yourselves together and practice if you can—just follow the names under the notes."

Brian promised that they would. Bowen sat and whistled to himself for half an hour, and then he went upstairs and had supper with Mag and sat with her on the sunporch again, still making up to her for the copies of the letter and no longer sure why he'd sent them out. There were other things he might better feel bad about, he knew: the nights he'd come home so drunk Mag had locked him out; the windows he'd smashed and the doors he'd broken; the way his daughters had fled across the fields to hide at the Wyatts' until he was sober enough not to smack them for not being sons; the sight of Hank brandishing a pan at him. But those were things long done, long consigned to silence, and it didn't do any good to dwell on them. He lit the kerosene heater and watched the snow fall on the frozen pond. Mag switched the TV on; Bowen asked her to turn it off.

"There," he said when she did. "Isn't it quiet? Isn't it nice? You can hear the water making icicles."

Mag gave him an odd look. A dog ran over the frozen pond, just a shadow under the moon, and Bowen said, "Look—doesn't she remind you of Ginger?"

"No," Mag said patiently. "That's an Irish setter."

The dog pranced on the light snow, burying her muzzle and then leaping up with joyful barks. Mag switched the TV back on. She was right, Bowen knew—the dog looked nothing like Ginger. Ginger was their golden retriever, who'd drowned in their pond one day when she'd fallen through a hole in the ice. The children had seen the dog go down and had run for him and Mag, but by the time Bowen had dragged himself up from the basement and found the shed key and gotten the boat, Ginger's howls were as faint as a passing goose and then she was gone. Ten years ago; another thing he never talked about.

"I'm going downstairs," Bowen said. Mag shrugged

and kept watching TV. As he left the room he tapped the door frame and heard Ginger under the ice again—*tok, tok, tok*—and when he did he thought how things like that wouldn't happen if he lived alone. His dogs wouldn't drown because he'd have no dogs; his children wouldn't grieve because he'd have no children. No Hank, tapping his way through life as lost as that dog; no Reba as cut off from him as if they'd never shared music; no Tonia born when Mag was too old to have a normal child. He'd live alone, the way his mother-in-law, Lily, did. It amazed him, still, what Lily had done when her husband finally died. Bowen had asked her reluctantly to come and stay with them, but she'd said no. She'd turned her tool-and-die shop over to her foreman, and she'd taken the insurance money and put it into winterizing her summer cabin at Whittaker Lake. Insulation, a new furnace, storm windows and doors—and there she was, with a place as tidy as a mole's burrow and no one to share it with but her cats. Him in this cramped house all this time, with Mag and the kids and the chickens out back—and Lily, alone. Sitting by herself at her plain pine table, a cup of coffee sending up soundless steam and no one to smell it but her, no one to break the morning's icy quiet, no one to shatter her dreams. The ice-fishing huts on the frozen lake silent too, the deer slipping softly through the trees while geese beat an unheard pathway overhead. When he thought of Lily he wanted to tear his own house down around him.

He'd live alone in a small shack deep in the swamp, he thought, like the one he saw when he was young and hunting with his father. They used to hunt woodcock once in a while, squirrel and rabbit off-season, pheasant occasionally, but what they really liked was hunting ducks, gliding through the wetlands just before dawn and hiding in the reeds. One day they'd found a shack in the giant wedge of swamp that stretched from their pond to the woods. The walls were made of jack pine slabs with the bark still on; the chimney, of rounded fieldstones. They peeked in one of the windows and saw a cookstove, a bundle of blankets, a frying pan, and a flute. Bowen had asked his father who lived in the shack.

"An old hermit," his father said, and Bowen hadn't known what that was until his father told him. They walked around the shack and behind it found a pile of cattails separated into roots and stems and furry spikes. Bowen's father said the man who lived there ate those and fish and squirrels.

"Will he hurt us?" Bowen asked. The swamp was noisy that morning with wind and birds; when the reeds rustled, Bowen thought he heard a bearded wild man watching him.

"I don't think so," Bowen's father said. "But we ought to leave him be." Bowen's father tapped the wall of the shack with his knuckles, the way he'd tap a log before the first cut, and then they headed deeper into the swamp.

Bowen never found that shack again. But all that week after his Cub Scouts came and went, he kept thinking how quiet and lovely that shack would be. How, if he could, he'd live like the man who'd inhabited it, hearing tree frogs, swamp songs, little sounds; how he'd get rid of these people, all this fuss, keep his ears to the ground and listen to ferns and weeds, like Friar Thomas. He opened his mail each day with a little jolt, waiting for a word he couldn't hear, and though nothing came and he knew dimly that his ten days had passed, he woke that last Friday feeling lucky. The sun was out and the snow was melting, burbling and chuckling under its crust.

The last of his chickens had died that morning, and so the plague was over. He gathered the bodies into a mound and burned them out back, where years ago his children had set a bonfire to spite him for something nasty he'd done, something he could no longer recall. His Cubs came at three, with their whistles and their music. Brian said, "We've been practicing," and the other boys smiled secretively.

"That's good," Bowen said, prepared to welcome anything. When he pinned the music sheets to the corkboard, he saw that the boys had scribbled all over them. "What's this?" he asked.

"You'll see," Brian said. "We changed some things, so you don't have to point at us. Just look for your name on the music, and give me your right-hand whistle."

Bowen handed it over, and Brian exchanged it for his high G. "Blow both whistles," Brian commanded. Bowen blew, hearing high C and G—a perfect fifth. The rest of the boys blew their pairs of whistles and all had thirds and fifths that were sweet together and weren't what Bowen had given them at all—he'd passed out the whistles in chromatic order. Mag came running down the stairs, a broken blender in her hands.

"Do you have to be so loud?" she said. "I can't hear myself think."

The boys kept tweeting; Mag had to shout for them to hear.

"Ssh!" Bowen told her. To the boys he said, "Let's play a song." When they started he realized at once what they'd done: they'd switched whistles so each boy had a harmonious pair and no one played twice in a row, and they'd juggled names under the notes to make it come out. They were right, of course—Bowen saw that this was a stroke of luck if not of genius. The notes floated up and down the string of boys like magic.

Mag stood on the stairs above them, watching and

shaking her head. The boys blew the melody and sometimes joined in groups of two or three; they'd penciled in
some chords just from hearing what sounded good. The
music blended with the noises Bowen carried around in
his head all day, and this made him feel wonderful. His
good fortune, he saw—that he could hear the secret harmonies made by whistles, ghost machines, snow, dead
dogs. Mag's face twisted, as if the boys were hitting sour
notes.

"What's wrong?" Bowen asked her, as if he didn't
know.

She shook her head and went upstairs. Bowen knew
he could send the boys home, climb the stairs, and make
his peace with her; that he could say he only played with
the boys to humor them. He didn't. He thought of Friar
Thomas out in the swamp with his cattails and his flute, of
the patients at the VA slowly copying his letter twenty
times by hand and preparing to return it to the world. He
thought of the days when Reba, just a girl, used to listen to
him explaining music theory. Melody, harmony, the circle
of fifths; the spicy addition of non-harmonic tones. There
were changing tones, he'd told her, a pair of notes on
either side of the principal tone, which give a sense of
motion without motion actually occurring. Passing tones,
filling a gap a third apart; escape tones leaping to a tone of
another harmony. Reba had sat beside him willingly not
ten years ago, her long hands spread on the organ keys.
And now she was grown.

He and the boys played the rest of the songs, until it
was time for the boys to go home. The creek that led from
his farm to the swamp fed into a small river, which led to a
larger one and then to another, branching and branching
until it emptied into the sea. Bowen stuck his father's

silver flask into his pocket and tucked his whistles up his sleeve. Then he forced open the bulkhead door, walked down to the pond, and headed south, across the swamp and away from the snow.

ANIMAL SOUNDS

B OWEN was gone. He vanished into the swamp as cleanly as if the sphagnum had swallowed him, and no one from Rockledge heard from him for months. But Reba knew he wasn't dead—if he was she'd have seen his shadow somewhere, floating over her scavenged furniture or ducking around a corner as she drew near. She knew for a fact that he'd simply left. She got her shadow-seeing eyes from him, along with her voice and her ears, and if she couldn't see him floating in space then he couldn't be gone. He'd cut loose, he'd set himself free, no more than what they all dreamed of doing. He was on a train somewhere, riding through British Columbia. He was on an island off the New Hampshire coast, at the Gulf watching seabirds, at Mount Rainier on a melting glacier. He was in one of the places Reba could only dream about, read about; but because he left, Reba had to go home.

"Half-moons," Mag said, when she called Reba at school in the spring of 1976 to tell her that Tonia had returned to Rockledge in disgrace after biting her teacher on the arm and being expelled from school. "That's what her teacher said—she said Tonia left half-moons of tooth-marks on her arm. I've got boys knocking on the door all day, wanting to know where your father is, and Tonia won't come out of her room, and Lily thinks all this is *my* fault—and I swear, if I had any sense I'd leave myself. . . ."

Hank called Reba that same night, saying he couldn't do a thing with either Tonia or Mag, and when Reba called her grandmother Lily in desperation, Lily said in no uncertain terms that these problems weren't hers. "I've got eleven cats that need me," Lily said from her cabin on Whittaker Lake. "Not to mention Max."

Cat lady, Reba thought; what she said was "Who's Max?" Not that it mattered—since Reba's grandfather Carl had died seven years ago, Lily had been as strange as sin. Prancing around in men's clothes, taking in strays, thinning her woods with a chain saw; as if all those years she'd acted like a normal grandmother had only been Carl, corseting her life.

"You know," Lily said. "The man I met at church?"

"How would I know?" Reba said impatiently.

"Well," Lily said. "I met him at Halloween. I had Tonia over to my cabin, and we were just sitting around talking to the cats and cutting out paper dolls. Tonia was giving me a hard time because I was blue that day, and she was wanting to know why I didn't go to the Senior Singles costume party over at the church. Aurora Swenson had been pushing me all week to go, and I kept telling her no —all these old biddies, and Pastor Sven running around with his silly face, and a couple of tired old codgers in the corner, picking at their drooping ears . . ."

"Is there a point to this?" Reba asked.

"I'm getting there," Lily said, her voice already fogged with sweet memory. "So anyway, Tonia got all excited about the idea, and I let her get me dressed just to kill some time. Next I knew, she'd decked me out in black tights, black shorts, a black leotard she striped with some yellow tape, and fake eyelashes. I was supposed to be a bumblebee. Who would believe it?"

"I believe it," Reba said tiredly. Since her grandfather's death, she'd gotten used to the sight of Lily in an old man's T-shirt with no bra on underneath, in bagged-out khakis and hooded sweatshirts, in torn long underwear. Whenever she mentioned Lily's outrageous costumes, Lily laughed at her.

"A woman my age," Lily continued. "Dressed as a bee. So I went to the party finally, and I wasn't there twenty minutes before Max came over, dressed as a box of Rice Krispies. White pants, white turtleneck, painted white face, white hair—and this handpainted cardboard box stretching from his chin down to his knees. He used to drive a North American Van Lines truck, you know."

"Good for him," Reba said. "Is he nice?"

"He asked me to dance," Lily said. "Me. And he brought me some champagne, and later we went to some movies and found out we both liked chocolate cream pie, and I met his fox terrier. And look at us now—he's the only one of you who can name all my cats."

"*I* can," Reba protested. "Suki, Pyewacket, Razznol, Wicker, Tibbs, Rowley, Thalassa . . ." Seven; she couldn't name the remaining four.

"See?" Lily said triumphantly. "You can't. But *he* can." She was silent for a minute, and then she said, "That's what you need, missy—a man who can name the important things in your life without thinking twice."

"Fine," Reba said. "I'll get right on it. But what are we supposed to do for now?"

"How should I know?" Lily said. "I'm going to be sixty-six next month, and I've got problems of my own. You'd better get your fanny home."

Reba hung up and went back to her dorm room, trying to think what she should do. No one could alter Tonia; no one would want to try. Tonia could read, slowly—she'd walk around for months carrying the same Nancy Drew mystery or junior high biography of some aging movie star. She could write in shaky capitals; she could cook fried eggs and make toast and tea. She managed fine in her own way, so long as someone was there to tuck her in at night, help her choose what to wear, wipe the corners of her mouth. Things Mag or Hank or Lily could do as well as Reba, except that, for whatever reason, none of them could just then. That was what they told Reba, and Reba believed them. She imagined Tonia grunting to herself in a corner the way she did when she was sad, and she decided to go home.

She told herself Tonia was the reason why, and she imagined that the relief flooding her when she made this decision had nothing to do with her loneliness or the way she'd failed to fit in at school, nothing to do with the sleepless nights she spent studying after finishing work at Nico's Pizza Palace. She went to the Dean's office in the same exhausted fog in which she did everything then, her skin greasy from bad food and lack of sleep, and only when he tried to convince her to take a leave of absence did she understand she wasn't coming back. The Dean had a small, pitying smile: A rest, he suggested. Some relaxation. As if she had the means to buy those things. She should quit her job, he said. Perhaps she was working too hard? He passed his hand over the dark waves of his hair, and Reba glared at him. Later, she'd tell people she left school because of money, that if one person had held out a hand, offered a loan, her whole life might have been different. She might have stayed in school; she might have paid someone to help Mag with Tonia or moved her whole family to Springfield. But none of these things were true.

She left because she needed to; she looked the Dean coldly in the eye and quit outright instead, leaving behind no one who mattered. She hadn't made a single friend.

It was June when Reba returned to Rockledge, and her house didn't look as she remembered it. During her stay in Springfield she'd airbrushed details from her memory: the way the shingles were cracked and moldy along the north side, the way the bushes grew over the windows, the way the pond scum turned the water green. Everything seemed to have gotten worse while she was away. No flowers out front where she remembered them; this year Mag hadn't planted a single thing. No screens up, no storm windows down, no lawn, no paint on the shutters, no hammock hung. Tonia ran wild through the knee-high grass, holding her hands before her as she directed an imaginary steed. No money anywhere—all the chickens had vanished with Bowen, and Mag in her first frenzy had sold off the barns and twenty acres for a song, investing the proceeds in a '65 Nova, an ancient Cadillac, and a '68 VW van, all of which clustered near the front door waiting for her to learn to fix them.

"I don't miss your father at all," Mag said. "I'm better off without him."

Inside, the house looked like a graveyard for dead gadgets. Toasters that had been around forever, blow-dryers bought with trading stamps, ashtrays with hidden fans for eating smoke. In Reba's absence, Mag had taught herself to fix the junk no one else would bother with. She'd put an ad in the *Pennysaver,* she told Reba proudly. She had customers. And on the basis of these she'd switched to part-time at the VA Hospital, acting as if they could live on the small change she was making with her hands.

Reba, walking into this and feeling mature and clear-

eyed, did what she thought any sensible person would: She
got a job. She looked around for two weeks and found that
no one was hiring, and finally she ended up at the VA, right
where Mag had spent all those years. They gave her a
desk, an office of sorts, and a plastic nameplate printed
"Reba Dwyer—Assistant Manager, Nights," none of which
made up for her dirty job in the basement running the
animal quarters where the doctors kept their experi-
mental stock. Rooms full of rat cages, rooms full of cats,
baying beagles, chortling pigeons, quiet rabbits. A goat, a
ram, and a ewe; six sad monkeys with plastic plates in their
heads. More smells than the Dwyers' old barn, worse
smells than a field full of cowflops on a summer day. In
place of theory and composition, counterpoint and voice,
recitals noon and night and piano lessons in-between, she
had animal sounds, a chorus of voices ringing off the cold
tile, shattering on the metal. Grunting, groaning, squeal-
ing, screaming, sighing, whispering. She'd have thought it
sounded like an army of men in love if she hadn't sworn off
men. Reba needed five hands—two to work, two to cover
her ears, one to hold her nose. And blinders for her mind,
so she couldn't think. After six weeks of sniffing manure
and hauling litter, she told her mother she had to quit.

"It's the pits," she told Mag late one night. "I can't
take it."

"Give it a chance," Mag said. "Maybe it'll get better
now that Aleks is gone."

"Aleks," Reba said in disgust. A one-armed Greek
who spoke hardly any English, he'd been Reba's only help.
He'd leered at her and crooned lewd foreign songs,
flashed his loose wet smile from doorways until the hairs
rose on Reba's neck. Reba had hated him, but his retire-
ment left her short-handed. "Worse," she told her mother

gloomily. "It'll just get worse. There's too much work already."

Mag scratched her black-and-white hair, picked up a wrench, and said, "So why don't we get them to hire Tonia? Kill two birds with one stone."

"Tonia?" Reba said.

"It's worth a try."

Reba took this to be a crazy idea, especially coming from Mag. Mag's hands might work, might even be quick and clever, but her mind was floating somewhere behind the husband she didn't miss. Mag took a screwdriver from the rack by her chair and pried open the belly of Joey Crane's radio-controlled model airplane. "Well," she said, peering into the tangled insides. "It beats working at the grocery store."

Reba had to admit that this was true. Mag had found Tonia a job stocking shelves at Bob's Red & White Grocery, but Tonia's doughy face had scared the customers away. They'd jumped at her big clotted squeals of laughter or fear, which almost anything could set off: dead fish arranged on ice, falling cabbage, breaking bottles. Bob had fired Tonia after a week. He said, "I can't have a kid doing this," and when Reba pointed out that Tonia had turned eighteen, Bob had only shrugged and said, "Irregardless." Reba and Mag told Tonia they needed her help at home, but Tonia wouldn't buy it. She wanted a real job, she said, one she left home for each day.

"You'd be together," Mag pointed out. "That's something."

"I'll think about it," Reba said. "But I'd rather quit."

"The money's good," Mag said. "And what else are you going to do? If we hadn't got rid of the piano you could give lessons. . . ."

Reba picked up a stray hair dryer and then told Mag

what she'd never admitted before. "I'm scared of the animals," she said. "You know?"

Mag hooted. "You?" she said. "After growing up here?"

"Me," Reba said, understanding her mother's laughter. She'd helped drown kittens when they overran the barn, helped Luke Wyatt gut turkeys for the holidays, pulled dead puppies from a pregnant dog. All this, all the animal life that goes on in a place like Rockledge, and she couldn't look a two-pound rat in the eye without getting the willies. The hospital seemed to turn the rats strange, the lights, the food, the noise getting to them the way something had gotten her father's chickens. She dreamed, sometimes, that the animals shrieked each other to death, that after she left each night they all stood in their cages and engaged in howling duels. The breeding rats got old and yellow and grew big fangs. The rat pups died of strange diseases; the cats drew Reba's blood with their razor claws. Reba worked in a cold sweat, nervous all the time and dreaming of animal revolts. She didn't think her feelings had anything to do with more than this job, didn't connect them with the fact that she'd lost her father and given up singing as a childish thing.

Mag, who'd always thought Reba's singing was foolish, didn't know any of this. She stripped the red coating from a piece of wire and said, "Tonia might help. She's always been good with the animals." And that was how they left it when they went to bed.

Reba went to work the next day thinking of Tonia, who'd never crossed an animal in her life. They used to find her out back, singing to the birds; the cats used to pile on top of her like she was something good to eat. She could call down swallows, talk to squirrels; she had the voice, the animal magic. A rat bit Reba that afternoon, and while she was soaking her thumb in Epsom salts she thought about Tonia home at night, wandering through the toasters that mined their living room. She went to the woman in Personnel and said, "Hey—how about we hire my sister for Aleks's job? She's good with animals, and it's only minimum wage. And who else are you going to get to do it?"

"Your mother already called," the woman said blandly. "It's worth a try."

She shuffled some papers and filed some forms, and the next Reba knew, Tonia was working for her. Tonia couldn't do what Aleks had done, couldn't lift heavy bags or haul litter or mix special diets. But she could mop the floors with disinfectant and clean cages and fill water bottles, and Reba was glad to have her. When Mag asked, a week or so later, how Tonia was working out, Reba said, "Fine. We're both learning."

She was telling the truth. Tonia changed the feel of that basement—with her there, Reba felt that the beasts were on her side. Tonia could move a nest of rat pups without making the mother crazy, separate two fighting dogs with a few soft words. She could hypnotize a cat by stroking a small patch on its belly. When the monkeys returned after a spell upstairs, Tonia groomed them until they stopped plucking at their pelts. She dyed her tan coveralls pink and tied her hair up with fat pink strings, and she lettered a sign in red marker to set on her desk when she went to the bathroom: BACK IN 5.

Reba was working harder than ever, but she felt good, she felt at home. Her stomach settled down and she lost the nervous sweats. She found that she almost looked forward to work; for the first few weeks she hardly minded that they never got out on time. They were supposed to punch out at eleven, but they couldn't go home until they were done and they were always late. Midnight, twelve-thirty, one; sometimes as late as two. Mag would grow nervous waiting for them. "Everything okay?" she'd ask. "Any problems?" "No," Reba would tell her. "Everything's cool."

And it was until the night she ran into Luke Wyatt. This was at the Rockledge Inn, on a cloudy evening when the stars poked through one or two at a time, as if someone were pricking the darkness with a pin. Reba hadn't seen Luke since she left for music school, hadn't run into him since her return home and wasn't even sure he was in town. His family's turkeys had died, she knew, hit by the same plague that killed her father's chickens. And his father had sold the farm to a developer named Simkowicz, who'd paved the hill and was building garden apartments along the crest. Luke told her the rest while he poured her a beer. "I moved into the top floor of my grandfather's house in town," he said. "I've been working as a carpenter's helper—odd jobs, this and that. You know. And paying on a little chunk of land I bought in Conway." He drew a complex map on a napkin, trying to show Reba where his land was. Then he said, "What are you doing back here?"

Reba explained about her father's disappearance and Tonia's return, carefully avoiding any mention of how hard she'd found school. Luke nodded and said, "I guess I heard that—I just didn't realize you'd come back." He paused and scratched his head, looking Reba over. "So listen," he continued. "How about you meet me up at my land Tuesday, around sunset. It's not so hard to get to, and it's really pretty—it'd be like old times down at the Gorge. I'll bring some beer. . . ."

"Can't," Reba said. "I have to work until eleven."

"So meet me after. Full moon's Monday—we'll have plenty of light."

Reba thought for a minute and then said, "Sure," partly because she hadn't had a date since she'd come home and she wanted to start small. She'd sworn off men but Luke was her friend and hardly counted as one. No big deal, she thought—she and Tonia would just finish up on time for once. No talking to the animals, no fooling around.

When Tuesday came, she told Mag they'd be home early. "I'll drop Tonia off right after work," she said. "And then I'm going out."

"Out? Where's out?"

"Out, out. I'm going on a date."

"Good for you," Mag said.

Reba shrugged and said, "It's only Luke," and when Mag asked how she planned to get done on time, Reba told her not to worry.

The next day, Reba sat Tonia down before they got started. "No fooling around tonight, okay?" she said. "I want to get done by eleven." She listed their chores on a neat chart and showed Tonia what she wanted done by when.

"Like a race?" Tonia asked.

"Like a race," Reba said, and with that she sent Tonia off and went to clean the rat cages. The rats snapped and chattered at her but she ignored them, moving up and down the rows of cages like an ox. Click, pull, empty, fill, click, move on to the next; tossing out the dirty litter and replacing it with fresh. A handful of pellets, clean water bottle, done. She wasn't thinking about Tonia or the animals or anyone but Luke, who'd looked much better than she'd remembered and was looking better each minute in her mind—he knew how she'd grown up and he liked her anyway. She was feeling pretty good by six o'clock. Efficient, organized, thinking how, if every night went like this, she might have a social life again. How she'd buy a used piano, start giving lessons, bang her life into some sort of shape; maybe take some night courses at the university. She finished the rats, thinking they might get done early after all. She'd do the food and water in the other rooms, have Tonia do the floors. She skipped off to the cat room happy and opened the door with a little flourish. Inside, a hundred furry heads and one blond one turned guiltily toward her.

"Tonia!" she cried. "Shit! I told you not to let them out!"

"But I shut the door," said Tonia, beaming. "See? They're all here."

All the cats were in the room, just as Tonia had said, but all the cages were empty. The cats swirled around Tonia, who sat on a broken bag of cat food in the center of the floor.

"I was *helping*," Tonia said, turning her eyes from Reba's face. "Once the bag broke, I thought it'd be smart to let them all eat here." A cat crawled under her chin and butted his head into the hollow there. Tonia arched her neck to cradle it.

"You're too much," Reba said. "How're we going to get them back in?"

"Don't be mad," Tonia said softly. "I can do it." She bent down low to the cats and began chanting something secret to them. Reba heard this:

> "Lawrenz Rat lives here,
>   he is the King of,
>   Rats! A crown he wears,
>   on his head. His eyes
>   are red and his teeth

will bite if you don't,
go in!'"

Any other night, Reba might have laughed; Tonia had been making up animal stories for as long as anyone could remember. There had been one, years ago, about a family of snails; one about the chickens, of course; another about three swans who lived beneath the pond. But this one was new. "Who's Lawrenz?" Reba asked.

Tonia rolled her eyes and looked mysterious. "Secret," she said. She made a clicking noise with her tongue and swept the cats back into their cages.

Reba shook her head, hugged her sister, and said, "Thanks. You love these little hairballs, don't you?"

Tonia draped the last cat around her neck like a feather boa. "Sure," she said. "You want to pat this one?"

"Later," Reba said. "Remember our race? We have to get back to work."

"The race!" Tonia said, and put the last cat away. "Let's do the floors."

Tonia grabbed a broom and swept so hard the litter flew into the corners. Reba gave directions step by step, knowing Tonia would be all right as long as she knew exactly what to do. When they finished, Tonia looked at the digital watch Reba had given her so she wouldn't confuse the hour and the minute hands. "Seven-thirty!" she sang. "Time for dinner."

Reba sighed and then walked Tonia down the hall to their shabby office, where they unwrapped their sandwiches and settled down to eat. At home, Reba knew Mag was stretched in front of the TV, eating the same things. Mag no longer cooked for herself.

A few minutes later, Tonia said, "Dessert?" and Reba, lost in a daydream, snapped at her. "You eat too fast!" she said, and then had to watch Tonia's face crumple in on itself, like the chameleon she'd once left in the sun. Tonia stuffed a lock of hair in her mouth and sucked on it silently. "It's okay," Reba told her. "Really. I'm sorry." She handed Tonia a brownie and said, "Eat this, and then we'll go back to work."

Tonia grabbed the brownie and stuffed it in. Reba had to look away. Tonia chewed certain foods with her mouth open and talked at the same time, so that food stuck to her chin.

"Here," Reba said. "Eat mine too." She'd lost her appetite. She cleared the desk while Tonia finished, hoping to discourage the giant roaches. And then she spread her list out, trying to see how they could hurry things. If she fed the beagles and the goat and the sheep, Tonia could finish the halls and help with the pigeons. They could still do it, Reba thought. Despite the cats. They could finish by ten and there'd still be time to get clean and pretty, still be time to dream. Reba showed Tonia what she wanted her to do.

"Just the halls," she said. "Understand? Don't go in any of the rooms."

Off went Tonia, serious and bent on doing good. Reba cleaned and swept, fed and watered, sang to herself and listened to the animals murmur back. She listened to the swish of Tonia's mop, moving away from her down the hall. Around nine, while she was tossing straw into the ewe's cage, she heard Tonia bellow her name. She flew down the hall, sure Tonia had been bitten, only to find Tonia in a pool of water by the tipped-over washbucket. Tonia bellowed louder when Reba reached her, looking over Reba's shoulder with a startled face, yelling and then laughing when the ewe who'd crept up behind Reba poked its dirty black nose in Reba's hair. Reba shrieked, scared half to death. Tonia thought Reba was playing and shrieked back. In another room the monkeys howled; Reba slipped and fell into the water and the ewe lay down beside them both, ending Reba's plans right there. They had to clean up the ewe and the floor and themselves, quiet the howling monkeys, calm the barking dogs. They had to sponge down the walls, feed the pigeons, feed the other animals; eleven-thirty came and went before Reba could send Tonia for her shower.

In their office, Reba slipped off her wet uniform and took some deep breaths to relax, wondering how she was going to survive another week, another day. Wondering how she was going to live. She put her head down on her desk and saw Springfield, her dorm room all her own, nice clothes, handsome men. All those girls from the suburbs leading tidy lives. Tonia came in half an hour later, flushed from her shower, and rested her hand on Reba's neck. She'd dried her hair with her head held upside down beneath the blower, so that it stood out around her face in a spiky globe. "Lawrenz Rat," she sang. "Lawrenz Rat, ate a cat, wore a hat, had a bat, couldn't sat, he was so fat, he broke his back. . . ." She rolled her eyes and looked at Reba, waiting for Reba to add a line.

"His head was flat," Reba said grimly. "Like mine."

"Why don't you go wash?" Tonia said. "It's late."

It was well past midnight when they headed home in Reba's rusty Cutlass. Tonia punched the radio buttons rapidly, catching parts of jingles and fragments of songs and singing these back to Reba. Reba wouldn't laugh; she was cold and her hair was wet. When they got home, they found Mag in the living room, surrounded by the pieces of an old space heater. The room was dark except for the small light near Mag's chair; Reba tripped over a blow-dryer on her way to the kitchen, just as Mag was trying to figure out the soldering iron.

"Jesus!" Reba shouted. "This place is such a pigpen!" She stomped across the linoleum and poured herself a drink. "Luke called," Mag said from the other room. "Said he missed you tonight."

"Great," Reba said. "Why didn't you ask him over? Maybe he knows how to use that soldering iron. Maybe he knows how to fix this house."

"Don't need to get nasty," Mag said. "Come sit."

Reba poured some juice for Tonia and then sat grumpily at Mag's knee, thinking that the living room looked like a battlefield strewn with blown-up tanks. Tonia took her juice without a word and huddled on a footstool, hunched the way she used to be when Bowen was in a bad mood.

"This has got to change," Reba told her mother. "I'm serious."

"What's the matter?"

"Tonia," Reba said, "Tonia . . ." She didn't mean to do it, but she started to cry, knowing she was going to blame Tonia if they didn't all change their lives. "The cats," Reba sniffled, hating herself. "And then the bucket, and the monkeys . . ."

Tonia hung her head and said, "I lost the race. Lawrenz Rat, his head was flat."

Mag laid her hand on Reba's shoulder, something she hadn't done in years. "So?" she said. "Wasn't it just a pretend race?"

Reba sighed and said it was. Tonia smiled.

"Besides," Mag said. "I made you both a present."

Tonia clapped her hands. Mag swept a curtain from the dark heap by her chair. "Ta-da!" she said. "Loomis dropped this off with the space heater—said it was only going to the dump otherwise. I fixed it up real easy."

Under the curtain was a cracked aquarium with a broken hood. Mag had sealed the glass with some sort of putty, glued the hood together and installed a new light. The floor was strewn with fine pink gravel.

"Fishes!" Tonia said. A swarm of neon tetras, striped red and blue, swam through soft green plants. "Where'd you get them?"

"Woolworth's," Mag said modestly. "I went into Northampton."

"Alone?" Reba said. "You went in alone?" Sometimes her mother amazed her.

Mag shrugged as if this were no big deal—Mag, who hadn't gone anywhere but work since Bowen left. Tonia swirled her pinky in the tank and crooned, "Fishes, fishes, fishes—come see Tonia." She made one, two, three small circles. The fish gathered around her finger.

"They're for your room," Mag said to Tonia. "We're going to do it over."

"We are?" Reba said.

"Don't you think it's time?"

"We could move the tools into the garage," Reba said.

"Paint the shutters," said Mag. "Do some things, get out a little—I asked Lily and Max over for supper, and I made plans with them to go to the fair, Lily and Max and all of us. I called Hank, and he's coming too. And I asked your friend Luke to join us. I never see him anymore."

"You what?" Reba said. For a minute, she'd forgotten Luke.

"You heard me," Mag said. "Time we changed some things."

Mag painted Reba's and Tonia's rooms, and she cleaned the house and dyed her hair. She had Lily and Max over for supper twice, and she made strudel. She said to Reba, "I'll look after Tonia more," and she kept that promise too, even telling Reba she could quit work if she hated it so bad. But Reba didn't quit, or not then anyway—although things went from bad to worse in the VA basement, one night following another in a string of animal catastrophes, she didn't see how she could leave until she somehow got Tonia settled.

She and Luke got together a couple of times, when they managed to mesh their days off. They had a picnic on his land, which turned out to be a big slab along the side of a rocky hill; they had hamburgers one night at the Rockledge Inn and lunch one day in Northampton, still just friends. Reba told Luke about Tonia and asked him what she should do. "Simple," he told her. "Find someone who likes Tonia, who can do your job as well as you do. Then leave. Get another job. Cut yourself a little slack."

"Easy for you to say," she said, thinking all Luke meant to give was his advice. She was surprised when he went further than that. He *did* know how to use a soldering iron, as things turned out; he also knew how to fix the leak in the basement and hang the screens and repair the broken toilet, how to flatter Mag and make Tonia laugh. Reba would come home from work and find Luke in the living room, cleaning cupboards or carving a sign for Mag to hang at the end of the driveway. The sight didn't please her as much as it might have, and she found herself asking him what he was doing.

"Just helping out," he told her. "What are friends for? I hate to see you working so hard." Some days he brought flowers; some nights he cooked; and all without pushing Reba for so much as a kiss. She was waiting for that, but she couldn't make herself take the first step. When she stood back a little she could see that Luke was good-looking: tall, slim-hipped, fair. His beard hid his chin and much of his girlish mouth. He was kind, he was gentle, his manners were good. He was as helpful as a Boy Scout in need of badges, and yet when she dreamed of him she dreamed him bodiless, just a head. She couldn't imagine him with his clothes off, barking and groaning like a seal. When he rested his hand on her shoulder or kissed her cheek, nothing stirred in her except gratefulness. She knew she had much to be grateful for—when things grew so bad at the VA that she was in danger of losing her job, Luke began coming in late to help. He swept and cleared with a vengeance, and he did more than that—he introduced Reba to a friend of his who had worked as a janitor upstairs for years, a man named Grey who thought Reba's job was worth having. Grey wore his silver hair swept back in a smooth wave, and he thought Tonia was wonderful. He said to Reba, "If you ever think about leaving here I wish you'd let me know—I'd love this job." He palmed two quarters and pulled them from Tonia's ears, causing her to squeal in delight. "Your sister and I would get along fine," he said to Reba. "You wouldn't have to worry."

Luke looked at Reba and mouthed "So?" but Reba shook her head; she liked her steady paycheck and thought she could live on hold, more and more aware of Luke's feelings for her, more and more tied by his help, without deciding anything. She drifted from day to day and night to night, letting Luke tidy up the frayed edges of her life. She went on that way until Labor Day, when Mag showed her the postcard Bowen had sent. On the front was a picture of a deep ravine, shadowed by tall trees and cut by a series of rapids. Rafts dotted the whitewater like floating rocks. On the back was a line describing the picture: "Ohiopyle, PA. Home of the World-Famous Youghiogheny River Gorge." No return address, no signature, no message other than a few terse lines. "Am well," Reba read out loud. "Took raft through rapids, camped in woods, saw stars. Unusual people. Men wear hats."

"Men wear hats?" Reba said to her mother. "Where the hell is Ohiopyle?"

"South of Pittsburgh," Mag said. "Almost in West Virginia. You can hardly see it on the map."

"We could call the police there," Reba said. "Maybe somebody's seen him . . ."

"What's the use?" Mag said. "Leaving home isn't a crime. And anyhow, the postcard's dated a month ago."

"Men wear hats," Reba said to Luke on their way to the fair. "You believe that's what he wrote?"

"Forget about it," Luke said. "Forget about him. He's gone. Let's have a good time."

At the first booth he showed off his throwing arm and won Reba and Tonia stuffed monkeys. He tucked the dangling monkey arms into the back of his belt, so that they hung behind him like a double tail, and then he reached for Reba and kissed her clumsily on the mouth. His lips were soft; his tongue was shy. He'd kissed her better that night in the parking lot, a year ago now, when she'd been about to leave town. He'd kissed her better when he was fourteen and exploring, and his clumsiness told Reba he was in love. Reba drew away from him and moved to another booth, still thinking about Bowen's card.

Max won Lily a Chinese mask, which Lily wore backward on her chopped gray hair, so that she appeared to have two faces. And then Lily kissed Max on the dirt path, possibly to mock Reba and Luke or maybe just to embarrass everyone. Lily teased Hank, watching openmouthed, about his own girlfriends; Hank, who didn't have a girlfriend, clung to Reba's side the way he had when he was small, and Reba let him since this kept Luke a body away. Luke took the hint. He hung back a few steps, and when they got to the sheds he offered to buy everyone a beer. "Let's go get a drink," he said. "Cool off a little."

Reba wanted to cool off away from him. She wanted to look at the animals; she wanted some time away from this group that was feeling too much like a family. She said, "You go ahead—I'm going to look at the pigs and maybe try some of the rides."

Luke shrugged and smiled and walked away. Mag and Lily and Max and Tonia followed him, leaving Hank behind with Reba. Together, Hank and Reba walked over to the livestock pens. "Some porkers," Hank said, leaning over the fence. He touched her hair with wistful fingers and then touched his own. "Look at this," he said. "Twenty-one, and falling out already."

"Think of it as a noble forehead," Reba said. "I'd give you some of mine if I could."

Hank smiled at her. "You all right? Seems like I've hardly seen you since you've been home."

"It's been pretty crazy," Reba said, wondering if Mag had shown Hank the card. "Between Mag and Tonia. Luke's helped out a lot."

"I noticed," Hank said. "You in love with him?"

"I don't know."

"So why'd you come back? Not that I'm not glad to have you . . ."

Reba shrugged. "Seemed like the right thing to do," she said. "Maybe it'll work out. Mag seems to be straightening out, and Tonia likes work . . ."

"Mag likes Luke," Hank said. "Tonia too."

"Everyone likes Luke," said Reba. "Even me. Especially me."

"Yeah, but . . ." Hank said. "If you want to get out of here for good and all . . ."

"I know," Reba said. "I don't want to stay, but I can't figure out how to leave."

"It's tough," Hank said. "Want to go for a ride?" Ellie Crane walked by with her four little boys and smiled at Reba, then looked again as if she'd mistaken her for someone else.

"How about a spin on that?" Hank said. He pointed to the ride nearest them, a huge tall pole with tiny planes suspended from long, thick rods. This was the ride he'd always liked best; Reba, afraid of most rides, had never been on it with him. But it was hot on the ground, and breezy up above. Reba, feeling courageous, said yes. They got in a blue plane with a lightning bolt splashed across its side. Hank took the seat with the steering wheel.

"Does it go fast?" Reba asked.

Hank shook his head. The attendant started them up and the children filling the other planes squealed as the pole spun, flaring out the long spokes so that they rose in a widening circle.

"Hold on!" Hank said.

They flew above the ground. Reba looked down and saw the Crane boys tormenting a cow, Aurora Swenson strutting the blue ribbon she'd won for her watermelon pickles. She heard pigs and cows and ducks and geese and horses and chickens; across the field she saw Luke handing Mag and Lily and Max and Tonia cups and cans. She tried to remember where Luke's family had scattered to, some to Gardner, some to Pennsylvania, some to Springfield, each flung in a different direction as if their farm had exploded when it was sold, leaving Luke alone among the rubble. Of course he was lonely; of course he wanted to graft himself onto some other family, even hers. Their

70

plane swerved and Reba gasped. It was connected to the supporting rod by some sort of bearing or joint, and when Hank turned the steering wheel they swung in toward the pole or out toward space, as if they might fly away. "Angels," Reba's father had once called all of them, even Luke.

"Look!" Hank shouted happily. "Look!"

He waved at the world beneath them. When Reba looked beyond the fairgrounds, she saw the Connecticut River, the Holyoke range, the cluster of squat buildings rising on Luke's old farm and mocking the families who still tried to make a living there. She looked down at the fair again and saw her family watching them—her family, her life. *We grew up like dogs,* she thought. Nice dogs ruined by bad training. Mag and Bowen, in their confusion, had dealt out pleasure and approval, permission to do certain things one day and denial of that permission another, punishment and anger and coldness as well, and none of it had seemed to bear any relation to what she and Hank and Tonia did. No causes, no effects—just random actions that fell as unexpectedly as rain from a sunny sky. *Men wear hats,* she thought. They'd never known what was allowed or disallowed, any more than Ginger had. Their household ran on a magnificent illogic, tempered only by Lily's exasperated efforts to set things in order, and the three of them had darted like lost puppies from one corner to the next, heads down, trying only to stay out of the way.

She watched as Luke bought another drink and handed it to Chloe McCarthy, an old classmate of his who'd walked over from the tractor pull and smiled at him. Chloe had dark hair and a darker reputation, and when she rested her hand on Luke's shoulder something fierce and nasty seized Reba's heart, which she tried to beat down. *What is that?* she thought. *What do I care?* If she didn't love him he must have the right to love someone else. Let him fix Chloe's basement, take care of Chloe's sister. She gripped the dashboard hard, trying to steady her whirling head. Her hands turned white and stiffened, until they felt like wood. When the ride stopped, she couldn't get up.

"Reba?" Hank said. "Want to go?"

She sat frozen, still seeing the fields spread out in a circling blur that held everyone and everything she'd ever known. Still seeing Luke and Chloe. She imagined that the scene around her was a photograph and then she snipped Luke away; the white hole where he should have been disfigured everything. Hank pried her fingers loose from the plane. "Come on," he said. "Time to get back."

When she stood she fainted dead away, as hard and fast as when she'd toppled from the bleachers at her high school graduation. She woke to find Luke bending over her, her family blurred behind him.

"Wake up," he whispered urgently. He'd turned the color of a lamb. "Reba? You all right?"

When he kissed her she felt as if she'd just been saved from an accident. For a minute she saw a dark road, late at night, strewn with bodies and broken cars. And then she saw Luke and she made a decision—not a permanent one, not for life, but just something to get her through the next few months or years. "Luke," she said. She wound her arms around his neck and kissed him back.

DISTANT
HEARTBEATS

I T was Hank's belief that his sister Reba slept with Luke Wyatt for the first time the night Luke torched the kitchen curtains. Hank was sharing Luke's apartment then—this was the winter of 1977, sometime after Luke had come back into the Dwyers' life, long enough so that when Hank got evicted from his single room at the Hillview, which had finally been condemned, it seemed natural for him to share Luke's place. It was big enough: the whole upper floor—kitchen, living room, three bedrooms and more—of Luke's grandfather's house on Main Street. And it was full that February night, as it was almost every night. Strangers, friends, and friends of friends sprawled on the floor and the furniture, drinking Pabst and eating popcorn. Luke was showing Hank how to swallow fire.

"Take the coat hanger, so," Luke said, deftly untwisting the neck and unkinking the bends. Hank stood next to him with another hanger, trying to do as Luke said, but his hands were twice the size of Luke's and he broke the neck right off. Reba, who was watching from the lounger, laughed and said Hank was the clumsiest man she'd ever known. Luke made a face at Hank and kept on going.

"Wad of cotton on the end, lighter fluid on the cotton . . ." Luke lit a match and touched it to the end. "Presto!" He tilted his neck and opened his mouth, as if he meant to chug a beer in record time. When he waved his wand everyone leaned forward; the women nearby screamed and jumped back when the flaming tip caught the curtains over the sink. They were made of something pink and soft that burned like paper, only faster.

"Hank!" Reba shouted. "The faucet!"

Hank turned on the tap and swatted the curtains down, but they broke into burning chunks that took off like butterflies. The guests yelled and stamped and poured beer on them; in a minute they were out and everyone stood staring at the charred remains and the ashes in the sink. Hank burned a hole in his favorite blue work shirt, but no one got hurt.

"Jesus," Luke said. "What a rush, huh?"

"No problem," Hank said. Reba laughed; some woman no one knew applauded quietly. Hank rinsed the sink out, thinking how the place always got trashed during these parties. He and Luke had furnished it half with Luke's grandfather's castoffs and half with his grandmother Lily's; in the six months they'd lived together, almost all the nice stuff had been destroyed. The curtains went the way of the rocking chair, the glass-topped table, the mantel clock, and the lamp, but Luke said not to worry about it and threw the curtain rod away as if he didn't care. The party broke up soon after that. Hank yawned his way around the rooms, tossing beer bottles in plastic bags and butts in a coffee tin. When he got to the extra bedroom and opened the door, he found Reba cuddling Luke and rubbing his hair the way she used to rub their cats.

"Sick?" Hank asked Reba. Someone always got sick at their parties.

"A little," Reba said. Luke just groaned.

Hank squeezed Luke's shoulder and looked at Reba, who made a face behind Luke's back. "You staying over tonight?" Hank asked his sister. "I can make up the bed." He hated for Reba to drive home alone so late.

Reba nodded, so Hank hauled Luke into Luke's own room and then got Reba settled. Toward morning, a noise woke Hank up. He stumbled out of his room in his shorts and his T-shirt and met Reba in the hall, wrapped in an old pink robe with a torn pocket that made her look about ten. She was tiptoeing out of Luke's room; her hand was still on the doorknob, trying to close it silently. She flushed brick red when she saw Hank.

That Luke and Reba were sleeping together was a revelation to Hank; he hadn't known they did, and in fact didn't know Reba had slept with anyone. But he didn't take this seriously. It was late; they were drunk; these things happen. Or at least they happened to everyone but him. He failed completely to realize what was going on, and so he was caught off guard in June, when Luke broke the big news.

Reba was over that night, making Hank and Luke grilled tuna and cheese on toast. Hank and Luke sat on the sunporch afterwards, watching the sky turn red while Reba did the dishes. They drank beer and looked at the trees and at the dark birds roosting in them until Luke cleared his throat and said, "You know, we're getting married."

Hank turned his head so fast his neck hurt. "You and Reba?"

"Me and Reba."

"How come?" Hank said. Which was not what he meant—anyone with any sense, he thought, would want to marry Reba. But he'd assumed Reba was visiting, just hanging around Rockledge helping Tonia and Mag while she figured out her life. Every month now, he'd expected her to leave. Luke or no Luke—they were old friends who'd gotten friendlier, was all he'd thought. Not this.

"She's pregnant," Luke said. "And we want the baby."

Hank felt his face go red. He thought of how Reba had been pale and slow the past few weeks, strangely queasy and more silent than usual. "Why didn't she tell me?" he asked.

"We just found out for sure—it's only since May."

"Jesus. Is it what you want?"

Luke looked out at the square, where a cloud of starlings was coming in over a cracked birdbath. "It'll be okay," he said. "It'll be good."

Hank excused himself and headed back to the kitchen, thinking how Luke had been through this three years ago when he married Sally Lambert, and how nothing had come of it. Reba stood at the sink washing dishes absently. "Hey," she said, when Hank touched her shoulder.

"Hey yourself. What's with the wedding plans?" A lock of curly red hair had escaped from Reba's braid; Hank tucked it back in absentmindedly and said, "Twenty's awful young."

"Not so young," she said. "It'll be all right."

"Would you do it if you weren't pregnant?"

She shrugged. "But I am," she said. Her face clouded over and Hank stole a look at her waist. Her jeans were fully zipped and seemed no tighter than usual. He patted her shoulder and she reached around for his hand. "It's okay," she said. "It's what I want."

Hank straightened up and made his voice serious. "I'll take care of the wedding, then," he said. "I bet Lily will help."

"Lily," Reba said. "Crazy Lily—I bet she will."

Halfway back to the porch, Hank turned and said, "Where will you live? You're not going to move Luke into the house . . ."

"Here," she said. "If you don't mind. It's cheap, and the three of us will be fine together, and Mag's been good with Tonia lately. I talked to her about it already."

"She knows?"

"Sure," said Reba. "I had to tell her. Typical Mag—she hardly batted an eye. So can I stay here?"

"Of course," Hank said, pressing his fist to his stomach to keep it from leaping about. In those days, Luke and Reba felt like all he had. "I'd just as soon keep you around."

Hank got lost during the party after the wedding. It wasn't his fault—he was drunk and tired and crazy, and the woods were dense and the moon was lost in a cloud. He'd been up since dawn, cleaning Lily's cabin at Whittaker Lake and getting it ready for the wedding. Reba wanted the ceremony small, so they had just her and Hank and Luke and Luke's grandfather; Mag and Tonia and Lily; Lily's Max and the minister. Ten minutes before the ceremony, Lily took Reba aside and tried to talk her out of going through with it, and Hank overheard them. He watched as Lily put her arm around Reba's shoulder, the two white feathers on her hat bobbing like moth antennae. "Don't do it," Hank heard Lily whisper. "You don't have to—you can just walk out of here right now, before it's too late. No one will mind."

"I *can't*," Hank heard Reba hiss. "Everyone's *here.*"

"Oh, the hell with them," Lily said impatiently. "They love you. They'll understand. And Luke will thank you someday."

"I'm pregnant," Reba said bitterly. "Understand?"

"Of course I do," Lily said. "You think I wouldn't help out?"

But Reba turned her back on Lily and went through with the ceremony. Afterwards, Lily turned her cabin over to a bunch of Hank and Reba's friends, so they could make a big party, and she locked her eleven cats in the basement so they wouldn't eat everything. This was August, stinky hot: the first thing Hank did was tap a couple of kegs, just to keep cool. Everyone drank except Reba, who couldn't because of being pregnant. She sat looking sleepy as a lizard from the heat.

By nightfall the party was out of control. Lily sat on the deck like a queen bee, holding hands with Max and watching calmly while people danced, fell into the lake, swam with their clothes on and off. Tonia sat by the edge of the water with Grey, her new friend from work; between them they raised a sand castle with towers and turrets and a wide moat and a drawbridge made from a shingle. Luke's tape deck blared out over the lake as they ate meatballs and salad and cold cuts and dip, and the carrot wedding cake Mag had contributed. Mag cried when Reba cut it. "It's a shame," she said. "A shame your father couldn't be here."

"Doesn't bother me," Reba said calmly. The knife sank smoothly through the icing, and Max brought out champagne for a toast. Hank drank everything anyone handed him and watched Luke and Reba together, wondering if Reba meant it when she leaned her head into Luke's shoulder. She looked calm and quiet enough, pleased if not exuberant, and when Lucinda Evans fell into the lake, Reba laughed so hard her eyes ran. Kevin Glover's sister, Jane, got drunk and sang songs on the stairs to the deck, and Lily liked that and the stars so much that she waded into the water right up to her sky-blue shorts, declaring that everything was just delightful. Around then, or perhaps shortly after, Hank stumbled into the woods, wanting only to take a leak—Paul Simmons and Patty Boyer had been in the bathroom for hours. And Hank got lost, right there in Lily's woods that he knew as well as anywhere. Lily had been out with her chain saw and had turned half the trees he'd used as landmarks into stumps; he tripped over a dogwood root and passed out right there. He woke hollering Reba's name as if he'd lost her in a fire.

Some friends came and found him, fifty feet beyond the cabin. He was crying by then, hunched over his knees. "Reba!" he called, sure she'd been drowned while he'd been lost. But his friends took him back to Reba's chair, where she was opening gifts and holding court, not drowned at all. Her girlfriends buzzed around, keeping track of who'd given what. Lily collected all the ribbons and punched them through holes in a paper plate to make Reba a crazy hat. Reba tied this under her chin, tilted backward so she looked like a donkey. Hank ran up to her and threw his arms around her, pleading with her not to go.

Reba smiled at him gently. "Hank," she said. "Really. You are *so* drunk."

"S'true," he said. "I love you."

"I love you too," she said. "It's okay."

Hank gave her a big wet kiss but only caught half her mouth; everyone cheered and even Luke laughed. Then Hank passed out on the deck. Later, Reba told him that she and Luke tossed him into their car when they went home.

81

Everything changed after the wedding, when Reba moved in for good. For one thing, Hank knew right away that they'd have to switch rooms. Luke and Hank had always used the small bedrooms in the back, leaving the big room near the living room free for parties and company. Hank hadn't counted on hearing Luke and Reba— whatever they'd done up until now they'd done when he was away, probably during the day when he was at work. But that first night they woke him and made him miserable. His head was popping when he shuffled out for coffee the next morning. Luke and Reba were up already, washed and dressed and eating pancakes, and they laughed when he came into the kitchen.

"You look awful," Reba said.

"Couldn't sleep," Hank mumbled. Luke brought him some coffee and loaded a plate with pancakes.

"Choke it down," he said. "You'll feel better."

Hank ate and drank until he did, and then he said, "Listen—would you guys mind moving into the front room?"

Reba blushed and Luke looked uncomfortable.

"You'll have more room," Hank said. "And more privacy."

Luke put his arms around Reba in a way that made Hank's chest hurt. "If you want," Reba said.

They moved Luke and Reba's stuff into the front room later that day and started settling in. Luke, who'd always done odd jobs, took steady work at Maglione's Nursery so he'd have money for the baby—he didn't like Reba paying for things and he made her quit working in the animal quarters, afraid that the fumes and strange diseases there might hurt the baby. Reba fussed about Tonia, but Luke took care of that too—he arranged for his friend Grey to take over Reba's job, which he'd been wanting for months, and Grey promised to take care of Tonia and did. As far as Hank could tell, Tonia seemed delighted with the change.

Their days fell into a quiet pattern. Reba napped in the afternoons and took her time shopping and cooking meals for the three of them. Hank cut back on his hours at Elzenga's print shop, so he could mess around the apartment and fix whatever Reba wanted—lights in the kitchen, shelves in the bedroom, a cabinet around the bare pipes under the bathroom sink. In the late afternoons he'd fix Reba a snack and then settle with her in front of the TV, watching reruns and game shows until Luke came home. Hank felt happy, then; those afternoons reminded him of certain bright days during their childhood, when he and Reba, home from school, magically had the house to themselves. Mag would be at work; Bowen, who was supposed to be watching them, would have crept off somewhere; and Tonia would be outside, pulling Jamie Rondine around in his red wagon. Inside, the house would be quiet, the only sound the soft, comforting buzz of the TV. He and Reba would curl up on the old red sofa and rest, just rest, their heads on the armrests and their feet in each other's laps. No one shouting, no one arguing, no one making them do things they didn't want. Small gray figures had flicked across the screen, consoling them then as they did now.

Sometimes they'd both be asleep when Luke got home, but Luke didn't seem to mind. The three of them had some good times until Reba got so big. This made her unhappy, and Hank couldn't blame her—one day she'd been herself except for a gentle slope of belly, and the next her face had coarsened and spread, her fingers had swollen, and she'd blown out like a sponge dipped suddenly in water. Her normal shape was sleek as a panther, long-limbed, small-bodied, with a pointed, catlike face and all that red hair. Now she looked like one of Mag's brioches, a knob perched atop a doughy mass. Luke leaned his head into her belly and said, "There's a zillion parts moving around in here. I bet it's twins."

"Feels like an army," Reba said. "He's kicking all the time." She was sure the baby was a boy and had even picked out a name.

"Twins run in my family," Luke said. "My great-aunt had two sets."

And sure enough, the next time Hank drove Reba to the Rockledge Clinic, the doctor heard two heartbeats. "Are you the husband?" he asked Hank.

"The brother," Hank said. "The husband's at work."

The doctor raised an eyebrow and said, "Well," but then he let both of them listen. Hank heard tiny tapping sounds, two threads beating like distant drums, calling and answering. African tribes sent messages that way, he thought. Hill to hill. Or was it the Indians, out west? Some strangers somewhere, who knew no English and had no phones and needed messages sent in a hurry. He couldn't stop listening to them; he only vaguely heard the doctor tell Reba that he was concerned about her blood pressure, which had risen a bit, and that he wanted her on a low-salt diet.

Reba was depressed on the way back home. "I look like a cow," she said. "Pretty soon I'll look like a hippo. And then *two* kids to take care of—Luke's going to hate me."

"You're crazy," Hank told her. He pulled into Friendly's and bought her a butterscotch sundae and more sauce and ice cream for home, figuring they'd celebrate after supper. Luke smiled and hugged Reba, as if this was what he'd wanted all along; he slipped pillows behind her back and treated her like she was made of balloons. Hank said he'd make dinners, so Reba could rest, and Luke said, "Good—I'll make breakfasts." When Reba went to bed that night, Hank and Luke sat at the table making plans and Luke, who was working a lot of overtime, told Hank he was glad he was there to keep an eye on Reba.

They took good care of her, but Reba didn't seem so glad. She kept on swelling, her fine features almost lost in the mask of her puffed cheeks, and she started snapping at Hank after the doctor told her she had to stay in bed. Her blood pressure went up and stayed up and she had headaches all the time; once a week she went to the clinic with Hank, where the doctor strapped a pair of transducers over her belly and then shook it as if he were trying to free a pudding from a mold.

"We're checking the babies' heart response to movement," the doctor explained in answer to Hank's bewildered gaze. "Hear how their hearts accelerate and then return to normal? That's good."

Hank could feel his own heart thumping with the babies', speeding in terror, slowing in relief. He wasn't surprised that Reba, enduring all this, grew bad-tempered. When he cooked her steak, she said it tasted like dirt without the salt and besides, he was making her fat. When he made her salad, she said he was starving her out. About this time, she started complaining to Hank of how food talked to her: the *slish* of ketchup sliding from the bottle, the malevolent crackle of dry English muffins, the sucking slow pops of lentil soup. Hank was careful not to look at her when she said these things, but he felt his stomach contract and then seem to lie over on its side. He played food games, trying to cheer her up; he sped soup to her on airplane spoons, zooming them into her mouth from above. Nothing seemed to make her feel better. One afternoon he walked by her room and found her staring into the mirror, and when he said, "What's up?" she threw her hairbrush at him.

"I hate this!" she wailed.

"Hate what?" he said. "Which part?" He thought she meant the doctors, the nurses, the tests.

"This belly!" she said. "It's up to my head and down to my knees, and I've still got weeks to go . . ."

". . . only twelve . . ."

". . . and the two of them rumble around in here like a couple of aliens. And I'm fat and ugly and everyone hates me. Look at my face."

"You look okay," Hank said.

Reba squinted her eyes at him. "I look like shit. And you and Luke are both driving me crazy—I wish you'd just let me alone."

"Whatever you want," Hank said. There was nothing he wouldn't do for Reba; although he couldn't leave her completely alone he started working more in the afternoons, to give her some space, and at night he went out or went into his room so she and Luke could act married alone. He did everything he could think of to make her happy; as far as he could tell, Luke did that and even more. And still, she got so bad by Christmas that he couldn't see what to do.

Luke told him it was just her hormones. "She can't help it," he said. "Her body's acting up, and she's mad at me for making her this way." Hank thought something else was going on—hormones couldn't explain the way Reba sat for hours listening to sounds only she could hear. Lately, she'd become convinced that the walls were full of boring bugs, termites or wood-eating wasps chewing their way through the beams. He remembered how, ever since Reba had been small, she'd had this way of acting mad about something she wasn't mad at, and then getting even madder at him for not guessing the real thing. This time, he couldn't guess.

They were alone on Christmas Day, because Mag and Lily and Tonia had all decided to visit Mag's sister in Chicopee and Reba couldn't make the drive. Luke and Hank cooked Reba a big dinner and then gave her presents. Luke had made a double crib and Hank had made a mobile of flying geese so the twins would have something to look at besides the ceiling during the long winter nights. Reba gave them both sweaters and said she was sorry for being so cranky.

"It's all right," Luke said. "I love you."

"Me too," Hank said.

Reba cried a little, and then they all laughed and told each other everything would be fine.

Reba went into the hospital the day after Christmas. Luke was working, so it was Hank who took her to her clinic appointment, Hank who drove her to the hospital after the doctor took Reba's blood pressure, jiggled the babies and listened to them, frowned and said, "That's it— I want you admitted today." Hank drove home and packed a bag for Reba; by the time he got to the hospital the nurses already had her in bed. The padded side rails were up, making Reba look as though she were trapped in a crib. A tongue depressor was taped to the wall behind her bed like a broken crucifix, and a plastic bag hanging from a pole dripped fluid into her arm. "What's going on?" Hank asked. "What's happening?"

The nurse looked at him. "Are you the husband?"

"The brother," Hank said wearily, reminding himself to call Luke.

The nurse looked at Reba; Reba nodded slightly. The

nurse said to Hank, "Her blood pressure's a little higher than it should be—Dr. Everitt wants her in bed here, where she can rest and where we can can keep an eye on the babies." Hank looked at Reba again: here in the hospital, she suddenly looked sick. Her face was enormously swollen and discolored against the sheets, even her fine nose gone thick and fleshy. Her hands might have belonged to a football player. Hank had never thought things were going so badly. Inside her head, perhaps. Or outside, on her skin. But not in the place in-between, not in her flesh. "Reba," he said. "How do you feel?"

"Headache," she said weakly.

"That's the hydralazine the doctor ordered," said the nurse. "It gives some people a little headache. But it's good for you, and good for the babies—you don't want to hurt those babies, do you? We'd like you to carry them as long as possible."

Reba moaned. "I'll call Luke," Hank said.

Luke came in that night in time to hear the babies talk—the nurse wheeled in a portable fetal heart monitor and wired Reba up, explaining that they'd be listening morning and night now. While Luke held Reba's hands, Hank stood across the room and listened to the two thready beats calling across space to each other, drumming messages. Girl drummers: the doctor had said they were girls. Reba and Luke had picked new names, Marisa and Marianne, and Hank liked to imagine them as teenagers in strange clothes, playing drums in a band. The heartbeats sounded faster to him than the last time he'd heard them.

The next day, and the day after that, Luke visited Reba morning and evening and Hank came by in the afternoons and sat with her, reading the paper or, sometimes, when no one else was around, singing old songs to her in his low voice and trying to get her to join him. Anything to cheer her up—he wasn't much of a singer but Reba didn't seem to care. Mag and Tonia came by on the second day, Mag with a mushroom brioche that Reba couldn't eat, Tonia with a pop-eyed goldfish in a plastic jar. Tonia started to cry when she saw Reba's face. "You got fat!" she wailed.

"Just for a few weeks," Reba said lightly. She held Tonia's hand to her cheek; when she took Tonia's fingertips away, a small dent remained there for half a minute.

Hank stroked Tonia's fuzzy hair and said, "It's just 'cause Reba's going to be a mommy—some mommies puff up before their babies come."

"Like the rats at work?" Tonia said hopefully, and Reba smiled for the first time in days. The truth, although Hank wouldn't have admitted this to anyone, was that Reba looked horrible; the truth was that she looked more and more like Tonia each day. He couldn't pronounce the word the doctor used for Reba's condition, but he could read faces and he knew from Reba's, and from the brittle smiles of the nurses around her, that things weren't going well. The first day the doctor had told them not to worry. "This isn't uncommon," he said. "Especially with a first-time mother having twins. As long as we can keep her blood pressure down the babies will be fine."

Luke and Hank went home that night and drank beer together in the kitchen, telling each other reassuring things. On the second day, when Reba stepped into the bathroom for a minute, Hank thought to ask the nurse what the tongue depressor taped over Reba's head was for. "It's just a precaution," the nurse said lightly.

"What kind of a precaution?"

"What we call a seizure precaution—there's a very slight chance, an extremely small chance, that someone in

Reba's condition could develop seizures, and we want to be prepared for anything."

Hank looked at the tongue depressor again, which was padded on the surface but hard beneath its deceptive covering, like the side rails on Reba's bed. Reba didn't seem to notice it—she lay beached on her sheets like a lost whale, and she wouldn't listen to the doctor or the nurses except to ask, morning and evening, if the babies' heartbeats didn't sound faster to them. She asked no other questions even when, on the last day of December, the doctor came in and said, "I think we need to get the babies out—they're showing some signs of distress."

"When?" asked Hank and Luke together. Reba didn't say anything.

"Tomorrow," the doctor said, still addressing Reba. "We'll give you some magnesium sulfate tonight—the hydralazine's not controlling your blood pressure as well as we'd hoped, and this will flatten you right out. You'll feel a little tired from it—maybe a little hot and flushed. We'll do a C-section tomorrow morning, once your pressure's down. I can't let you carry the girls any longer."

"It's too early!" Luke said. "They're not due for eight weeks."

Hank knew he ought to leave the room. Reba wouldn't look at him or anyone; Luke was clenching and unclenching his hands and walking around in tight circles. "We don't have a choice," the doctor said, his voice still calm and reasonable. "We have to take the babies out tomorrow. Reba? Do you have any questions?"

She rolled her head toward him. "What did I do?" she asked. "Why is this happening?"

The doctor touched her shoulder lightly. "You didn't do anything," he said. "This just happens sometimes. But you shouldn't worry—everything's going to be fine. This is just a normal complication."

When he left, the nurse gave Reba a shot and then placed the transducers on Reba's belly for the last time. Together, Reba and Luke and Hank listened to the babies' joined heartbeats. They were very fast; very far away. They were complex and irregular, as if the girls had learned to speak and were using their new knowledge to send a last message to each other and all of them. It was perfectly clear to Hank that hearts were breaking all around him.

Hank might have suspected what was coming next— all through their childhood, the way Reba had dealt with the worst that had happened was to hide out, hole up, refuse to talk to anyone. In this way, she was not unlike their father. Still, she caught Hank by surprise. She stayed in the hospital for a week after the surgery, not talking to anyone while she mourned the girls. They were delivered dead, which Hank had known would happen from the night they'd drummed their good-bye to him, and which he suspected Reba had somehow known all along. What could they say to each other after that? Almost nothing— when she came home, the three of them tiptoed around the apartment, wept in separate rooms, tried to talk about other things. Luke put the cradle and Hank's mobile and the baby clothes downstairs, in his grandfather's closet. Reba shrank back to her normal size almost immediately, as if what had swollen her had only been air. Much of her hair had fallen out; she cut the rest and then, at the end of January, she asked Hank to move.

"*Move?*" he said. Somehow, even after all that had happened, he'd thought the three of them would continue together forever.

But Reba set her jaw stubbornly. "Please?" she said. "Just move, okay?"

She burst into tears; Luke came in just as Hank was saying no. "What's wrong?" Luke asked.

Hank was all set to tell him when Reba grabbed Hank's arm and pulled him toward her. "He's *moving,*" she said to Luke. "And it's all your fault."

Hank couldn't tell whether he or Luke was more bewildered. Luke looked at Hank and said, "You don't need to go . . ."

"He does so!" Reba said. "He can't stand the way you yell at me . . ."

"I never yell at you!"

Luke was right; he never did. Hank said, "Calm down, Reba. I'm not going anywhere." He thought she was just hysterical.

Luke wrapped his arms around Reba and looked at Hank bitterly. "So go," he said. "Go ahead."

"I don't *want* to—she doesn't want me to either." Hank didn't expect Luke to understand. No matter what happened, he knew Luke would never know Reba the way he did. He stood there waiting for Reba to straighten things out, but she didn't say anything.

Luke led Reba into her room. "I'll help you pack in the morning," he told Hank. He closed the door and Hank heard Reba crying.

Hank went out and got ripped that night, not so much because he wanted to as because he couldn't stand hearing Reba. He started out watching hockey at the Chesterfield Inn, and ended up playing pool with his friend Kevin Glover at the Empty Bucket. Kevin told Hank that he was nuts.

"Come on," he said. "Get real. She's just going through a phase right now—she'll come out of it. As soon as she gets pregnant again, she'll feel better. If you don't want to move, then don't."

They were drinking shots of tequila with beer chasers, and Hank felt as though he could light his breath with just a spark. "Have to," he mumbled.

"Why?"

"Why, why—sometimes there isn't a why."

"Yeah," Kevin said. "Well, don't go getting all philosophical on me."

What Hank wanted to do just then was hit Kevin, or anyone, start a big brawling rumble that would end up in the parking lot. What he wanted to do was break someone's nose. He glared at Kevin. "You wanna fight?"

Kevin laughed at him. "Don't be an asshole," he said. "It's not *my* fault, what's going on."

Hank stuck another quarter in the pool table, and then he broke and started clearing by himself. He sank two bank shots and then a tough combination, playing the way he only could when his mind was somewhere else. He was thinking about the nieces he'd lost, the girls that might be as close as he'd ever come to children of his own. He thought of his big ears, big nose, huge palms and short stubby fingers; none of these seemed insurmountable to him but they, or something he couldn't determine, had so far kept all the women he'd longed for away, even as they seemed to draw the women he didn't want.

Kevin came over and picked up a cue. "You want to stay with us?" he said. "The couch pulls out."

Hank shook his head. "I'll stay with Lily for a while."

It was past three before he crawled home; in the morning he told Reba he was leaving. He packed his van, feeling the lost twins between them like an army. When he looked back, he saw Reba at the window. He waved and tried to catch her eye, but she dropped her head and turned away.

Hank stayed at Lily's cabin for a week and then moved into a room on Main Street over the hardware store, not far from his old room at the Hillview. He started working longer hours at Elzenga's print shop, and he bought some things to add to the bed and dresser he'd taken from home. He had a hot plate, a coffeepot, his bed and a half-size refrigerator; he thought that, all things considered, he wasn't doing bad. He was sane, he hardly ever cried. And in February he started seeing Lucinda Evans, the girl who'd fallen into the lake at Reba's wedding. Lucinda was company, but nothing more than that, and Hank missed Reba all the time. When he woke each morning, he wondered how Reba was and if she was eating right. At night, when he watched TV, he wondered if Reba was crying in her room. He got a telephone and gave Lily his number, so she could give it to Reba if Reba wanted to call him. But it was Luke who called, two months later, to ask him over for Easter dinner. "Lily and Mag and Tonia are coming too," Luke said. "Sort of a family reunion." There was an apology buried somewhere in his voice.

By then, Hank was ready to take whatever he could get, and so he told Luke he'd come. He washed a shirt and pressed some pants, so his family would think he was doing okay, but when Sunday came he got cold feet and asked Lucinda to come with him. He picked Lucinda up at two and drove to Luke's grandfather's place. It was raining; they got there just in time to see Lily creeping out of her car with a newspaper over her head. Under it she wore an Easter bonnet, a real, old-fashioned hat with a twist of fluffy stuff at the base and crisp silk roses.

"God," Lucinda said to Hank. "Your grandmother's something else." Hank looked at her with a spark of interest, but her mouth was pursed and he could tell she'd missed the point entirely.

Lily waited for them at the upstairs door; when she saw Lucinda she sniffed and pushed her way inside. Reba was standing there, as pale as when she was first pregnant. "Here," Lily said to her. "Happy Spring." She held out an aluminum bowl full of plain white eggs. "They're hard-boiled—I thought we'd do them up to celebrate."

Reba took the bowl with both hands and ducked around Lily awkwardly, all the time looking over Lily's head at Hank. He could feel her eyes skidding away from his. "Hank," she said.

He moved forward to kiss her cheek and stumbled over Lucinda's shin. Reba blessed him with a smile. "Still clumsy?" she asked.

"Always," he said. When he got his balance he waved at Lucinda. "You know each other?"

Reba and Lucinda nodded, and then Reba's face stiffened up again. In the living room, Lily snapped at Luke when he tried to take her coat. "Don't fuss," she said. She draped the coat over the back of a chair, tugging at the undershirt that stuck out from the neck of her dress. Mag and Tonia were inside already, curled together on the couch; Tonia was telling Mag a story about her rats, something about a King Lawrenz Rat and his eight rat helpers, sneaking up the stairs at night and into the upper wings of the VA. "He can see at night," Hank heard Tonia say. "Also he can read." She unfolded the napkin she'd pleated between her fingers, and she read this:

> "Lawrenz Rat puts out his face
> to say good night, he makes a noise

like this: Kiss. Why do that with
two faces? He makes a noise like
kiss to all his rats. Kiss,
he makes, to Reba Queen,
who is not there."

"Can I see that?" Hank asked. Tonia smiled at him,
crumpled the napkin, and stuffed it into her Sprite. Hank
shook his head and looked at Mag, but Mag smiled as if
nothing unusual had happened. Figures, Hank thought—
that was Mag through and through, ignoring the strange
things thrust in her face. All the time he was growing up,
Mag had stayed locked in her own world no matter what
Bowen or Lily or Tonia might do. She never interfered
more than to spirit her children away when Bowen raged;
as far as Hank could tell, she prided herself on being able
to ignore almost anything.

Luke fixed Hank and Lucinda drinks, and then they
all stood around not knowing what to say. Hank heard
Reba swear in the kitchen, as if she'd burned herself or cut
a finger. He spilled his beer when he jumped up.

"Leave her alone," Luke said softly. "She's okay—
she's just nervous cooking for company."

"We're not company," Hank said.

"That's right," Lily added. "We're all just family."

Reba called them into dinner then. They sat at the
table, stricken by quiet, until Reba brought the roast in
and started carving clumsily.

"Here," Hank said. "Let me do that." When they'd
lived together he'd always carved, and he thought he still
knew how. He laid out slabs of meat and Reba dished out
vegetables.

"Well," Lucinda said brightly. "Everything's deli-
cious."

Hank was glad she could be polite; the food was terrible. The meat was undercooked and the potatoes were lumpy, and Reba looked about to cry. Lily and Luke got to talking about some project for Lily's cabin, and since Hank couldn't figure out what to say he looked around instead. The walls had been painted, as if Reba meant to erase every mark of their life together. He looked at Reba, meaning to say something, but Reba crumpled her napkin, rose, and said, "Excuse me for a minute, would you?" Tonia started to complain but Mag hushed her up; as soon as Reba left, Lily started telling old family stories. Luke and Lucinda, who weren't family and didn't know any better, listened politely. Hank knew he was going to break a dish if he didn't talk to Reba, so he mumbled something and slipped away.

Luke and Reba's room was empty; so were the extra bedrooms. The bathroom door was closed and he heard water running. "Reba?" he said, tapping on the door.

"What is it?"

"Can I come in?"

"I guess."

He opened the door a crack and found her crouched on the floor with her back against the hamper, the faucet gushing full on hot and the room so steamy he could hardly see. Reba was holding a baby blanket in her arms, pressing the soft nap to her closed eyes. The blanket was yellow, and divided into quadrants—one with a soft doll baby that slid into a pocket shaped like a crib, one with a mirror surrounded by petals, one with a cloud made of something white and fuzzy, and one with a plaid puffed dog waiting to squeak when squeezed. The girls had been meant to lie on it, entranced by the textures and shapes.

"Reba?" he said.

She looked up tiredly. "Where's your girlfriend?"

"At the table, listening to Lily's stories."

Reba smiled at that; Lucinda didn't know how to cut Lily off, and they both knew she'd be stuck there for hours. "So what's up?" Hank asked. Reba's hair was stringy from all the steam; Hank reached over and tucked a wisp behind her ear. His mouth was full of questions choking him like marbles, and he didn't know what was okay to ask so he spit out the smallest one. "Thinking about the girls?" he asked.

Reba squeezed the plaid dog, which let out a plaintive squawk. "Of course I am," she said, and shook her head. "What do you think? I always am. About them, and everything that's happened, everything I did. . . ."

"What everything?" Hank asked carefully.

She waved her hand vaguely in the air and let it fall to the furry white cloud. "You know," she said, brushing the nap with her thumb. "Stuff. Like whether I should have married Luke, or come back here, or taken better care of myself—everything. Like how come I didn't want the babies at first, and how they knew that; how I even got pregnant. All the things I did with Jessie and nothing happened, and then a couple of nights with Luke and— wham! Like I wanted it to happen, like I wanted them— maybe I did, but I didn't think I did, and that's what they must have heard, that's what they must have thought . . ."

She paused and then said, "Doesn't the water hitting the sink remind you of the way their heartbeats used to sound? I swear, sometimes I hear the two of them talking to me."

"Reba," Hank said helplessly, wondering where Mag was. She was the one who ought to be here, comforting her daughter. Women's problems, women's talk—how was he supposed to know what to say?

"Listen," Reba said.

Hank closed his eyes and listened. At first he heard only a steady pounding, but gradually the stream of water seemed to separate into two and the drops to separate within the streams until he could hear the drumming, hear the girls again, the two of them calling in the dark. He looked into the blanket's plastic mirror and thought he saw their shadows as he listened quietly. "It wasn't your fault," he said, reaching for Reba's hand.

"I know," she said. "Not exactly. But everything was sour from the start. I never told Luke about all those men. I hardly told him anything. He doesn't even know me."

"Sure he does," Hank said. And then he thought and said, "What men?"

"When I was hanging out with Jessie Thayer. All that stuff."

Hank wasn't sure what Reba was talking about, but he knew enough to move delicately. Those men—which men were they? Who cared? He didn't need to know their names to know Reba. "Luke doesn't need to know everything," he said. "He still knows you."

Reba shook her head. "I ruined everything," she said. "I thought if I kicked you out, Luke and I could be like a family somehow, with no one watching. I thought I could see what was happening if you left."

"So?"

"So what was happening, *is* happening, is nothing. We can't hardly say a word to each other. I tell him it was all my fault for not wanting them to start, and he tells me I'm crazy, that it's not, and I try to tell him what I feel like and I can't, and you're gone and Tonia's gone and Dad's gone, everyone's gone . . ."

"We're all here," Hank said. "Except Dad. Give it some time." On his battered dresser, in his room on Main

Street, lay the postcard Bowen had sent to him at work. "The Cheat River," read the title on the back. "Wild, Woolly—West Virginia!" The handwriting was Bowen's, although there was no signature. "Big water," he'd written. "*Really* big water. Big trucks, brown dogs, women with strings of pale kids. Am well. Have rented a canoe." Hank had puzzled over this for a week, finally deciding not to show it to Mag or Reba. They'd all seen the first card; they all knew Bowen was alive. But Reba had brooded over that message for months, and Hank couldn't see that this one would be any help. *Brown dogs*—what would she make of that?

"Sing to me," Hank said. He was thinking how, after the fair but before she'd gotten married, Reba had once tried to explain to him what music school had been like, how she couldn't say anything to anyone and had to sing instead. "Sing to me," he said again. "If you won't talk."

"I don't sing anymore," Reba said gloomily. "My voice has been gone since my fourth month."

"Just sing anything," he said.

She sighed and then, in a voice no more than a whisper, all breath, no sound, she sang an old Pete Seeger tune that she and Hank used to do together. She stopped when Lucinda tapped on the door and asked if they were ever coming out.

"Lily's setting up to do Easter eggs," Lucinda called to them. "She wants you to help."

Reba looked at Hank and made a face. "We'll be out in a minute," Hank said. Just then, he didn't mind leaving Lucinda alone; Lucinda liked his ugly hands and disapproved of Lily. Reba inched her way over to Hank and put her head on his shoulder. Slowly they began to breathe at the same speed, their heartbeats quieting. When Lily came later to get them, they were almost asleep.

THE SKY IS
THE COLOR
IT USED TO BE

ALL through the summer, Reba dreamed of plane crashes, terrorist attacks, crazed fundamentalists bearing arms. She woke in the night and felt the floor to see if it was hot; she called Tonia and Hank every afternoon to make sure they were alive. A wall as strong and transparent as glass had grown up between her and Luke, and their conversations took on a deranged feel, as if they were diplomats from different cultures forced to deal without an interpreter. They spoke in phrases they might have learned from Berlitz tapes, courteous, thoughtful, false; no possibility of either misunderstanding or truth. And a whole land of words became forbidden territory for them. *Child, girl, baby, twin, family, love, hope*—the closest Luke could come was to say, "Do you want to try again?" while Reba could manage only a single word: "No."

Reba looked for a new job, needing desperately to get out of her haunted apartment, and when she did she ran into Nelson Callowell the way she might have driven into a tree. She made her way to a cramped office in a low concrete building, at the same university her father had attended briefly after the war; but she went expecting only regular hours, a salary above minimum wage, and some decent benefits. Interesting people, maybe; a chance to meet someone new. Ten minutes into her interview, Nelson, the Director of Public Relations, finished reading her application. She raised her eyes and looked into his, praying he wouldn't ask her to take a typing test.

"Don't," Nelson said. "I can't concentrate." He gave her fair warning but she crashed anyway.

"Why not?" she said innocently. And her comment *was* innocent—this was in the fall, nine months after she'd lost the twins, when she still felt fat and ugly and lost and had no sense that the slim, unmarked woman looking back from the mirror was her.

She looked into Nelson's eyes again; he looked into hers. For the last six months, Luke had looked past her neck. "Your eyes," Nelson said. "They're somethin'."

Reba dropped her eyes and blushed. If she'd been older, she wouldn't have taken the job—it was nothing more than clerical work with a fancy title, "Assistant to the Director of Public Relations." But she wasn't older. She was not quite twenty-one when she met Nelson, with an unhappy husband she couldn't reach, and a mother and sister who both needed help, and a stack of hospital bills that still, nine months after they'd let her out, continued to trickle in. Bills for lab tests, radiology, anesthesiology, her room and a TV she'd never used, prenatal exams, postpartum counseling. She and Luke had no health insurance, and that was one reason Reba wanted this job—that, and the fact that she could take courses free at night if she lasted out a year. So she said yes to what Nelson offered, and went to work in an office full of women.

Nelson hid behind her in a walled-off cubicle; the women, four including Reba, sat at desks in the outer room. Part of Reba's job was to guard Nelson fiercely as a lion, but instead she found herself quaking before Lorrie and Wilma and Sarah, who reminded her of the girls with whom she'd briefly gone to music school. They were older than her, in their mid- or late twenties, and they thought Rockledge was nothing more than a park for cows. They shopped in Springfield and dressed sharp and talked easily on the phone, and they treated Nelson in ways that Reba found hard to understand. She watched as Wilma mothered him and Sarah teased him and Lorrie baked him cakes; she stood aside as they flirted with him over coffee and then worked around him as if he didn't exist. The way they split the office responsibilities left Nelson with only public functions, speeches and campus meetings to which he waltzed off alone in the afternoons. In his absence, the women churned out press releases and course catalogs and donation appeals, never consulting him until whatever it was was done. And still, Reba was fooled: because everything passed over Nelson's desk, Reba thought something happened there.

Reba thought Nelson did something to everything—certainly he did something to her. In Rockledge, men who were forty were wrinkled and old and had bellies they lifted with one hand to sling over their belts: like Reba's own father before he ran away. But Nelson, at forty, was as red-haired as Reba, slight and very fair with an elf's smile. He had a dimple that flirted just west of his chin when he told Reba stories. He opened doors and lit cigarettes and never sat while Reba was standing; once, although he was quite small, he half carried and half dragged Reba over a big puddle. Something about being from the South made him seem even more exotic—he never said where he'd grown up, but he mentioned Kentucky and Tennessee, teaching somewhere in Maryland, a job once in Virginia. As if to prove it, he refused to catch on to the local ways. He had a wood stove at home, but he drove a car fit only for Florida. He wore an enormous down jacket and no boots; an L.L. Bean sweater and no undershirt. Reba, who found this charming, took it upon herself to help him out. She made his phone calls and straightened his files, told him where to buy snow tires and how to choose a cord of wood. Each morning, she went into his office and asked him whose work she should do first. Was he grateful? Of course he was. From her very first week he took her out for long lunches filled with wistful stories.

In those years there was a restaurant near the university that specialized in odd salads and oversized, exotically flavored popovers served with hot butter. Nelson often took Reba there; he'd tear into a popover with his small hands and then, over the cloud of scented air it released, start weaving his web. When he wasn't talking about the South he talked about books: poetry in particular, Elizabethan poetry especially. "Where is the lost charm," he would say, "of the Elizabethan songwriters? Where is that poise, that lyrical ease?" He'd recite sonnets while Reba stared in utter dazzlement. He gave her Marvell and Donne; he said he'd been an English teacher before he fell into public relations, and that for years he'd been working on a book of criticism. Sometimes he hinted that he was thinking of working on it again. "Now that you're here," he'd tell Reba. "Since you are such a help." And then, somewhere after the popovers and tofu salad, before the coffee, after the wine, he'd shift the conversation to Reba, almost as if he thought she wouldn't notice. "Tell me about your parents," he'd say, as though he found these stories charming. "About your family." He acted as though the place where she lived, that pocket of land halfway between the Berkshires and the Connecticut Valley but part of neither, was a triangle of weirdness worth exploring.

Reba found it hard to understand what he wanted from her—who would want her life? And she was cautious, too, after her experience in music school. But she had no one else to talk to, and slowly, over the winter and fall, she leaked out bits and pieces to him, just enough to keep him happy. She didn't mention Mag, now fixing cars at Conrad Sprengler's garage; she didn't mention the chickens or Bowen or Tonia, still feeding rats. She talked about Lily and Hank, mildly eccentric. She told him a story about Max and Lily's eleven cats. But she also told him how Luke grew up on a turkey farm, and she knew from the way Nelson leapt on that that she needed to be careful. "It's like the Bermuda Triangle up there," he said, apparently both repelled and fascinated. At least he was not completely repelled.

This was okay, that wasn't; as she sorted through the contents of her mind she watched his face and learned to build a picture of her life that someone like him could stand to hear. Decked out, tricked up, bent toward charm and humor—really, she wanted to talk about none of it. Not Rockledge itself, in all its tired squalor, not how she came to be married a year out of high school. And not, especially not, about the twins, who still floated a foot above her head like balloons or guardian angels. Nelson thought of her as a girl, she knew. But there hadn't been anything girlish about that pregnancy, and anyway she didn't want to talk about the things she knew. She wanted to talk about the books Nelson gave her and about why all day, every day, she waited for the time when everyone left the office but them. She wanted to talk about the sudden hard thump she got in her chest each morning, when she parked her rusty Cutlass next to his blue convertible.

She wanted to talk about whether this thing she had for him was love. She thought it was—although she dreamed about him at night, she never went farther than imagining a kiss. This was more than the hots, she thought; she knew what that was. It was all she'd ever had before Luke, and Luke was something else again. No, what she had with Nelson was real, what happened in books. She lived on occasional long glances, an accidental brush of her hand, a walk across campus alone. She went everywhere she could with Nelson, in a state of perpetual blush. At home she mooned about, ignoring Luke and cradling the cat Lily had given her in one arm and a book of poems in the other. Luke, lost in his own daze and still mourning the girls, was so far away from her that when he said sometimes, "What's wrong? What is it?" she had only to look at him in a certain way to shut him up, to make him think what was wrong with her was what was wrong with him. Which it was, would always be; except that now there was also this other thing as well. She felt no need to explain to Luke why she began styling her hair, which had finally grown out. At work, she started drafting Nelson's reports. Grateful, always grateful, Nelson praised her conciseness and style, her wit and her legs. She took to wearing shorter skirts.

Winter came; misery. A year since she'd lost the twins. Luke bought a pair of cross-country skis and began spending long days, sometimes nights, gliding through the swamp. When he came home his beard and moustache were solid ice. Reba went to her mother's house when Luke was gone and watched TV with Tonia; Tonia bought gerbils who made baby gerbils who escaped into the walls, where they made a smell. Nelson began asking Reba if she was happy, married so young; then he began to mutter about the trials and responsibilities of his long marriage and fatherhood. But he looped around when he did this, never complaining outright or slighting Ginnie, his wife.

He'd fill the office with implications and then he'd say, "Darlin'—don't you ever wish you were free?"

"Free?" she'd say. "Me?" The ties that bound her to Luke and her family seemed like cables woven in a tricky pattern of nets and traps, and she couldn't imagine ever breaking them. She didn't think she knew much about marriages then, except that hers had been derailed and held her pinned beneath the wreckage. She thought Nelson complained because he was unhappy and that she was unhappy with her life. When Luke made love to her he was as distant as the moon; she closed her eyes and thought of other things until the night when, lying beneath him, she tried and failed to imagine Nelson in his place and then, despite that, made up her mind to give Nelson anything he asked.

But Nelson didn't seem to want anything more than to go on talking in the late afternoons. Reba had seen Ginnie by then, and couldn't imagine that Ginnie was why: she was broad-hipped and messy, perpetually trailing the golden children who only made her look faded. It seemed obvious to Reba that Nelson should want to shake Ginnie off, and yet when Ginnie came by the office Nelson always welcomed her into his cubicle, where Reba could hear them chattering. Later, when Nelson led Ginnie out, Ginnie would sit down in the outer room as soon as Nelson shut his door, and then she'd gossip about him with the other women.

"You sleep late this morning?" Wilma would ask. "Nelson's wearing different-colored socks again." If Nelson came out the women would hush and then talk about recipes until he left. Reba always typed during those conversations, the cool rhythms of the letters blanking out her mind. She didn't want to know Ginnie or the other women —she was at that stage where her feelings flashed like traffic lights, so tongue-tied she couldn't talk anyway. She stopped talking to anyone about anything, forgot to call her mother or Lily or Hank, hardly ever checked in on Tonia at work. When the phone rang at home she'd answer it and forget to say hello, her mouth open while she listened to the wire's hum. Lorrie asked her more than once if she was all right.

"Me?" Reba said. "I'm fine."

Reba's obsession with Nelson—for that's what it was, as she recognized later, obsession futile and dark with all she didn't know—lasted through the long winter and into spring. Nelson filled her mind, pressing everything else from the dark closets and corners there and expanding like foam into the spaces in which she might have thought of other things. Like her family, like her music; like her marriage or her life. All that was gone now, and Nelson filled her like helium. And this kept her from seeing things she might otherwise have noticed, such as the gesture Luke made in March, when he brought home a section of tree trunk from the great oak felled in the common, and made it into a coffee table for her.

Some part of her saw him lugging and sanding and varnishing, taking pride in the top's silky surface against the rough bark of the sides. But she didn't see the loneliness behind Luke's gesture, or the wish that it would bring her back from wherever she'd gone. Instead she noticed, as if in a dream, the small cones of sawdust that appeared around the table's perimeter in April, and the pencil-sized holes that began breaking through the bark on the table's sides later that month, as if things were eating their way out from inside. Things were: early in May, a swarm of two-inch wood-boring wasps launched themselves from the burrows they'd grown in and filled the apartment, hurling themselves at the dark wainscoting and lowering themselves down, their long ovipositors spinning like drills as they laid fresh eggs. She went into the bathroom and watched as Luke rushed around trying to kill the bugs with his shoes, with her books, with any weapon that came to hand. She was hardly able to comfort him when he pounded the walls in frustration.

Who talks to him? she wondered then. *Who says his eyes look like green lakes?* But when she touched him he wrapped around her like wisteria and she had to move away. "I have to start working extra hours," she told him then. "We're on a big project till June." Luke nodded and went to their room. Through the closed door she could hear him whistling mournfully; afterwards, she would sometimes think that if he'd danced out instead, a smile on his face and a demand that they do something together—instantly, suddenly, now—on his lips, she might have knocked down her half of the fence and everything between them might have been fine.

But Luke retreated even farther after that, and one afternoon, soon after the bugs hatched, Nelson took her with him to a committee meeting. They walked the long way to the library, near the edge of the woods and past practice rooms sending out sounds of cornets and saxophones. Nelson touched her hand and then held it, saying she felt cold, and this was the first time he touched her on purpose. Something swelled inside her chest so that she could hardly catch her breath. She thought she knew what this was: the torn fabric of her life, packed into an acorn like a set of magician's fine silk scarves and suddenly ready to be released. Nelson might have asked her anything then; she would have told him. But all he wanted to know

111

was why she was shivering. When she blushed he said that young girls were sweet in the spring.

"Want to skip the meeting?" he asked, stroking the top of her hand with his thumb. "We could walk in the woods instead."

"Sure," Reba whispered.

With his other hand, Nelson reached out and touched Reba's mouth. He looked at her for a long time, and she read wonderful things in his silence. Then he patted her hair as if she'd suddenly turned into a golden retriever. "Not today," he said. "Maybe some other time."

Reba tried not to look disappointed. They went to the meeting, where Nelson jiggled chairs so he could sit next to her, his knee pressed into her thigh. She took notes, as always, but all her concentration was focused on the dime-sized patch of flesh that connected her to Nelson. When the meeting was over they walked back the short way, not touching or talking. Reba sat down at her desk to sort through her notes and found she couldn't read them at all. And then Nelson poked his head around his door and asked if Reba could come home with him after work.

Reba nodded yes; her hands shook as she cleared her desk. Lorrie, who'd been watching her, asked what was going on.

"Nothing," Reba told her, lying as easily as she had at sixteen, all her old forgotten habits slipping back into place. "Just some extra work we need to finish up—something for the catalog."

"Want some help?"

Reba told her no, but she couldn't keep from smiling. This was what she'd read about and waited for, the fate of young women in offices. She dreamed about the long, dark ride in Nelson's convertible, and although she couldn't see farther than that, she called Luke to tell him she'd be very late.

Nelson came out once the office was quiet, buttoning his sweater. Together, he and Reba turned out the lights and walked down the empty corridors. Nelson tucked Reba's hand into the crook of his arm once they were outside.

"All set?" he asked.

Reba, past speaking by then, could only nod. The sky was still light and was planning to stay that way for hours, but Reba shook as if someone were blowing on her and wished for dark. In the car Nelson turned and, instead of kissing her, said, "Why so quiet?"

She took a long breath, hoping for inspiration. Nothing came but the same tired words. "I love you," she said, forgetting everything she'd learned during her years with Jessie, forgetting that this was the easiest way to scare someone off, the hardest way to keep him. In the backseat she could feel the shadows of her twins looking at each other, horrified, as if she was only supposed to speak this way to their father.

Nelson drew back the arm he'd stretched along the car seat. "Lord," he said. "Lordy, Lord." He shook his head and favored Reba with half a smile. "Y'all are so *for*ward up here."

Reba dropped her eyes, feeling as clumsy as her brother. Nelson hummed something to himself and then waved at the woods. "Look," he said, and then he spoke a strange line, framing it in invisible quotation marks. "On a long spring evening, the sky is the color it used to be in the South."

Reba stared at him dumbly. The line sounded like a quote from a real song but was, more likely, from a song the Callowells had made up themselves to sing at home.

Because they were that kind of a family, Reba knew already—so wrapped up in themselves, so pleased, that they'd have a family song the way they'd have a family bird, movie, flag; family jokes, family tales.

"Aren't those trees somethin'?" Nelson continued. "If we were home we'd sit on the porch, drinking bourbon and watching the sun set."

What home? Reba wanted to ask. *Which one?* She couldn't keep his stories straight. Nelson patted her knee and she thought, for a minute, that there was still hope. If she drew back she might still get lucky; she might still think of the right thing to say. She tried to look shy.

"Let's go," Nelson said. "Ginnie's making us dinner."

Reba was too startled to move. Ginnie, making dinner —and she'd imagined a dark, hushed house, free not only of Ginnie but of her blond children. A fire, perhaps some wine; a low, soft sofa. They drove through campus quietly, turning a few minutes later down a village street to stop at a small white house. Ginnie, framed in the tiny door, kissed Reba's cheek and led her through the narrow hall. Nelson kissed Ginnie and whispered something; Ginnie laughed and rested her head on his shoulder. Reba followed them blindly into a kitchen hung with copper pots. While Nelson made salad, Ginnie poured Reba some wine and showed her around the house. It was full of cracked antiques and much too small for them.

Nelson filled Reba's glass again when they came back. Reba could hardly look at him, but he smiled encouragingly and guided her to a table made for six, where the seven of them crowded together. Nelson avoided Reba's knees this time, but he kept her glass full and made fun of her rosy cheeks. Across the table, Ginnie ignored them and talked to her children. By the end of the meal, Reba was just able to offer to help clean up. Ginnie turned her down.

"Sit on the deck with Nelson," she said. "Watch the sun set." As Reba turned to go, Ginnie gave her two clean glasses, a bucket of ice, and a bottle of bourbon. Reba left her scraping plates.

Behind the house the deck stretched out, overlooking the yard and the maple trees. Lawn chairs, tables, and potted plants dotted the redwood planks. Nelson pulled two of the chairs together and sat Reba down next to him. From the basement beneath them, his children slipped out into the yard. Reba snaked her hand through the side of her chair and touched Nelson's thigh, still ready to tell him anything.

"More bourbon?" Nelson asked, moving his leg. He topped Reba's glass off without waiting for an answer, and then he said, "Watch," and pointed to his children. "Aren't they somethin'?" He sat back in his chair and folded his arms, as if he were viewing a play he thought Reba would like.

Nicky, Nelson's son, set a white cardboard target against the hedge separating their lawn from the neighbor's. He paced back across the grass until he reached some point that made sense to him, and then he sent a cluster of rubber-tipped arrows flying into the center of the target. Holly, Nelson's oldest girl, sat under an apple tree braiding her golden hair. The two youngest, Maggie and Carolee, jumped behind Nicky like puppies. They had hair the color of marigolds and dimples like Nelson's; Carolee wore a yellow rain hat set on backward and Maggie gravely turned circles of cartwheels, rounding off each circle with a split. Even Reba could see that they were lovely children, although of course not so lovely as her own twins might have been.

She closed her eyes and saw Marissa and Marianne as they'd been for that one second in the hospital when, unzipped from the neat wound on Reba's belly, they'd been pulled out as small and inert as footballs. Reba wasn't supposed to see them but she had, just a glimpse of their frosted skin and transparent nails and soft, sparse hair, their heads tipped back as the green-clothed people surrounding Reba tried to breathe life back into them. Too late—she'd felt them leave her as the nurses rolled her down the hall. As they'd floated away to rest above her head, she'd seen their lives as they might have been: two red-haired girls, chrysanthemums rather than marigolds, crawling, walking, talking, growing up together. Going off somewhere to do the things Reba had never done, because she wouldn't have let what had happened to her happen to them. Their house would have been calm and orderly; they would have done their homework each night. They would have sung in junior high musicals and had clothes that matched. Somehow, Reba would have kept them safe. To Nelson, who was looking at her expectantly, Reba said, "They're lovely." She felt the twins on her arms like water wings, keeping her afloat.

"You ought to have some," Nelson said blandly.

Reba stared at him, wondering how he failed to sense the twins. The time she'd spent all fall and winter talking to him inside her head, opening doors and showing him around—how was it he couldn't see the biggest thing there?

He smiled, pointed at Carolee's mismatched skirt and socks, and said, "Such a ragamuffin. Did your mother let you dress like that?"

Of course, Reba thought. Worse. She opened her mouth to tell Nelson what she'd worn, done, been, and from the yard, Maggie's shrill voice floated up.

"Daddy!" she called. "I'm stuck!" Caught in her last split, she was pinned to the grass like a broken pair of scissors.

Nelson vaulted the deck railing and jumped down to the yard. The evening redness left the sky as Reba watched him pull Maggie up; in a minute the children's gold hair flattened and turned gray. They leapt on Nelson and pulled him down, shrieking and giggling. Nelson laughed, and then it was dark.

Ginnie slipped into the chair beside Reba and lit a rose-colored candle. The lawn went black, shut off from their circle of light. "Aren't they funny?" she asked, waving a heavy arm over her family. "I love to watch Nelson playing with them—he's like a kid himself." She leaned over the candle and lit a cigarette. "When we lived in Virginia, they'd play like this until the moon set." She reached over and tousled Reba's hair. "Cheer up," she said. "You shouldn't take him so seriously—he's always like this in the spring. Haven't the other girls in the office ever told you that? He's such a flirt."

Reba shook her head. Flirting, she suddenly remembered. Play for the sake of play. "I don't talk to them much," she said.

"They've all been through it—just humor him, it'll pass." She laughed softly and then added, "I've been lucky —these things come and go with him like chicken pox and don't hurt anyone, and he's sweet enough to bring you all home. Are you twenty yet?"

Reba nodded. "Twenty-one."

"Children?"

Reba frowned and shook her head.

"Ah," Ginnie said. "You ought to have some."

Reba couldn't think of anything to say. As much as she would have liked to hurt Ginnie, break her sweet, sunny face between her words, the fact was that Nelson hadn't done anything she knew how to explain. Everything had happened in the pauses between his words, in her readings of his odd lines of poetry and fragments of songs. She shut her eyes and saw the Callowells camping somewhere along the eastern shore of Maryland, two golden parents with their four glinting offspring, safe within the circle of a fire they made in a certain way.

Ginnie went into the house for more ice. On the dark lawn the children had Nelson pinned, one to each limb.

"Mommy!" Carolee called out. "We caught Daddy!"

"That's nice," Ginnie called from inside.

Before Ginnie could come out again, Reba slipped over the deck rail and into the night, the twins' shadows bobbing behind her like water lilies. She ducked around the corner and started her long walk back to the university and her car. Above her the tree peepers screeched their song, filling the sky the way they had summer nights at the Rockledge Gorge.

For two days Reba stayed in bed with the covers over her head, wondering if it was possible to die of humiliation. "I love you," she'd said to Nelson, and worse than that—looking back over the winter and fall, she saw that she'd dribbled out enough of herself to Nelson to constitute a flood; enough, almost, for Nelson to know her. She shredded the hem of her blanket and refused to tell Luke what was going on. He tiptoed in and out of her room, bringing tea, lemonade, ice cream, books, the cat, a radio —anything he thought she might like. She wouldn't eat, and she wouldn't talk to him. She concentrated all her energy on putting the twins to rest, as she knew she should have done months ago. She couldn't let them go completely, so she took a huge breath and drew their shadows into her lungs, where they could rest against her heart and be comforted. When she exhaled, she felt her breath cold and sharp as winter on the creek.

That was what she needed to cast the Callowells from her. As she lay in bed, her mind threw out a picture she hadn't seen in years. Back before she knew Jessie Thayer, and when Luke was no more to her than one of the band of children with whom she ran shrieking through the woods, she used to spend her winters skating. There was a creek deep in those woods, which ran smooth and quiet toward the swamp and froze solid most winters, forming a silver corridor through the iron-gray trees. The creek was shallow and quite safe; almost all the children she knew were allowed to skate there. After school, in the brief hours before darkness fell, Reba and Hank, Luke and his brothers, Sally Lambert and Sue Keefe, Matthew and Ben and Joshua Gamble, Kevin Glover and his sister Jane, the Elzengas, the Weisses, the Ryders, and more, had all gathered on the banks of the creek and strapped clumsy, double-bladed skates over their boots. These were skates of a kind seldom seen anymore, small silvery platforms adjustable in length, with a metal toe-cup and a complex system of red straps holding them in place—so cheap that even the worst-off among them owned a pair. Equipped identically, as for a crusade, bundled into handed-down coats and stained mittens, the army of children shuffled and slid each day in groups of three or four, following the creek toward a point over the horizon they could never reach. Reba's chief joy then, a joy as fierce as singing, was to glide with them down that silver street, her arms linked with whoever was her best friend that year.

Into her last winter on the creek had come three new children by the name of Bonfrere, transplanted in from Kentucky. They had sandy hair and hazel eyes; Adele, the oldest, who'd entered Reba's fifth-grade class after the school year had begun and would leave before the year was out, had a collection of fossils she kept in plastic boxes. Trilobites, she told Reba proudly. Ammonites. The Bonfreres' place was as warm and comforting as Reba's was cold and strange, although the whole family, all five of them, were crammed into the four rooms they'd rented in a house on the square. But they'd tacked plastic over the windows to keep out the drafts, and when the children went home their mother made them popcorn and helped with their long division. Reba would have moved in there if they'd let her: Adele's family was as exotic to Reba as some new fruit—a kiwi, say, or a tangelo—and Reba responded to Adele's brief overtures with all the ardor of her ten-year-old heart. She gave Adele an enormous bottle of Emeraude for Christmas, which Adele promptly shared with her sister; for Valentine's Day she sent a huge lacy card inscribed "Your Friend Reba, Forever." On the banks of the creek the three Bonfrere children sang the mountain rounds their mother taught them, their high, nasal voices floating over the snow. They couldn't skate until Reba taught them. For a few weeks after that, while their ankles strengthened, Adele seemed to welcome Reba. Then she firmly, kindly rejected her, skating off into the woods with her own brother and sister.

The day this happened, Reba skated home by herself, so unhappy that she forgot to unstrap her skates at the end of the creek and clumped through the woods on her double blades. She headed for her father, in whom she still found some comfort. Mag was in the sunporch, reading something to Tonia; Hank was still skating on the creek. Reba found her father in the barn, sitting on an overturned pail and reading an old book by the dim yellow light. When she came in he looked up and blinked twice, his face naked and distant. This was back when he was beginning to separate himself from them, during that stage when he forgot his children were children and treated them kindly, curiously, as alien adults. Reba threw herself sobbing at his knees, trying to tell him what was wrong, and he responded with some tale he'd pulled from Thoreau or Emily Dickinson, something about rushing into the house of love too fast, throwing open the suitcases of your heart and unpacking all the treasures there, only to find that you'd entered the wrong house and that, quickly and with embarrassment, you had to jam everything back in and flee. "The wrinkles shake out," Bowen told Reba kindly, while the chickens rustled and clucked in the background. "In a few weeks you'll have everything all re-packed, and you'll be as good as new." He might as well have been speaking French for all Reba understood—all that spring, until Adele's father's business failed and the Bonfreres vanished as quickly as they'd arrived, the sight of Adele gave Reba such a pain she could hardly speak. And yet Bowen was right; by summer Reba had forgotten Adele.

Now, recalling her, Reba could see that Adele's family had formed the same tight bud as did the Callowells, petals turned in toward each other with no room for anything else—the kind of family she and Luke might have made if the twins had lived. Reba lay as still as the wasps inside her coffee table while she considered this and repacked her heart. When she was done she decided she wanted her job, and she returned to work determined not to give Nelson so much as a smile.

"You all right?" he asked the day she came back.

"I had the flu," Reba said coldly, and that was as much as they ever talked about the night at Nelson's house. They stopped talking books in the afternoons and started talking business, which is how Reba found out he didn't know anything. She began eating lunch with Lorrie and Wilma and Sarah; eventually she told them about the twins and Luke, although she never mentioned her absent father. Hank had finally shown her the postcard from West Virginia, and now she imagined Bowen floating from river to river, exploring a wilderness long since mapped and searching for the sky of his dreams.

"Can't you move?" the three women asked her, when Reba described the snow, the smells, the isolation of Rockledge to them. "I can't believe you live up there."

When she said, "I can't—my family's there," they shook their heads and said, "Well—at least you don't have to *dress* like you live there." They took her shopping and showed her how to drape a scarf, and they taught her how to do their work and how to handle Nelson.

"Just ignore him," they said, when Reba asked them what work Nelson should see. "He doesn't care so long as it all gets done." Reba typed and wrote and proofread catalog copy the way the other women did, and she managed so well that, when Wilma left a few months later, Nelson had to promote her. Reba and Sarah and Lorrie got to watch him interview women for Reba's old job. He must have seen twenty before Isabelle walked in; when she did, Reba knew the search was over. Isabelle was tall, quite slender, and quietly dressed, with green eyes glowing behind her glasses. She blushed furiously as she walked past the three women, and they smiled at each other as soon as Nelson closed his door.

"Really," Lorrie said. "Really, now. She can't be nineteen."

Sarah pinched her nostrils shut with her fingers.

"Hmm," she said in Nelson's nasal drawl, which Reba suddenly heard as very much like that of the little girl from Kentucky. "The sky, hmm, the sky; your eyes, the sky, your eyes . . ."

DREAMS OF LIFE

WHAT Luke remembered of his job at Maglione's Nursery were the towers of red clay
pots, rising above his shoulders like the legs
of dinosaurs. Sand and rocks and tools and
dirt and bags of peat and humus; and him, trapped under a
sweating glass roof between the towers, tamping dirt
around two-leaved transplants. Begonia, begonia, begonia; freesia, freesia, freesia; fern, fern, fern; palm—that's
what his two years there had been like, with his mind
drifting up near the ceiling vents and dreaming a life
while his hands sifted dirt.

He hadn't minded at first, not while Reba was pregnant and he could feel he was working for something
worthwhile, the lives of his children germinating as dark
and secret as seeds. But after the twins were lost he could
hardly stand it. He was alone in the greenhouse except for
Noreen Unehauser, who had control of the radio by virtue
of her twenty years' seniority and who always played a
country-music station that gave him headaches and drove
him to thinking about the twins. Once he'd listened to
those mournful tunes with a sense of calm pleasure, of
danger overcome and himself and Reba safely ashore. But
the songs seemed to change after Reba lost the girls, so
that all he heard were phrases about babies drowning or

falling down wells. He'd fight all day not to hear them, and then he'd go home to a Reba who was bitter some nights and as distant as a comet others. There she'd be on the sofa, playing her father's scratched opera recordings over and over again while a voice plaintive and yearning as a cat's filled the apartment with liquid syllables. He couldn't understand the lyrics but he heard the message: *I miss, I want, I hurt.* That was Reba all over, and always had been; part of her charm was the fierceness of her longings. But to hear them made public, naked and unadorned—no, it was too much, worse than country music. "How can you stand that stuff?" he'd ask Reba, but she wouldn't answer him.

When Reba got her promotion that summer, Luke quit. "Assistant Manager of Annual Giving," she announced one night, with an odd smile.

"Same office?" he asked, hoping she'd say no. She hadn't gone to work early or stayed late since the May night when she'd come home as stunned as if a car had hit her, radiating fear and misery. "What?" he'd said then, wrapping his arms around her stiff body. "What is it?" Something had happened to her at work, but she wouldn't tell him what it was. "I miss the girls," she'd said. Lying. He knew she was. He'd feared something else—that she'd failed at her job somehow, been humiliated or repri-manded. And yet here she'd been promoted.

"Same office, different job," she said now. "A girl named Isabelle took my job, and I took Wilma's." Her eyes were quiet, not lit the way they usually were when she was excited. A shell seemed to have hardened around her since that May night, distancing her from Luke in a way that even the death of the twins had not.

"I'm glad," he said. "I'm proud of you."

She shrugged and picked at her nails.

A week later, Luke left Maglione's and went back to

work outside, framing houses and laying roofs with men he'd known for years. Champoux, Ribideau, Scarpatowski; he didn't think Reba would mind. New jobs for both of them, almost as though they'd started new lives. *I'll wait six months,* Luke thought. *Until we're both settled. And then I'll talk to her about starting a baby again.* He saw the two of them sitting in a rocker on a quiet porch, their arms entwined around each other's waists. A gentle rain would be falling around them, enclosing them in a world of their own. "So what do you think?" he'd say to her softly. "Want to make a baby?" She'd smile at him and rise from the rocker and lead him to the bedroom, right then. . . . B A B Y, easy enough to hum in the code that Reba had invented. Even his cracked voice could manage it.

Six months, he thought. *She might be ready then.* Kneeling on a gable, Champoux passing him shingles that fell into place under the steady rhythm of his wrist as he dreamed of Reba—that was work, that was doing something, and if he didn't earn as much as he had before, at least it was quiet and his hands looked like his again, brown and nicked and strong. There were trees to watch, and the complex movements of clouds. His mind was free to dream all day, and at night he drew plans for the cabin he wanted to build on his land in Conway. Posts and beams, a plank floor, perhaps a skylight. Reba took a second job.

The cabin was for Reba, or so Luke thought—when he pictured it, he always saw her inside on a soft chair, an afghan drawn over her legs and a smile on her face. With this in mind, he persuaded her to funnel the money from her second job into the mortgage, which he could no longer cover himself. The new job was Mag's idea, not his —Mag had fixed up and sold the three old cars in her front yard with her friend Conrad Sprengler's help, and she'd liked doing that so much that she'd quit the VA altogether and gone to work at Rad's service station full-time. She'd roped Reba into doing Rad's books for him on Saturdays, saying it would give Reba some extra money and get her out of the house, and Luke didn't mind this at all. He and Rad had known each other casually for years, and he found that he liked walking across the square on a warm Saturday, buying an Orange Crush from the soda machine in the office and shooting the breeze with Rad while Mag bent over an old Ford truck and Reba frowned at the scrolls of paper tape spewing from the adding machine. Sometimes Hank would drop by, sometimes Tonia; sometimes Rad's wife, Linda, would bring their little boy Brian and set him on the hood of someone's car. Rad had a beaked nose bigger than Hank's and a collection of shaggy-dog stories that kept everyone entertained. Sooner or later Rad would pause between stories and then Luke or Hank would run over to the Red & White for a couple of six-packs and a carton of sandwiches.

"Kicks are for Trids," Rad would say, when Brian thrashed his feet in the air. An old line from an old joke that always made all of them laugh. Afterwards, Luke and Reba and Rad and Linda might go bowling or have dinner together, and Reba would laugh with the men while Linda cooked. Luke could see the way Reba bloomed in this company, touching Rad's wrist lightly as he made a joke, and he was grateful that she'd made a friend.

Some Saturdays Luke couldn't join everyone because he had to work. On one of those working days, when he was rushing to finish a roof before the persistent drizzle turned to rain, he ran home at lunchtime to pick up his coat and found Rad and Reba instead, Rad wedged uncomfortably into the corner of the couch and Reba with her head on his shoulder. Because the living room was set slightly off the entrance hall, Rad and Reba didn't see Luke at first.

Reba was crying; Rad's head was bent low over her and he was stroking her hair with his right hand. *They've done this before,* Luke thought, pierced by the sight of Rad comforting her. No one was laughing now. *She tells him things she doesn't tell me.* "It's all right," Luke heard Rad say. "Can you tell me what's wrong?"

"I *hate* this," Reba sobbed. "Everyone else has a place to go. You have Linda and Brian, and Nelson's got Ginnie and all his damn kids, and Lily's got Max and Mag has Tonia and I don't have *any*thing. . . ."

What about me? Luke thought, and Rad, as if reading his mind, said, "What about Luke? Luke loves you more than anything."

Reba raised her head and blew her nose into Rad's handkerchief. "You don't get it," she said. "You don't understand . . ." And then she saw Luke.

"Hi," Luke said awkwardly. "It's rainy. I came home for my coat."

Rad and Reba drew apart. "I didn't hear you come in," Reba said.

Luke made a face. "I know. What's going on?"

Rad bent over and tightened the laces on his boots. "Nothing," he said to the floor. "Just talking."

Reba looked over Luke's shoulder and sighed. "Nothing," she said. "I'm just having a bad day. I woke up feeling shitty and then I screwed up the payroll and then Mag started giving me grief about not spending more time with Tonia . . ."

"Let me stay home with you," Luke said. "I'll call Champoux and tell him I can't come back this afternoon."

"Go back to work," Reba said quietly. "I'm okay—I was just heading back to the garage myself."

"Reba," Luke said. "Give me a break." But then he clamped his back teeth together so he wouldn't shout. That was one of the rules he and Reba had made, after growing up loud and violent: that they wouldn't yell, throw things, nag and pick the way their parents had. He couldn't say anything he wanted to in front of Rad, but his forced silence left him feeling as though he might start bleeding from the ears. "Jesus," he muttered. "I'll see you tonight." And then he stormed down the steps, as angry as if he'd found Rad and Reba in bed together.

Rad came running after him. "Hey," he said, resting his hand on Luke's shoulders. "Listen, Luke—I don't know what you're thinking, but nothing was going on in there. She was upset all morning, and I was just trying to listen to her."

"That's my job," Luke said fiercely. "Mine."

He shook Rad's hand off, and Rad stepped away. "Anyone can listen," Rad said softly. "No big deal."

Luke went back to work and spent the afternoon pulling old shingles like teeth. *Anyone can listen,* he thought. But no one listened to him. Champoux, Ribideau, Scarpatowski—the three of them talked to each other all day while their hands were busy, but they talked about baseball, basketball, bars in town, work and bills and cars. And he talked the same way to them. He'd never dream of talking about Reba, about his life—his life was private, his problems his own. Only women talked about those things. Sometimes he envied them—the women he saw in the supermarket, their carts gathered by the broccoli while they whispered in each other's ears; women he saw in small clumps on the streets, at Lily's house, behind the counter at the hardware store; the women he imagined surrounding Reba at work. All of them discussing secret things, in a language closed to him. When he'd married

Reba he'd thought that world might open, that she'd act as an interpreter. Instead, she talked to Rad.

Reba was waiting for him when he got home that night, her face pale and distant. He waited; she served him dinner. He waited some more; she cleared the dishes. When he still didn't speak she sat down beside him, wrapping her hands around a mug.

"I'm sorry," she said quietly. "How much did you hear?"

"Not much," he said. "Just enough to know you were talking to him like you never talk to me anymore."

"It's . . . different," she said. "Because Rad and I are just friends. Remember how you and I used to talk before we got involved, when I'd come over to see Hank and then you and I would end up talking about everything?"

"Of course it's different," Luke said. "We're supposed to talk *more* now. We weren't in love then."

"That's the point," Reba said. "I could tell you anything then, because you didn't take it personally. We weren't involved."

"You could tell me now," Luke said. "Tell me anything."

Reba shook her head.

"You mean you talk *about* me," Luke said, his skin shrinking with the thought. "You talk to Rad about us."

"Not exactly," Reba said.

She fell silent, but Luke could almost hear her thinking. She didn't need to say she didn't like sleeping with him—he knew that, he always had. Just like he knew it was nothing he was doing wrong, nothing he could fix. *Some smell I have,* he thought. Some way my skin falls or doesn't fall, some way my arms hang from my shoulders. Some lack of the mysterious chemistry that streamed from her to him but had never streamed back. She only made love to him easily when she was half drunk or half asleep. *When I'm not me*, he forced himself to think. It wasn't that she didn't have a wildness, only that the wildness wasn't for him. He'd known that when he'd married her, and had thought he could change it, and had been wrong. Sometimes he could feel her fighting with herself, trying to make herself want him. But a flicker of moonlight along his flank would never stir her the way the same flicker on her would drive him mad. She'd never stand in the hallway and study the back of his neck; she'd never dream about him the way he dreamed of her even as she lay there beside him, breathing quietly in and out in the cool silence of early dawn. In his dreams she came to life, yearning after him with eager hands. He couldn't bear to think of what Rad might know.

The shadows under Reba's eyes were as gray as mice. Below their window he heard a gang of boys shrieking as they hurled themselves into a pile of leaves, and for an instant he saw himself and Reba in another leafpile years ago, huddled there with his brothers and Tonia and Hank, all of them still on the same side. He leaned over the back of the sofa and watched the boys as Reba tried to explain why she'd been so upset. The sky went from gray to black as she talked; the boys went home. Reba bit at her nails. "I hate this town," she said. "I hate this place." The clouds gathered and then it rained again, and the lighted windows around the square danced in the dark like fireflies. Luke watched the night pass, unable to look at Reba. His skin felt broken and stripped.

"I'm so bored here," she said, and then she started to cry.

Luke put his arms around her. It wasn't the scene he'd imagined: no porch, no swing, although the rain was falling. "Let's have a baby," he whispered to her. "That's

what we need to fix us." *Child,* he thought, silently working out the tones in Reba's code. Not much of a tune. He
whistled a handful of notes.

"Are you crazy?" she said, crying harder. "Why are
you whistling at me?" Luke held her head to his chest and
tried to take comfort from the fact that she cried in front
of him.

That winter, Reba started taking courses part-time—a
music course, piano lessons, beginning biology. She swore
that what she and Rad talked about was never Luke, and
although Luke didn't believe her he was afraid to say
anything, afraid to find out what would happen if he dis-
turbed that friendship. *She needs it,* he told himself. And
he thought that Rad needed it even more. Some days,
when Luke joined them in the garage, he caught Rad
looking at Reba as he told her jokes in a way that reminded
Luke of himself. *He's in love with her,* Luke thought then.
At least a little. He couldn't blame Rad—there he was,
Saturday after Saturday, with a Reba who stuck out in
Rockledge like a diamond in river gravel. Almost, Luke
felt sorry for Rad.

Luke never said a word about this to Linda or anyone
else, and he and Reba and Rad and Linda continued doing
things together. The four of them got along well enough,
except that Rad got quiet and sulky when Reba talked
about school. Luke thought Reba's courses were what was
bothering Rad—Rad had always hated the university, and
he'd made fun of Reba's job before. "What is this horse-
shit?" he'd mutter to Luke. "What's she need all this
school stuff for?"

But Luke didn't want Reba to stop—her courses were
free and they made her cheerful again, almost the way
she'd been when they were first married. All through the

spring semester she leapt from bed each morning and fixed Luke French toast or eggs, and then she vanished until late at night and came home smiling.

Maybe it's time, Luke thought. *Maybe she's ready now.* He imagined Reba cradling a new baby in her arms, and he was so convinced this was what she needed that he'd almost made up his mind to take care of things himself if she said no. He'd take her camping, he thought. And make sure she left her diaphragm at home. Or he'd take a pin and poke tiny holes in it, invisible but effective.

The more Reba smiled, the more Rad sulked. Luke said to Rad one night, "What's your problem, anyway?" and Rad stared at Luke, pointed to Reba singing in the kitchen, and said, "Why do you think she's so fucking cheerful?"

She's pregnant, Luke thought triumphantly, but he didn't want to tell Rad. "She likes school," he said, but Rad gave him a scornful look that sent a sick shiver down his spine.

Luke watched Reba closely for the next few weeks, and he began to notice the care with which she dressed for work. Stockings and high heels where she used to wear pants; a little more makeup than usual; perfume and earrings and silky scarves. "My friends at work," she said, when he commented on her appearance. "They're trying to clean me up." She'd started working late again the nights she didn't have classes.

"We're busy," Reba told him the night Luke asked what was keeping her at work. "We got this big project, and the personnel office dumped a new guy in with us, who I have to train. Robbie. Robbie Calkins."

"Oh?" Luke said. He felt a warning prickle along the back of his neck. "Is he married?"

"Sure," Reba said. "Two kids."

And Luke relaxed a little. Another Rad, he thought. Another friend. He could almost stand the idea that she was confiding in someone else. But Reba had never dressed for Rad, and the more Luke watched Reba, the less he was sure he understood whatever was going on. One night, when she came home at eleven, he asked her carefully, casually, if there was anything she wanted to tell him. The next day he returned from work to find the apartment torn apart. Reba's clothes were gone, and most of her records, and most of the pots and pans. She'd left him their cat, Zozie, and a note she'd written on music paper in the sphinx code she hadn't used for years. *She must have heard my whistling after all,* Luke thought, his heart pounding with hope and fear as he struggled to turn the notes back into words. And then his heart stopped. Translated, the note said, "Sorry. I need to be by myself for a while."

No signature, no explanation, nothing else. Rad got only a note, which he wouldn't show to Luke, and when Reba didn't come to the garage for two Saturdays Rad sulked about as pale and worried as if Reba had been his wife and not Luke's. It was Rad who managed to find Reba down in Sunderland, Rad who gave Luke Reba's phone number. When Luke called, the first thing she did was ask him for the car.

"I need it to get to work," Reba said nervously.

"Forget work," Luke said. "Forget the car. What about us?"

But she wouldn't tell him what was happening, other than to mumble that she was restless and lonely and wanted to be closer to school. "Closer to work," she said. "Closer to the practice rooms."

Farther from home, Luke knew she meant. Farther from the village where they'd both grown up. She'd always wanted to cut herself off from who she was. He was the one who wouldn't let go, when anyone might have heard what she was saying. He closed his eyes and saw Reba wading in the pond near her parents' house while the fat ducks circled around her, quacking and carrying on as she sang to them. Her voice flowed like honey and her red hair flamed with the last of the sun, binding her to him along with a thousand other scenes. Reba under a railroad bridge, along the creek, deep in the swamp; pale in his father's barn, her mouth turned up to his; rising above the fairgrounds in a blue airplane. He thought of living without her and it was like living without his lungs.

"We'll share the car," he pleaded. "Let me move down with you."

"I have to be alone," she said quietly. "I need to sort out some things."

"Well, shit," Luke said, his voice rising despite himself. "What do you *want* from me?"

When she didn't answer, he said he'd be around if she needed him and then he settled in to wait. He built a shed for the Pitagorskis; he hammered his thumb and turned his nail black; he stepped on a spike that drove right through his shoe and into his foot. He called Reba every week to say he loved her and find out how she was, but she never told him anything more than the useless facts. She was fine, her job was fine, she had enough money; no she didn't need anything he could give her. He found out, when she stopped letting him give her things, how much he'd relied on that.

Summer came early and hot that year; at night, he and Zozie would sit in the living room with the windows open, panting in the close thick air and longing for Reba. She called periodically to ask for things she'd forgotten, books or cushions, a flowerpot, her father's binoculars, but her voice was distant and she always managed to pick these things up when Luke was out. He let her have the car after all; the apartment grew emptier each week, until there wasn't much left but Luke's clothes and tools and a few odd pieces of furniture. Luke threw the mattress on the floor, where it was cool.

Luke was so lonely that he took to meeting Rad after work for a few hours at the Rockledge Inn. They didn't talk much about Reba then—Rad blushed and got cranky whenever Luke brought up her name. They talked about the Red Sox instead, or about Mag and her cars, or about Linda, who was pregnant again. They played a lot of pool and watched a lot of TV. Luke had trouble working without a car and couldn't afford another one, but he borrowed some money from Rad and always told Reba he was fine, so she would want him back. He watched his life narrow to a thin line of working, eating, sleeping, and he began to wonder if asking Reba for explanations had been a mistake, something it wasn't fair to do when he'd married her so young.

It was Sally Lambert, in part, who got him thinking this way. He hadn't thought much about Sally in years— she'd come and gone before Reba had even left for music school, and Luke had shed their brief marriage the way he'd shed a layer of skin. One day, during the heart of his lonely summer, he hitched into Florence to see a friend about some wood. When he was done he treated himself to pie and coffee at Flo's Diner, and from the window he saw a sign advertising cheap haircuts that reminded him how shaggy he'd become. He went into the shop and found a young woman with bleached hair shaving a small boy's neck, and he'd already said, "Do you think I could get a trim?" before he recognized his ex-wife. A little girl, not more than two and a half, stood behind Sally's legs. She popped her head between her mother's knees and looked Luke over.

"Hello," she said severely. "You know my mommy?"

For a brief second, before the years and reality caught up with him, Luke thought the little girl might be his. He opened his mouth and the little girl opened hers, waiting for his next move.

"Luke," Sally said, as calmly as could be. She looked him over for a minute and then introduced her daughter, Pearl.

"You got married again?" Luke asked.

"I didn't," Sally said.

"You didn't," Luke echoed. And then he took another look at Pearl, at her smooth beige skin and curly eyelashes and frizzy cloud of light-brown hair, and he whispered, before he could stop himself, "That is no way Dale Gorman's baby," Dale being the man Sally had left him for when it became apparent that their marriage had been a mistake.

"True," Sally said calmly. "Dale and I broke up after I quit at the dentist's office and moved to Springfield."

"You were in Springfield?" Luke asked. "So close?"

"Beauty school," Sally said. "By the time I was licensed I was pregnant with Pearl. Remember Henry Cardoza? From Leeds?"

Luke shook his head.

"Well, anyway. He's long gone."

"Huh," Luke mumbled, and looked at Pearl again. She was as beautiful as any child he'd ever seen, and she might have been his—she was what he'd dreamed about during those days at Maglione's. Before he knew what he was doing he'd invited Sally and Pearl for a picnic and then, embarrassed, realized he didn't have his car.

"That's all right," Sally said. "We'll take mine."

While he was still regretting his impulse, she packed a huge satchel with juice, a pillow, a blanket, a stuffed bear, and a storybook, and then she stood waiting expectantly, Pearl's hand in hers. Her striped skirt waved around her legs, echoing the bright stars and streaming comets that speckled Pearl's shirt. Luke straightened his old pants self-consciously and then ran out to the corner store and picked up some cold cuts and bread and wine, wondering how he looked in Sally's eyes. Worse? Better? His beard had filled out since she'd seen him last and his arms were tan, but his sneakers had holes in them.

Half an hour later they were deep in the woods, on a road that reminded him of his own land in Conway, which he hardly ever saw. Pearl pointed out every flowering bush they passed and shrieked when they reached the crest of the hill and saw the glittering array of Maglione's greenhouses below. "I used to work there," he told Pearl, touched at Sally's gesture.

"I didn't know that," Sally said. "It's just a hill I like." She spread a blanket on the flat ledge and then tied Pearl to her with a harness and leash made of thin blue webbing, which Luke fingered in amazement. This was what he'd missed, he thought—leashes and Pampers and baby food and miniature sweaters, denim overalls small enough to clothe a cat. This, and all the rest of it. Sally pointed out Pearl's neat, tiny feet and graceful neck, saying, "She's going to be a dancer" with a note of pride that reminded Luke of how Sally had once dreamed this for herself. He could just remember her dancing the part of a moth in their sixth-grade musical. Below them, the shrubbed borders glowed green and gold near the pond where the water lilies grew. Luke looked down at the fields and wished he'd never left, thinking maybe Reba wouldn't have taken off if he'd stayed.

They must have been near a swallow's nest; all afternoon they were dive-bombed by sharp-winged, slate-blue
birds. "Plane!" Pearl shouted each time one swooped by.
Luke and Sally and Pearl ate their lunch on the ledge and
watched the ants carry away their crumbs, and when Sally
asked him how Reba was he told her she was gone. Which
didn't seem to surprise Sally half so much as it had him—
she knew things about Reba that he'd never guessed.
Pearl napped, wrapped in the blanket, and Luke and Sally
made their way through the bottle of wine while Sally told
him some of what she knew.

"What did you expect?" she asked, touching his leg
the way she used to with her creased white hands. "After
all the stuff she did with Jessie Thayer. . . ."

"What stuff?" he asked, and then frowned. "Jessie.
What a jerk."

Sally shrugged and drew a crude star in the dust beside her. "You know," she said. "Everyone knew. Or at
least some of us did—all those guys they went out with,
sneaking into bars and staying out all night and then singing in choir like butter wouldn't melt in their mouths . . .
who'd they think they were fooling?"

"Me, for one," Luke said, breathing slowly and wondering if Sally had any reason to lie to him. "Reba and I
didn't see much of each other when she was hanging out
with Jessie."

"This is news to you? You've known each other since
you were five or something. . . ."

"Not then," Luke said. "Remember? I was with you."
As he spoke he saw them at the party after their graduation. Him in a baggy blue suit he'd borrowed from Hank,
Sally in a pink gauzy something-or-other, cut low over her
bony chest and then draped and tucked and spangled and
frilled, a girl's dream of elegance. Her hair, dark then, had

been piled into an elaborate cone with ringlets coiled beside her ears. Homely—there was no other word for her then, although she'd grown into a pleasant-looking woman. That night she told him she was three weeks late, and a few days later they drove to Springfield and got themselves married. They'd stayed together only three months and had parted easily.

"Sure I remember," Sally said, and tapped him lightly. "We were so stupid—anyway, all I'm saying is that Reba did a lot of running around before you two finally got together, so maybe it's not so surprising she's running around again."

"I'm not sure she is," Luke said. "She seems to want to be by herself."

"Sure she does," Sally said. "Like a pig wants wings. Why don't you ask her what she's up to?"

Rad's advice, Luke thought. And look where it had gotten him. He kissed Sally, just to remember what that was like, but it only made him feel sad.

He slept poorly for the next three nights. When he shut his eyes he saw Reba everywhere, with everyone, her big green eyes gazing at another face, her hair spread over someone else's pillow, a hand other than his tracing the long columns of muscle that rolled down the river of her spine. He dreamed of her turned into Sally, Pearl into their child, and when he woke he flopped around restlessly and saw himself and Reba walking his land three years ago, when he'd been more in love with her than he'd ever been with anything. They'd sloshed through the mud in their rubber boots, and he'd showed her the spring and the jagged cliff, the maidenhair ferns and the valley. The spring trickled through stones that hid red salamanders, and when he'd asked her to marry him she'd said yes. He'd thought then that he knew everything about her—what could be better than marrying someone he'd known all his life? He'd dreamed out loud of a small cabin, a fireplace, a well out back; no electricity, not at first, but maybe later when they came there to live. She'd never said she wouldn't.

His land—that was what he wanted to comfort him. He called Hank one evening and asked him to drive him out to Conway after work. The land looked hot and dead that day, the spring gone dry and the animals in hiding. The path he'd started to cut the year he married Reba was mostly overgrown, as was the site he'd marked out for the cabin. He and Hank climbed the hill in the amiable silence they'd fallen into since Reba had thrown Hank out, and it was work for Luke to bring up Reba's name. "What's going on with her?" he asked.

"I don't know," Hank said. "She never talks to me anymore. I'm not sure she talks to anyone."

"She sure doesn't to me."

"You try?"

"Every week," Luke said.

Hank shook his head. "Nothing you can do but let her be," he said. "She'll come around in her own time. When we were kids she used to pull away like this, not talk to anyone till she'd worked out whatever was bothering her. Look how she was with the twins."

"That's true," Luke said. "But then we knew why."

Hank shrugged. "But now we don't." He picked up a splitting twig and said, "Go talk to Mag—maybe she knows something we don't."

And so Luke took to walking over to the Dwyers' house on the nights he didn't see Rad. He always took his tools; he always fixed some little thing when he was there, a broken stoop, a torn screen, a leaky toilet, as if he could conceal what he really wanted, which was to be in a place where Reba had once been, to hang around people who were hers. Some nights Hank came over, some nights Lily and Max, and Mag fixed them all sardines on toast or macaroni and cheese.

Mag didn't seem to hold it against him that Reba had taken off, and Luke was long past blaming her for bringing Rad and Reba together. He felt comfortable there, in the forest of dirty clothes and tools and broken machines. Tonia liked to show him the aquariums lining the walls of her room, and while Luke watched the darting silvery fish she'd talk about work and the animals, and about the endless story she was writing regarding the lives and loves of her rat colony. Her friend, Grey, had stolen a black-bound, red-cornered laboratory notebook for her, in which she wrote with a green felt-tip marker. Her large wobbling capitals bulged above and below the ruled lines.

"Listen," she'd say, standing with her back against the wall while Luke sat across from Mag and handed her tools. The story, or poem, or whatever it was, seemed to have no beginning or end. It ran day by day, episode by episode, rat soap opera. Each night Luke visited, he heard a new installment. He couldn't keep the characters straight—there were kings and queens and murderers, witches and princesses, monsters in the shape of cats and monkeys, fairy godmothers in the image of Reba. One passage she showed him went like this:

> "Lawrenz Rat sits all alone, he has
> a hurt on his,
> head. No one plays with, him.
> Then comes Reba Queen, with
> red hair. Lawrenz! she says.
> Waves her wand, made of
> jewls. Tells him little storeys,

one starts like this.
Little boy, my little joy,
you are my, little smile.
Anyone so angel lovelyness
and cute, I love you.
Come out and play,
on the fram."

"It is a poem," Tonia said gravely the night he heard that part. "All this, it is a poem-story for Reba, when she comes back."

"It's beautiful," Luke said, and touched her furry head. He looked over at Mag, wondering why he couldn't dream a Reba to comfort him the way Tonia had. After Tonia went to bed, Luke helped Mag rewire a waffle iron. Mag said, "Do you want her back?"

"Of course I do," Luke said, and that's when Mag told him to be flexible. "Give her some room," she said. "She's like her father—keeps everything important to herself. And she doesn't know what she wants right now. Whatever's going on now, if it's anything, doesn't mean much."

"You think?" Luke said, remembering what Sally had told him and wondering how much Mag knew.

"She'll always come home," Mag said. "If you let her. Just humor her for a while. When she was a girl, we'd have these awful fights and then she'd go hide in the woods for so long I'd be worried sick."

Lily was there that night, and Lily disagreed. "That girl doesn't love you," she told Luke sourly. "She's just lost. You'd be better off to let her go."

But Luke ignored Lily, and within a month he thought he'd found proof that Mag was right. In August, when his and Reba's third anniversary rolled around, he steeled himself, bought a huge bunch of irises, and went to visit Reba. All summer he'd pictured her alone in a tidy place, spare and bright, and he was horrified when she opened her door. Her apartment was in a basement, a string of cramped, badly laid-out rooms meandering through the bottom west corner of an old brick building and making way for furnaces and ducts. Her pictures lay against the wall in forlorn stacks; the walls and ceilings were peeling paint and the high-set windows were filthy. Above his head ran a network of rusty six-inch pipes, carrying heat and water to the rest of the building. The place was miserable, and so was Reba. Her hair was as dry and listless as reeds and she'd lost weight.

"Luke," she said, when she let him inside. Her gaze was as helpless and bewildered as it had been the day she'd fainted at the fairground. She took the irises and said, "You want to stay for dinner?" While she cooked Luke washed the windows and the floor and hung three pictures, all of which made Reba cry. They had a bottle of wine with dinner and Luke told her about visiting the land and how much it had made him think of her. Before he knew what was happening, they were together in the narrow bed Reba had borrowed from her mother.

In the morning Reba asked him if he wanted to move in. "Of course," he said—nothing else seemed important then, not his job or his friends or the fact that he hated this valley where Reba had chosen to live. That night he drove back to Rockledge and picked up his clothes and the cat, and that was when he promised to build Reba a study she could have to herself. Not a cage; that was never what he had in mind. Something the opposite of that, a nest, a home for her alone.

He spent the early part of the fall painting the walls and ceilings white and the steam pipes a cool bright blue, and then he went to work on his big project. The apartment's only charms were the huge, oddly shaped closets tucked into its twists and turns, and he set about to renovate one of these. Each day, after Reba left for the university, he'd strip down to his shorts and unlock the door to the huge closet off the living room, and then he'd start ripping and banging and hammering as if the work could make sense of their lives. He was happy Reba had taken him back—happy, happy. And yet sometimes he was so worn out with caring for her that he dreamed of floating away in a boat. *Caught again,* he thought, pushing that away as fast as it entered his mind. *And just when I was beginning to learn to live without her.* That wasn't true— he could never learn to live without her. But when he remembered his picnic with Sally it began to seem more appealing than it had been when he was living it. Before he'd shared Reba's bed again, there'd been nights when he'd dwelled on Sally's kiss, and when he stopped working on the study for half an hour and sat in the dark kitchen, he sometimes thought he almost hated Reba for the hold she had on him. *It's not her I hate,* he told himself then. *I hate loving her so much.* He pushed that thought away too. What he hated was this basement apartment twelve miles down in Sunderland; what he hated was being out of work. He hated what Sally had told him about Reba and Jessie.

We're never going to have another baby, he thought. *Never be a family.* In his worst moments he felt as though he didn't know Reba at all, and the only way he could calm himself was to measure and plan and build. He'd bring a lamp in from the living room and spread his stuff out on the floor—wood, tools, screws, nails, oil and rags and hinges. The closet was too small to work in, although it was plenty big enough for the desk and bookshelves Luke had planned, plenty big enough for Reba the way he dreamed her. Still, her back straight, her hair red and smooth and glossy, reading quietly the way a child might on a rainy afternoon. Peaceful, the way she hadn't been in years. She'd started taking piano lessons as if these could save her life, and Luke dreamed of scraping money together for a used upright, which he could fit in next to the desk. For now, Reba could only play in the university's practice rooms—one of the reasons, she said, why she was away so much. Sometimes Luke found her drumming silently on the fake keyboard she'd sketched on the window ledge, and when he did he'd take her in his arms and promise her everything.

He was working on the legs one November Saturday, planing some pieces of clear dark oak he'd scrounged and telling himself that this was fun, that he didn't mind working alone. He tried not to watch the sun pass the living room's one high window, tried not to dream about the hills back home or the leaves falling on his land. The dark rich mud that covered the valley was as unlike the sparse soil of Rockledge as anything he could imagine—fine for farming, good for asparagus, tobacco, and celery, but otherwise humid, flat and bare, full of colleges and snotty kids. It seemed to him that anyone smart would live up in the hills, and yet here he was. All part of being flexible, he told himself. And although Reba lied to him occasionally, and he was almost sure she knew he knew, he shut his eyes to that as well. That was part of being flexible too—not always needing to know the truth, deciding that being with Reba was more important than anything. She had a core to her about which he couldn't be fooled; he knew her, he must. And so he refused to wonder where she might be or why she'd started playing her father's old records again. *"O salce, salce, salce!"* he heard despite himself. The willow song; *salce* meant willow. Desdemona mourning Othello's desertion, Reba said, her eyes gone misty and dark. What did a willow have to do with anything? He hated that music; he drove it from his mind and told himself he was just hanging out, working so hard his mind went blank and he forgot everything. He forced himself not to worry, to forget the time of day, and so he didn't notice at first when someone opened his door. He'd left it open to get a little cool air, and Rad startled him.

"Reba?" Rad called down the stairs. His voice echoed along the walls. Reba had gone back to work for Rad in October—part of patching up their lives, she said. They needed the money. And although Luke hadn't seen him since he'd moved, he shouted "Down here!" and pulled his pants on, ready to welcome him. Rad seemed surprised to see him in a closet, half naked and covered with sawdust. Rad was in his working greens himself, black and greasy to the elbow.

"Luke," he said. "What're you doing?"

"Not much," Luke told him, waving his hand over the surrounding junk. "Just messing around."

"Not working?"

"Naah." Luke didn't want to say he hadn't worked steady since he'd moved.

"That's tough," Rad said. He took off his cap, leaving a warm wet ring below his matted hair. "Hot down here. How's Reba?"

"Fine," Luke said. He cleared off the file cabinet, so Rad had a place to sit.

"Reba!" Rad bellowed down the hall.

"She's at the garage," Luke said. "Didn't you go in?"

As soon as he said that he knew he shouldn't have—Rad hadn't gotten that dirty working at home.

Rad sat down and scuffed at the oak curls on the floor. He drew a little face there with the tip of one boot, and then he said, "Shit. What the hell is all this?"

"The desk I promised Reba."

Rad shook his head, and Luke knew he was thinking how he promised Reba too much. "Why do you put up with this?" Rad had asked after she'd moved out, and Luke hadn't known what to say. He'd loved her when she was growing up and told him everything; he loved her even now, when she was secretive.

"She called in sick," Rad said morosely. "Mag had everything under control at the garage, so I thought I'd stop by and cheer Reba up."

He dug his toes into the oak curls again and they stared at each other until Rad mumbled something Luke couldn't catch and kicked at the hinges on the floor. "You turkey," he said more loudly. "She doesn't need a *desk*— it'll just make her want to keep going to school."

"Want a drink?" Luke asked.

Rad nodded, and Luke fetched the bottle of Four Roses from under the bathroom sink. On his way back, he grabbed a couple of Dixie Cups.

"Let's see what you got here," Rad said.

Luke filled the cups and handed one over. "This lip, here—this fits over the molding along the back wall and holds up the edge. These are the legs."

"Nice," Rad said, stroking the length of one as if it belonged to Reba. "Looks like a lot of work."

"Sure," Luke said. "But it'll be a nice surprise."

Rad lifted an eyebrow, and Luke knew he was thinking how often it was that Reba did the surprising. "So where'd she go?" Rad asked, his voice as sharp as if it was Luke's fault Reba wasn't at home.

"I don't know—maybe she went shopping."

Rad snorted into his Dixie Cup. "To the dentist's," he said.

"Her brother's."

"The Laundromat."

"A haircut?"

"Naah."

They both laughed then, but not very hard. Luke picked up one of the desk legs and then started rubbing it with linseed oil. "Remember the summer?" he asked.

Rad nodded and settled his face into unhappy folds—they both knew what happened when they asked Reba too much. Luke looked at Rad's drooping head and knew he should say something. "Maybe she went to the doctor," Luke said. "And she didn't want to worry me, so she said she was going to your place instead." For a minute he almost believed this himself—perhaps she was pregnant after all, and wanted to find out for sure? But as soon as he thought this he knew it wasn't true.

Rad shook his head and said, "Don't bullshit me."

"I'm not," Luke said. "I'm just thinking."

He never lied to Rad if he could help it, but sometimes he found it hard to comfort him and still tell him the truth. It was as if Rad wanted him to hit her, or yell at her —and yet if Reba had been Rad's, Luke knew Rad would have done the same as him. Which was nothing—anything was better than losing her. He reminded himself that Rad didn't know Reba from before, when anyone could see that the sun streaming in through the red church window was centered on her. *History,* he thought. That was worth something.

Rad picked at the grease beneath his nails and stared at Luke, who could feel him wanting to ask a million things. Relax, Luke wanted to tell him, breathing deep himself. Be flexible. Rad kicked one of the steam pipes and said, "Why do you bother?"

"Because," Luke said, as a vision of his life without Reba opened before him. "Because I don't know what to do." The years he'd spent without Reba had passed like a bad dream, even the time he'd spent married to Sally. He could remember having his eyes and ears checked then, thinking the muted fog he made his way through had a physical cause. He'd stopped drinking altogether, but the feeling of perpetual hangover never left. And anything was better than that, even the last painful summer. Even this.

They heard the door open together. Like guilty boys, they emptied their Dixie Cups and hid the Four Roses bottle under a drop cloth. Reba called, "Luke!" down the stairs, but Luke didn't answer right away.

"Ask her where she's been," Rad said, and Luke knew Reba wasn't talking to Rad anymore.

"Luke?" Reba called.

"In here," Luke said, remembering how they used to call each other that way when they hid in the swamp, and wishing things between them could be like old times. But they had several different kinds of old times to choose from, and it wasn't clear, even to him, which old times he wanted back. The *old* old times, probably, when they could tell each other anything. The times back before Reba's father left, back before Jessie Thayer. Sometimes it seemed to him that that was where everything had gone wrong, not so much when Reba met Jessie as when he'd been unable to let her tell him about the things they did. That was the corner where he'd let her pull away; that was how they'd reached this point where she couldn't say anything about whatever was at the heart of her life.

When Reba came into the living room and saw him and Rad together, she stopped short and leaned her head against a pipe as if she'd suddenly grown tired. *Anyone so angel lovelyness,* Luke thought. *I love you.* He kissed her and pointed her toward the kitchen. She hung in his arms for a minute, and he felt her waiting for him to ask.

"Go make some coffee," Luke said, as gently as he could. "You'll spoil your surprise."

She left quietly, turning her head from the unfinished study. "Come on," Luke said to Rad. "Help me get this stuff back in the closet. I don't want her to see it yet." *I should leave,* he thought. *Just leave.* He knew he couldn't.

Rad looked at him. "You're such a jerk," he said, his face blotchy from the whiskey. "Why don't you ask her?"

"You do it," Luke said. "If you have to."

For a minute Luke wondered if Rad were fool enough. She'd tell Rad, Luke knew, as easy as she'd tell him. She'd throw it all away before she'd tell an outright lie. Did that make what she was doing his fault? For a minute he imagined what his life might be if she cut him loose. The kettle hissed in the kitchen and Rad snapped his cap back on his head.

"Shit," he said. "You two settle it—I'm going back to work. You want to get together later?" He said this as easily as if they'd been meeting every week, as if he hadn't been avoiding Luke since Luke's move to Sunderland.

"Sure," Luke said.

Rad nodded and left without saying good-bye to Reba. "Luke?" Reba called from the kitchen. He could hear her drumming on the windowsill. "There's coffee."

Luke finished cleaning and shut the closet door,

knowing he wasn't going to ask Reba anything. They had a quiet dinner and talked about Reba's job, and later Luke went out with Rad and watched a Celtics game on TV. The ball swished through the net as if it had a life of its own.

THE APPLE PICKER HITS THE ROAD

REBA'S new piano teacher, Mrs. Koerami, proved as fierce and demanding as Reba's father had been when she was young, or as her old voice teacher, Mrs. Barinov, had been later. *"One* and *two* and *three,"* Mrs. Koerami tapped, a human metronome. Reba took lessons from her all during that long year when she'd moved out on Luke and taken him back and then drifted away from him again, and when she played badly, which was most of the time, Mrs. Koerami struck at her like a cobra on speed. "That is not *mus*ical," she'd hiss, clicking her tongue against her teeth. "Can't you *hear* what he meant?" Her gray hair swept back from her face in wiry wings. She never played for Reba, although she'd once been quite famous; arthritis had crippled her hands into hooks. She'd pace the room instead and sing the melody in her cracked voice, while Reba repeated the offending phrases. "Too much ru*ba*to," Mrs. Koerami would say in despair, nibbling on a square of Belgian chocolate or one of the dry French biscuits that seemed to remind her of her time in Paris. "You are *ru*ining the line." She cursed Reba for playing the early romantics like a barbarian, and she set her to Bach and Haydn as a cure. When Reba complained that her life was chaotic and kept her from practicing, Mrs. Koerami laughed and made her a present of a small biographical dictionary called *Lives of the Composers.* "All musicians have troubles," she said. "Look at Mozart. Look at Liszt."

Reba was half in love with her. That dry, spare body, the coarse hair, the crippled fingers—all that seemed attractive to Reba, evidence of a life given over to something cool and disciplined. Mrs. Koerami had no lovers, Reba knew; if she had a husband, Reba was sure she didn't sleep with him. A single bed with spooled posts and starched sheets awaited her somewhere. She'd sleep on her back, Reba thought. With her mouth closed and her arms folded across her chest, not limb-sprawled and tossed as Reba did. In Mrs. Koerami's studio were no stray papers, no lost books, no unfiled sheets of music. Her Belgian chocolate sat in a drawer near her blue teapot. She wore black silk, black wool, black cotton dresses and black shoes with heavy heels. If she had a family she never spoke of it to Reba; no pictures adorned her clean white walls and Reba had no idea how she was ever going to play well enough to please her.

Reba had seven hours allotted to her each week at the university practice rooms, and it wasn't nearly enough. Scales, arpeggios, left-hand exercises, and then a nibble at her music and the time was gone, the notes still whirring in her head. She played on her desk at work and on her kitchen windowsill at home, having read in Mrs. Koerami's book that Chopin practiced this way. Luke watched her; Luke encouraged her. And when Luke's grandfather died late in November and left them his house in Rockledge, the first thing Luke did after they moved back was to sell the big clock in the dining room and buy Reba a used upright that had been in the Elks' Hall basement for thirty years. Someone had driven thumbtacks into the felts to give it a honky-tonk sound, but once Reba pulled these out and had it tuned it played well and Reba knew she owed Luke. She thanked him, but thanking him was nothing.

Luke moved the piano into the first-floor apartment for her, and he started knocking out the wall sealing off the stairs to the rooms he and Hank and Reba had once shared. "Wait," he told her, full of enthusiasm now that they'd left the valley and come home. "It'll be great. I'll make you a studio down here, and you can give piano lessons and stop working full-time and go to school more."

"I'm not good enough," Reba said. "I'll never be good enough." But she was touched by his gesture and by his faith in her. He'd never asked her where she'd been that Saturday six weeks ago when he and Rad had waited for her, or if her absence was connected with the reason she'd first left. In his patience, and in his promises, Reba thought she saw a vision shimmer. Mozart rather than Liszt, clear cool order; a passionless life that would leave her someday like Mrs. Koerami, her heart displaced to her fingertips. A house looking out on the square, neat and organized; crickets chirping summer nights; some useful work and a few small pleasures as harmless as Belgian chocolate eaten one square at a time. Rows of polished pots and pans and food simmering on a bright stove, her family eating a roast chicken sprinkled with herbs while she played Bach in another room.

So much more attractive than her own confused ways! On a sheet of paper she listed what was wrong with her life: two jobs, a husband she couldn't love enough, no time to practice; a father whose idea of a Christmas greeting was a postcard from the famous dam on the Gauley River, on which he'd written, "Headed for Kentucky. May be there for Christmas. Tamaracks are turning yellow." Not to mention the affair she'd been having for ten months with Robbie Calkins, which made her dreams of Nelson Callowell seem like an honest mistake. She imagined herself old and dried and purified, and she set out to do what she thought Mrs. Koerami would. She quit working for Rad, and although she couldn't make herself enjoy touching Luke she let him talk her into applying for a loan to fix the house. The bank wouldn't give them a loan without a co-signer—she and Luke were as broke as they'd ever been and no one in Reba's family was able to help. "Not to worry," Luke said, convinced he could get his father and uncle to co-sign the loan if he offered them an interest in the house. "They'll do it," he assured Reba. "I'll go spend a few days with them in Gardner, convince them what a great investment this is. The house'll be worth some money once we fix it up." *And you'll love me,* Reba heard him thinking. *You'll love our life, and you'll love me.*

"You think?" Reba said.

"Sure," Luke told her. He still wasn't working steadily, but he was as full of plans as if he couldn't see how they'd turned from a struggling young couple into shabby adults. He'd been making some oblong cherry-and-maple boxes he called slit drums, and he'd sold a couple at a crafts fair and another at a show. Now he thought he had a business. "I'll set up a shop in the basement," he told Reba. "Really go into production." He had a dry glitter about him in those days, and a need to make wild promises that almost corresponded to Reba's need to hear them.

Only one thing stood then between Reba and her new life, and that was Robbie Calkins. Robbie was the reason she'd left Luke in the spring and the reason she'd taken him back; he lived in Chesterfield, a few miles north of Rockledge, and he'd worked in the physical plant at the university until he hurt his back. Reba had glimpsed him once or twice while he was changing light bulbs or fixing tiles, but she'd never paid attention to him until the Personnel Director dumped him in their office in March. "Use him however you can," Nelson had told her and Sarah and Lorrie, and he'd waved his hand over Robbie as if Robbie were so much meat. Reba and her friends had put Robbie to work stuffing envelopes, sticking labels on fund-raising letters, recording checks as they'd trickled in. Robbie smiled and did whatever they asked. He was brown-eyed and big, six foot three, two-thirty or so, and running a little to fat, which Reba had never liked in a man before but didn't mind in him. He had beautiful hands and a smile that seemed to say everything was easy, and although he was only twenty-eight he had two kids and a wife and a beat-up car with a baby-seat in the back.

And he had more than that—he had a laugh that lit up the office and an endless flow of jokes, a good-humored charm that took the sting from deadlines and from the endless overtime they worked as the annual report came due. Out of his tan uniform and spruce in a pink shirt, he was so sunny and broad and warm that he made Reba catch her breath some days. She found herself drifting toward his desk more times than she needed to, searching for witty comments that would make him smile and dressing with more care than she had in years. Talking to him was easier than talking to Rad—Robbie didn't know anything about her family or Luke or the twins, and she could make him believe she led a normal life. She fell into the habit of eating lunch with him at his desk, and while they picked at their dry sandwiches she'd gazed into the big picture frame he'd propped against the wall. The frame held a blue cardboard mat dotted with oblong cutouts; in the cutouts were pictures of Robbie's family. His wife in a wedding dress, his daughters, Wendy and Jane, alone or together, he and his wife at a high school dance, their mouths wide in laughter. With the smallest bit of encouragement he'd gone on about the pictures for hours, and when Reba had leaned over his shoulder to look more closely she'd caught a smell of soap and shaving cream and starch that had filled her throat with longing.

She hadn't been able to stop staring at him; when he looked up and caught her she'd blushed and then he'd winked at her. A droll wink, flirtatious, nothing more than that, and it might have ended there if they hadn't worked late one April night after everyone else had left. "You hungry?" he'd asked her when they'd finally finished up, and when she nodded he took her to a bar in Hadley that she'd never seen before. The Starlight Lounge—small white bulbs flashed around the door and, across the parking lot, around the sign of a run-down building known as the Starlight Motel. The motel had orange metal doors opening onto the metal mesh walkway that framed the second floor.

They'd split a pitcher of beer. Robbie told her four dirty jokes in a row, leaning closer to her each time and touching her arm for emphasis. Her common sense split off like a shadow and floated away on a river of alcohol. The waitresses were laced into flowered dirndls with thigh-high skirts, and despite them Reba hadn't been able to keep herself from coming on hard to Robbie. *Not what I mean,* she thought, as the words left her lips. She'd meant to invite him home to meet Luke, to invite herself over to his house to meet his family. She'd meant to keep things light and flirtatious. Her mouth kept moving, framing an invitation she couldn't stop. Some old Everly Brothers tune blared from the jukebox and kept Robbie from hearing her.

"What?" he'd shouted, and so she had to make her

offer again. *A cure*, she'd said to herself then, thinking how she woke each morning next to Luke with Robbie on her mind. *One time and that'll cure me. One time.* Beneath his shirt he might be soft and pale. Clumsy, perhaps; or too familiar, not familiar enough, too rough, too gentle, stupid. Anything might save her. *It'll be terrible*, she'd thought. Half wish, half fear. *And then we can go back to being friends.* She'd set her glass down hard and spilled most of her beer on the vinyl-topped table. A waitress flounced by and wiped it up with a rag, her thighs in Robbie's face.

"No," Robbie had said, when he finally understood what Reba was suggesting. He drew away from her and curled his hands in his lap. "I can't. If I was free, then sure. But I'm not." He paused and then said, "And you're not either."

By then, Reba was so drunk and humiliated that she wanted to cry. *But I am*, she wanted to tell him, thinking of the way her skin shrank when Luke touched her. Sometimes she wondered if she and Luke had simply been imprinted on each other, the way goslings imprinted on rubber-booted farmers or baby monkeys fell for terry-wrapped boards.

Robbie had refused her again, more nicely this time. "I've got kids," he said. "Responsibilities. You understand?"

She'd nodded and asked if they could go. *Don't laugh*, she thought. *Just don't laugh.* She could hear the girls in Springfield laughing at her when she'd misjudged them the same way. Robbie walked her to her car, and when they got there she whispered, "Would you just kiss me good night?" A flash of inspiration that hit when she remembered how she'd stared at him all those days and caught him looking back; she knew what she was doing, and it worked. As soon as he kissed her she could feel his good intentions floating down the drain. They had just enough money between them to take a room at the motel, and after that they'd met once or twice a week on days so bright, it seemed criminal not to be out. He'd brought a six-pack or a bottle of wine and she'd brought a couple of joints; in the bright light they'd talked and touched and talked again until Reba fell in love with him and couldn't stop listening. Robbie brought a grace to her body she'd never felt before, not with Luke, not even with Jessie's boys, and the feeling terrified her. She'd been unable to understand how anyone kept from seeking this over and over, what kept the world from dissolving into an avalanche of need. Under Robbie's hands, the swamp where she'd played as a child returned to her.

His touch had been a dogwood setting forth its symmetric blooms, a chorus of bullfrogs on a steamy night. When she'd closed her eyes she'd seen soft-crowned rushes, the silty shore, a caddis fly's house slowly built from grains of sand and twigs. She'd heard a flock of red-winged blackbirds lifting off a fence, and she'd remembered how she and Luke and all the others had summoned each other with imitation birdcalls, which she hadn't tried to make in years. *O-Ka-LEEE*—that was blackbird's call. She'd tried it out on Robbie and he'd laughed. He laughed at everything once they started sleeping together, and he wasn't comfortable unless both of them were giggling. "Lighten up," he said when she sighed. "Stop being so serious. I'm just another dink with ears."

Robbie's third daughter was born the week Luke went to Gardner to find money for the house. Reba had been prepared for the news and was convinced she wouldn't care—she had a house, a husband again, a shadow of a life. But when Robbie called the office that December Monday, Reba found herself spinning into the vacuum she'd inhabited, on and off, since the day she'd first seen him. She hung up the phone when Robbie finished talking and rested her head on her desk, and when she could move she told Nelson she was sick and needed a few days off. Then she drove home to Rockledge, dug some clothes from the rubble of drywall and plaster littered everywhere, and headed for the Starlight Motel. She skipped her classes; she skipped her practice sessions and canceled her lesson with Mrs. Koerami. She blessed the stroke of luck that had pulled Luke out of town and kept him from seeing her like this.

She brought with her some rum, a little money, a few joints rolled in a plastic bag, her phony ten-dollar Walkman, and no plan other than to shed Robbie for good. As soon as she checked into the motel, she closed the curtains, covered her head, and slept. She dreamed of Robbie. She dreamed of his wife. She dreamed she *was* his wife, listening to the lies he'd told all spring, part of the summer, part of the fall. She woke weeping at four in the morning and remembered how, each week, Robbie had told her what lies he'd told his wife and then, as often as not, said he couldn't see her anymore. But each week he'd crumpled after a couple of days of her staring at him and him staring back at her. He couldn't seem to stay away from her, but he told her he wasn't in love or anything else and he didn't mean for her to fall in love with him. "It's like basketball," he'd told her once. "I do it for the exercise." And then he'd smiled. Another joke.

She walked to the nearby McDonald's for breakfast as soon as it was open. The sky was gray and smelled of snow; Reba wore her radio and listened to a piano trio, which made her feel as though she had three ears. Cello in her right ear, violin in her left, the piano spiking through the center of her head. She reminded herself that, thanks to Luke, she had a piano at home. She reminded herself she had a home.

"Egg McMuffin," she told the waitress. "Coffee. Extra cream."

"Hash browns?" the waitress bellowed, as if she had to scream at Reba because of the radio. Reba remembered how Lorrie and Sarah and Nelson had yelled like that at work, when she'd started wearing the radio after the first time Robbie had dumped her. It had kept her from hearing him on the phone.

"No thanks," Reba told the waitress. She ate by the window and tried to remember things she liked to do. She couldn't think of anything except singing and playing the piano, and she couldn't sing anymore and couldn't play well with Robbie on her mind. She'd been working on a Bach suite and a Beethoven sonata and three Gottschalk songs since summer. During the odd times things had gone well with Robbie, she'd begun to see how these pieces might be played. But in between, when things fell apart, the notes had shattered under her hands and dropped to the ground like flies. "You are to feel the *music*," Mrs. Koerami had hissed at her then. "What is in the com*po*ser's heart, not yours."

She went back to bed. On Wednesday she got up and went to the Rite Aid for some cigarettes. A big display of Diet Coke towered near the door—cases of bottles, cheap. She bought a case and some ruby-colored nail polish, because she felt like drinking rum-and-Cokes and doing her toes. Not much, she knew. But at least she felt like something. Near the nail polish was a stack of fat manila drawing pads that reminded her of Tonia, shaping her alphabet with her tongue between her teeth. Reba liked the way these looked so much that she bought three. She bought some felt-tipped markers as well, sixteen colors sealed in a plastic envelope. The snow started to fall before she was done, and she stopped on her way back to the motel and watched the fields turn white, remembering how she'd once liked the snow. She still had a tiny scar at the outer corner of her left eyebrow, from the time she and Hank had sledded into a tree. Robbie had never asked her about it.

When she got back to her room she made herself a drink and then opened the bag of markers and took out the first four—black, blue, silver, gray. She thought she might look out the window and draw the snow on the fields, and she didn't know until she started that she was going to draw the stars, the water, and the bridge. She drew them the way they'd been her first night at the motel, when she and Robbie had been giddy from too much wine and sore from too much messing around. They'd wandered out to the creek behind the parking lot and the footbridge that crossed it. The sky was very black that night and crammed with stars. They'd stood on the bridge and looked for the Milky Way, but they hadn't known where to look or what to look for.

Robbie had waved his hand and said, "Look—the Big Dipper."

She'd looked and thought she'd seen it, but when she looked again she'd seen dippers everywhere. "What's that?" she asked, pointing to another group of stars.

"I don't know," he'd said. "Looks like a bear."

"A bear with a broken leg, maybe."

They'd laughed and then stood there for half an hour, naming the rest of the sky. "Barn Owl," Robbie had pointed out. "Bicycle, Lizard, Apple Tree."

"Miner," Reba had showed him. "Cat. Cow."

"Swallow," Robbie had said.

Oh, there must have been something to him. When he'd touched her she'd felt like a child again, as if she'd been handed the key to the locked desk drawer where the adults hid their secrets. New news, the sort that Jessie had once brought her. Reba had sat on the four-inch railing guarding the bridge and leaned back into Robbie, drawing her feet up so there was only him between the water and her. He was as solid and warm as an elephant's leg, and when he'd made a move to tip her over she'd let herself go, knowing he would catch her. "You're so trusting," he said. He'd tipped her again and again and still she hadn't resisted, and they'd made love on the planks of the bridge and then gone back to their cars.

He'd been nothing like Nelson, with all his feeble courtliness; nothing like Luke. When she slept with Luke she felt like she was sleeping with her brother. She'd driven home to Luke with her toes in knots and her eyes so wide she could hardly see, and a few weeks later she'd left him and moved to Sunderland. Six months ago; she hadn't been able to give a thought to what she was doing to him, and she'd left him a note as senseless as the post-cards her father mailed to her. All she'd been able to see was a bed of her own and a door that locked. She hadn't bothered fixing up her new place because she'd thought all she needed was Robbie—him filling the doorway there, lumbering down the stairs, seizing her in the bare dark living room. She'd bought a vanilla-scented candle to put near the head of her bed, but Robbie had visited her only once, and only after she'd lured him there with promises of her claw-footed tub. Her place made him nervous, he said. Anyone might visit. After that, they'd gone back to the motel.

She drew the stars silver in a jet-black sky, the bridge

black and gray, the river black and blue. She drew them exactly as they'd been, not as she'd seen them on the bridge but the way they were before she fell in love. On the bridge she drew a pair of shoes she'd lost that evening, when Robbie had carried her down the metal mesh stairs so her thin blue heels wouldn't stick in the grids. Her shoes had fallen off, but before they did she'd had this one clear moment when Robbie was just a hot body she'd slept with and she still had a chance. Somewhere between losing her shoes and naming the stars she'd fallen in love with him, bump, thumpety-thump, like falling down those stairs, and after that she'd never seen him again the way he really was.

After she drew the stars she wanted to use some other colors, so she drew the cows she and Robbie had once seen browsing along the river. She drew the cows brown, like big brown dogs—she'd never been able to draw and these drawings were only sketches. The mist she drew yellow, with the sun shining through. Willow trees she drew lacy green, bark brown, river blue. She didn't draw Robbie and she didn't draw herself; she drew what was there before they'd made it into background. She drew with her radio on and listened to Christmas carols, humming along with the ones she knew. "Silent Night" reminded her of stars— she wedged the star picture into the mirror and admired it. She leaned the cows against a chair. She fixed another rum-and-Coke and listened as a choir of little boys' voices brought her peace on earth, goodwill toward men, joy to the world. They sang the way Luke used to sing, before his voice cracked. "And this shall be a sign," they sang. She saw the things she'd drawn as road signs she couldn't read until she drew them—"Go Slow," "Stop," "Do Not Pass." Somehow, Robbie had made her blind.

On Thursday, Reba woke full of energy and returned

to the Rite Aid for some thumbtacks. She picked up breakfast at McDonald's again, returned to her room, tacked
her drawings up, and smoked a joint. When she bit into
her Egg McMuffin, she suddenly saw the egg that had
rested on Nelson's desk a few weeks after the first time
Robbie had dumped her. When Robbie had found out Lisa
was pregnant, he'd stretched out on the bed, not on this
one but another, with his face gone yellow and his hands
clenched up. *Two other daughters,* he'd said. And a too
small house and not enough money and Reba—some time
for him to be having another kid. He'd lain there waiting
for her to comfort him, and she'd said the first thing that
crossed her mind, the worst thing she could have said.
"I'm falling a little in love with you," she'd told him, and
then she'd waited for him to say something back.

"I gotta go," Robbie had said, after a long pause.

He'd leapt up, stuffed his wide feet in his shoes, and
taken off. *Your wife did it on purpose,* Reba wanted to call
out after him. *Can't you see?* When she pulled herself
together and followed him it was pouring rain, and she
hadn't seen his message until she'd turned on her wind-
shield wipers and found a white envelope ticking back and
forth. She'd turned the wipers off, pulled the soggy envelope inside, and read his cold words. "This has to be it,"
he'd written. "I love messing around with you, but it's just
messing around. I have responsibilities."

And yet he'd come back within a couple of weeks. "I
act like a shit sometimes," he'd told her over lunch. "I
know I do. My friends used to say my middle name was
asshole, and I still turn my head when someone calls that
out in a crowd." Then he'd told her a joke and smiled
winsomely, as if that should be enough for her to forgive
him. She hadn't said anything and he'd tried again. He'd
let his mouth droop at the corners, and he'd said, "You

don't know what it was like going home the night we split up. I got there wanting some peace and quiet, and Lisa handed me a raft of shit like she hadn't done in years. 'Cut me some slack,' I wanted to tell her. 'I just broke up with my girl.' But I couldn't say anything. She took the kids and ran off to her mother's for the night, and there I was with no her and no you, watching baseball on the cable till dawn. And then I came back to work and there you were, staring down at your desk like someone had taped your eyes there. It just killed me."

That week Holly, Nelson's oldest daughter, brought an egg into the office to show off. The egg was floating in a jar of vinegar, soaking there for some science project. All day, Reba and Lorrie and Sarah and Nelson had watched the acid eating away the shell. When Holly came in late that afternoon to see how it was doing, Nelson had lifted the egg from the jar and held it up for their inspection. The shell had disappeared and the insides had jiggled, held together only by a tough membrane. In the light the yolk had bobbed dreamily, and Reba had thrown up in front of everyone. She'd seen Lisa, stomach swollen, when Lisa had come to pick up Robbie, and her own breasts had grown and she'd puffed up, as if she were carrying the twins again. She'd cried and craved strange foods at night and missed a period, but it had all been just her body's joke, its way of saying how stupid she was.

She put down her Egg McMuffin and drew the soft membrane, the cloudy white, the sunny yellow yolk. And then she kept on drawing, whatever she could think of. She drew the tobacco fields across the river, the way they'd looked the first time Robbie had come back. She didn't draw him, but she drew the acres of white gauze shading the plants, the poles suspending the gauze, the green leaves underneath. She drew tractors in other fields.

She drew her desk at work, Lorrie and Sarah, Tonia and Hank, Nelson surrounded by his golden children, Mag, Zozie, Bowen at his organ, Luke working on that study in their basement apartment, which he had never finished. She drew Lily in an undershirt, on a couch heaped with cats. She drew all she'd lost since she first slept with Robbie, when she'd started seeing the world through Vaseline.

Reba stayed at the motel until Friday night, which found her standing at the front desk and trying to persuade the clerk to turn on the phone in her room. The clerk wanted ten bucks as a deposit.

"I'm just making a local call," she told him. "Just one."

He picked at his nails and said, "Those are the rules. If you want to leave a credit card I'll take that instead." Then he smiled, knowing Reba hadn't checked in under her name.

Reba gave him the money, which left her with four dollars and a little change, and then she called Robbie's house for the first time ever. "Just come for a drink," she said when he picked up the phone. "I'm at the motel." She could hear his two older daughters playing near the phone and his mother-in-law screeching at them.

"Well . . ." he said. He waffled a bit and then he came, the way he always had. She knew he didn't have the willpower God gave a goat.

When he hung up, Reba combed her hair and changed her shirt. She got ready for Robbie the way she always had, but when he knocked and she opened the door she saw right through him. She looked and saw the door frame, the dark sky, the champagne bottle he carried. He didn't block out the rest of the world the way he had for months, and that made Reba think she had a chance. She saw a shadow, standing there as stiffly as if he'd never opened a motel room door before to find her inside.

"Room twenty-three," he said, smiling the smile he used whenever they'd broken up and he wanted to come back. He wore the pink shirt Reba had always loved, fresh with the smell of a hot iron. "Didn't we have this one before?"

"Sometime in August," Reba said. "Remember the smell?" She did—she couldn't forget it. The last time they'd had this room had been right before her third anniversary, right before she'd asked Luke to come back. The Slukarskis had been spreading manure in their celery fields, on the rich bottomland across the river. Reba had opened the windows that day, and the room had smelled like a barn. They'd smelled everything from these motel windows, and Reba remembered it all—cucumbers rotting, apples, asparagus in June. This was the room with the flowered bedspreads, the broken towel rack, the bug-eyed kitten pictures on the walls. The room where Robbie had said he was bored, and where she'd once decided never to see him again. The drawings she'd tacked up on the walls had changed the room a little, and Robbie raised an eyebrow when he came in.

"Jesus," he said. "What have you been doing here?"

"Nothing," she said, lying easily. "Just killing time. Luke's been away this week, so I had our new place fumigated." *Bugs*, she thought. *He's dumb enough to believe that.* He'd never been curious, never wanted any more of her than she'd chosen to give. She knew he would have taken less if he'd known how.

Robbie held a bottle out. "I thought we'd celebrate."

"There's glasses in the bathroom," Reba said. Her left hand practiced scales on the night table, making a sound someone might have confused with nervous tapping. But

it wasn't that at all—Mrs. Koerami had said Reba's left
hand was too weak to do justice to Beethoven and needed
constant practice.

Robbie moved past her, his eyes drifting to the sheets
of paper tacked to the walls. When he came back he sat on
the bed and popped the cork. "To Amy!" he said, clinking
his glass to Reba's.

"To Amy!" Reba echoed. She looked at Robbie's huge
shoes, thinking how he was acting happy over this newest
daughter of his because he had to, because he didn't remember she'd seen his face when he first found out Lisa
was pregnant. Only a fool would have taken him back
after he'd dumped her that first time; she'd taken him
back three times and wasn't even sure she knew why,
except that being with him was like smoking, hard to quit
even after it stopped being fun. And now here he was
again, stretched out on the bed with his shoes kicked off,
being careful not to touch her.

Reba didn't touch him. She passed him a joint and he
chattered away, as he always did when they hadn't slept
together for a while. *I, me, me, I, my;* his wife, his children,
his house, his life. Each time he'd decided they shouldn't
be lovers anymore, he'd talked to Reba as if he didn't have
another friend in the world, as if they'd ever had something in common besides going to bed.

Always, Reba thought. *He always does this, talks himself into touching me again.* One day he'd spent half their
precious two hours together talking about his father's apple farm and how he'd liked picking apples there better
than almost anything. The apples grew in groves, he said,
split by rolling hills. His friend Rick had helped him, and
together they'd watched over the Jamaicans who helped
with the harvest. At night they bought bags of homegrown
from the pickers and smoked it down by the river. *Every-*

thing was easy then, he'd said, his voice grown wistful. *Get up, get high, get laid, get paid, get some sleep.*

That ease was what Reba had thought she was getting when she took him. But when she'd asked Robbie where all that had gone, his voice had turned bitter as he described how he'd gotten Lisa pregnant and married her. Rick had died when he crashed his brother's truck, and his father had sold the apple farm to some developer. *Summer's nothing like it used to be,* he'd mourned, as if all this had happened just to spoil his dreams. And yet it was summer then—he and Reba had been lying in a streak of sun when he told her that, but he wasn't thinking about her at all. She'd wanted to punch him, to ask if he thought these things happened only to him.

He went on and on about Lisa's labor, never asking Reba what those drawings were doing on the walls. *Figures,* Reba thought. He'd never wondered; he wasn't in love. His world was solid and all of a piece and nothing like hers, and the worst he ever got was wistful for that apple farm. *I dream about it all the time,* he'd told her once. In his dream he was playing basketball in an orchard that was paved between the trees. That was one of the times she'd taken him back—when he talked like that she couldn't help but love him, even knowing that part of him was no more than a stick of cinnamon buried in a pie. He'd said she smelled like an orchard in full fruit to him, and yet he hadn't meant anything. His biggest talent seemed to be for liking what was; hers seemed to be for loving what wasn't, and that was no talent but just something to get rid of.

"I took her to the hospital then anyway," said Robbie, interrupting Reba's thoughts. "And it's a good thing, because we hadn't been there an hour before she really got going. They had to call the doctor in from rounds."

"Really?" Reba said. She knew how to humor him; she nodded as if she were interested and then tuned out again, knowing he couldn't tell.

"Amy popped out in ten minutes," Robbie said. "You should have seen that wrinkly face."

As if I would want to see, thought Reba. He was always talking about his girls, about the apple trees he'd planted for each one, the sandbox he'd made Wendy, the way Jane had danced around the yard in a Bruce Springsteen T-shirt, denting a scrap of wood with a ball peen hammer. Sometimes he wrenched her heart so hard, it seemed to lodge in her throat instead. This time she tried not to listen, tried not to watch as he loosened his tie and unbuttoned his shirt partway. He'd told her over and over again he'd never leave his wife, and she'd said "Fine" but hadn't looked ahead because there wasn't anything there. She'd looked for the little things instead. When they left work each day, she'd looked for morning. When they left their rooms at the Starlight Motel, she'd looked for the times they'd come back. When he talked to her and then fell silent, she'd waited for him to talk again.

Robbie droned on and Reba stared at the pictures she'd tacked to the walls. Robbie started explaining how Wendy and Jane had helped him decorate the baby's new room. "I made it from a closet," he said, and Reba thought of Luke tearing apart their new house. "The room, I mean. And the girls drew some pictures and we hung them all over. Looks funny—sort of like in here."

He scanned the drawings on the walls, but they weren't signs for him and didn't mean anything. All they did was remind him of his daughters. *Maybe that's all I did,* Reba thought. Robbie had once said that she and his daughters all reminded him of deer.

"I didn't know you could draw," he continued.

"That's pretty cool. The girls drew a bunch of cards for Lisa and we brought them in yesterday."

Robbie paused for a minute, and Reba knew she should say something. "I'm glad things are going well," she told him. He was just a stranger by then, slightly drunk and lying next to her in bed—what she'd always been for him but never seen. He unbuttoned the rest of his shirt but still didn't touch her. She lit the joint again and passed it to him.

Robbie talked about his wife some more, but he was flushed and drunk and horny and high and began to forget his lines. When she touched his ear and whispered, "Make love to me?" she knew he wouldn't say no. He was counting on her to tide him over, knowing he wouldn't get any at home for six weeks. She knew Robbie. She knew he wanted her to want him the way she used to, wanted to make her crazy at his touch.

"Well," he whispered. "Maybe one last time." She knew he'd said that so often, he didn't believe it himself.

Reba let him touch her and take off her clothes; he had to take his off himself. When he started in with his standard tricks she waited to see if her drawings would vanish and the room grow gray. Nothing happened. *No more Robbie,* she thought. *No more of this.* His fingers reminded her of celery, his smell of fresh-turned fields. Dried bugs jumped in the ceiling light when he moved, and she found that by pleating two parts of the bedspread together she could turn two anemones into a rose. She let him heave and toss and sweat and try to make her come, and she lay there, just a body, hearing the Beethoven she was supposed to be practicing. She thought of that clear, cool house looking out on the square, the rows of polished pots and pans she'd never owned but might. A cold fuck was what he'd always wanted: no emotions, no strings. She gave him snow. Cold sheets, cold skin, what she got from Luke and all she'd have now. Mrs. Koerami's life.

Robbie lifted his head above her. "What is it?" he asked. "Don't you want me?"

She did, but just to feel what it was like not to want him. She touched his back, amazed to find it only flesh. Like a dream, she saw the apple picker that had once been him leap up and take off without a backward glance. He was slim, still, and his arms were filled with apples, and he didn't give a shit about anything. He was laughing; he was gone.

She didn't have to say she wouldn't see him anymore. She made herself a drink and drew his head as it had looked when he was passing out the door. She drew the door, and then she went outside and sat on the cold metal stairs and tried to imagine Luke in Gardner, calling her every night and hearing the phone ring in the empty house, wondering where she was.

O MY CHARMER,
SPARE ME

ANK didn't make his way back into Reba's life until after the noise was over. The hammering and sawing and drilling sounds from Luke's grandfather's house floated across to Elzenga's print shop, where Hank still worked, all winter and into spring; the Wyatts' backyard butted up to the scuffed, muddy lot behind the shop. When the presses were running Hank couldn't hear anything, but when they stopped he heard sporadic crashes and steady taps, occasional curses. The work was going on inside, where he couldn't see it—those first few months after Luke and Reba returned, Hank met them only at Mag's.

He never saw Reba at Lily's, where he spent much of his time; Lily was furious with her. "She had her chance," Lily told Hank one afternoon, when they were looking out on the frozen lake. "She finally manages to pull away from Luke, and what does she do? Takes him back and ignores the rest of us. I swear, she deserves whatever she gets."

Lily had Razznol and Rowley on her lap, Pyewacket on her right shoulder, Wicker around her neck, but Hank saw nothing strange in that. What was strange was how mad she was at Reba. "Just because you warned her not to get married," he said. "You gotta give her credit for trying to make it work."

"Huh," Lily grunted. "Don't gotta give her credit for anything." She messed a spoon around in her bowl of butter brickle and then lifted her chin at Hank. "Look at you—you grew up the same way, and you haven't been so dumb."

Haven't had the chance, Hank wanted to say. Lucinda Evans had vanished after that Easter dinner at Reba's, and since then there'd been only an odd evening here and there with girls who were friends of his friends. Pale girls with limp hair, chunky girls with glasses. Girls who liked to bowl. Sometimes he thought he should just settle down and choose one, the way Reba had settled for Luke or their parents had settled for each other. But Lily always told him no. "Wait," she said. "You'll know when it's right."

Meanwhile his life was wearing away. Setting type, running the presses, writing out invoices and making deliveries, Sunday dinners with Mag and Tonia, evenings with Lily and Max. His hairline creeping back to the crown of his head. Going nowhere, he thought, and he stopped Reba one day on the street and said, "So when are you going to let me see the house?" Enough of this estrangement shit, he thought. He'd been watching her for weeks. The noises had stopped early in May, and when they did he'd noticed that Luke had begun leaving early each morning but that Reba seemed to be around much more. In the afternoons, when there was so little work at the shop that Hank's boss took off and Hank stretched what there was out like toffee, he'd heard Reba playing the piano. And in the evenings, as the days grew longer, he'd walked by and seen her outside, planting lilacs and begonias in the dim cool light.

"The house?" she said, the day he approached her. "It's a disaster. Trust me—you don't want to see."

My sister, he thought, a little bitterly. She'd withdrawn behind a wall of secrets as thick as any other married woman's. And yet she must have heard him—one afternoon a few days later, when he was sitting at the table behind the print shop eating his lunch and tossing the scraps to the squirrels, Reba opened a gap in the hedge between them and invited him through.

"Want to see the house?" she asked, as if the house were not a mystery to her whole family. Things were suspended in midconstruction, and Hank picked his way gingerly through the rubble. The living room and the kitchen were almost finished; Reba's piano stood in a niche near three new windows still sprouting pink frills of insulation. Plastic sheets draped the hole where a wall had been knocked out to expose the stairwell. The dining room was a jumble of boards and Sheetrock and cans of paint, tools and putty and tape, and as for the upstairs—"Don't bother looking," Reba told him. "What a wreck—we ran out of money, and Luke ran out of time and energy." Hank took a quick peek, ignored what he saw, and praised the work they'd done downstairs. Could be worse, he told himself. Could be a hole in the roof.

"How come you're home?" he asked her. "No work?"

"I quit taking courses for the summer," Reba said. "And I switched my job to part-time for a couple of months, so I could concentrate on my piano. What about you?"

He made a face. "Nothing to do half the time over there," he said. "Everything's dried up."

"You could come visit me," she said. "Listen to me practice. I could use someone with half an ear—Luke's no help these days."

And so Hank took to dropping by almost every afternoon and listening to her play. In between the pieces she talked about composers and theory until he thought he was almost learning something—him, the one with the bad voice, the one Bowen had given up on in despair. He and Reba hadn't spoken about anything important since she'd thrown him out of the upstairs apartment, but now she started talking again, sandwiching stories about herself in between musical tales. Reba, Mozart, Reba, Bach. Sometimes she told him more than he wanted to know, which is how he found out about Jessie Thayer.

He and Reba were sitting on the couch one day, with Zozie between them, when Reba set down the music she'd been showing him and wiped her temple. "God, it's hot," she said. "I can't remember a summer like this since the year I met Jessie. Remember her?"

"Jessie Thayer?" What Hank remembered was a blond girl he saw only at school, always with Reba. And how Reba had changed after meeting her. Most days she went to Jessie's after school; when she didn't she'd come home and do odd things, shorten her skirts or fuss with her nails. No more touch football, no more hide-and-seek. Jessie had long, shapely nails, polished and smooth; Reba had soaked her bloody, bitten stumps in baby oil in hopes of imitating them. "Look at my cuticles," she'd once mourned to Hank. "All ragged." He'd nodded, thinking she meant the ridges of crisp flesh that rimmed her gnawed-off nails. Girl things—that's what Jessie brought to mind. Girl talk.

"Yeah," Reba said. "Jessie Thayer. I never brought her home much, but we were real close for a couple of years."

She looked down at her hands and Hank, just making conversation, said, "Money, right? I remember her clothes. And that carriage they used to walk her baby brother in."

"She was crazy," Reba said. "I taught her to sing, and

she taught me everything else. We used to sing in choir high as kites."

"Come on," Hank said.

"True fact," Reba told him. "She always had great dope—I don't even know where she got it from. And wild —there wasn't anything she wouldn't do. We used to sneak out her window weekend nights and run all over."

She stared out the window, a slight smile on her face. "There was this bar . . ." she said, and while Hank sat frozen she told him about the parties, the boys, the liquor they stole, the hash they smoked at dawn; the Pepsi and the dark cars. *Where was I?* Hank wondered. *How'd I miss this?* He searched his memory and saw himself hiding in the woods, fighting with Bowen, feeding the chickens and watching Tonia. Aware that Reba was never around but with no sense where she was. And he had meant to take care of her. *Watch your sister,* Mag had said. He'd been four, maybe, and Reba had been two, and there was a yard behind the house then, not a field of weeds. No fence— Bowen had tapped four stakes into the ground, at the four corners of the yard, and told Hank to imagine something filling the gaps, a wall of stone, a wall of air. It was Hank's job not to let Reba pass beyond the stakes. A clothesline ran from the corner of the house to a locust tree, hung with worn sheets and obscuring the children from Mag's view. Each time Hank looked down for a minute to find a stick or pick up a beetle, Reba darted for the woods. In the end he'd tied a piece of string from her arm to his.

Reba fell silent and looked at him. He swallowed hard, his mouth filled with bitter fluid, and he said, "What did Luke think of all this?"

"He never knew," Reba said simply. "Still doesn't, as far as I know. By the time I got back from music school all that was over, and by then I couldn't stand to tell anyone."

All those men, she'd said to him years ago, when they had crouched together in the bathroom. *When I was hanging out with Jessie.* Finally he knew what she meant. For almost three years she'd hardly spoken to him, and then one day she'd parted the arborvitae with her long hands and asked him through, to tell him this. Something even Luke didn't know. It made him uncomfortable, and yet it filled him with a certain pride as well.

As the summer wore on, the stories Reba told him grew more and more personal, as if, by listening to the first one, he'd given her permission to tell him anything. At first all her stories centered on her time with Jessie, but later she worked her way around to Nelson and finally to Robbie and Mrs. Koerami.

"When?" Hank said in confusion. "When was this?"

"Just this year," Reba said. "I finally got rid of him right after we moved back here. You know my teacher, Mrs. Koerami—I kept thinking how I'd like to run my life like hers, all smooth and cool, and this was how I figured out to do it. Cut that part of me right off—for this." She waved at the plastic sheets and the drywall.

"You did the right thing," Hank said, although he wasn't sure.

"Did I?" she said moodily. "Sometimes I feel like I cut off my foot. I swear, if I didn't have my music . . ."

At night, Hank would go home and try not to imagine Reba doing the things she'd done, but her stories stabbed him like needles. The more she told him, the more his memories of their childhood together sharpened. Once she'd met Luke she'd turned to him instead, and then to Jessie after Luke. Never to Hank—when Lily took them to her cabin for the weekend, Reba sat sullen and buried in a book while Hank and Tonia played with Lily. Soon it was Tonia Hank held on to, rather than Reba; but he'd never meant to let Reba out of his sight. She'd been in the swamp the day they all got lost; at the creek when they were skating and at the Gorge on the summer days when all of them gathered there. At the Gorge they'd broken into groups as separate as species—the younger girls, eight and nine, splashing in the water; the small boys, Luke and Hank among them, playing with the girls sometimes but sometimes, already, pulling off into caves and tree houses where girls were not allowed; on the rocks, stretched out in the hot sun, the twelve- and thirteen-year-old girls flaunting their new bodies while the boys that age stole hot glances and tried to act cool. He'd been in one place; she'd been in another, leading a life as secret as a plant's.

She might still be leading it, for all he knew. There was the Gottschalk question, for instance—they'd been talking for several months before Reba showed him the program for her first recital. He recognized almost everything on it, except for the last entry:

O Ma Charmante, Epargnez-Moi! Louis Moreau
(O My Charmer, Spare Me!)   Gottschalk
           (1829–1869)

Hank didn't catch the dates at first; from the way Reba's hands trembled, the way her heels clicked across the floor as nervously as an antelope's, he feared at first that this was another lover, someone who'd written a song just for her. It was possible, he knew: around her, anyone might do anything. He caught the dates before he made a fool of himself, and then he asked Reba who Gottschalk was. He was expecting one of her clear, precise musical lectures, but Reba only smiled and said, "Hardly anyone knows him—he spent a lot of time in the West Indies. He's sort of a favorite of Mrs. Koerami's."

"Yeah?" Hank said. "So play the song for me."

"Not until the recital," she told him. "I want it to be a surprise."

Hank shook his head, not saying the whole recital *was* a surprise. He knew there was no talking Reba into something she didn't want to do. "So how come you want to do this recital?" he asked.

She set her jaw and said, "Because."

"Because why?"

"Because it's a good idea. I'll play, and then I'll announce that I'm giving lessons this fall, and all the mothers will sign up their kids."

"Right," Hank said. "You're going to dazzle them?"

"That's right," she said. "I am. I need to make some money of my own, and this is how I want to do it."

She planted her large, long, fine-boned hands on the couch, framing Hank's knees and confronting him again with that amazing, batlike stretch of skin between her forefingers and her thumbs. She'd had those hands even as a girl. "You'll print up the programs?" she said.

Hank sighed. "If that's what you want," he told her, and then they got down to business, which consisted of his trying to convince her to photocopy the eighty copies of the program she wanted, and her trying to convince him to print them on a wildly expensive deckle-edged paper. They compromised on a lightweight pearl-gray bond, and Hank asked her again about the Gottschalk song. "What's the point?" he said. "Playing something they've never heard—it's not like you'll convince them."

Reba smiled. "What the hell," she said. "It's worth a try. It has this feeling to it, sort of sad and restless and wild all at once, that brings back Jessie for me. I want to play it."

"Your choice," Hank said.

A few weeks before the recital, Reba took off on a nine-day trip. "I won the lottery!" she told Hank one day, waving a strip of paper in his face.

Hank sat down hard. "The Massachusetts lottery?" he said. "You won a million bucks?"

"The *university* lottery," Reba said impatiently. "The Director of Employee Relations thought this up—it's supposed to help staff members get to know each other better so we work together better—something like that, I don't know. Anyway, we all got to put our names in and they picked ten people, and I was one."

"So what did you win?"

"A camping trip!" Reba said. "Can you believe it? Ten people from all different parts of the university, and two trip leaders, and they're sending us in a van to *Maine*, with six canoes. We're going to paddle through this chain of lakes and sleep in tents and stuff, and they're paying for everything and taking care of all the food and equipment. Doesn't even count as vacation time."

"Sounds strange to me," Hank said. "You sure you want to go? Camping with a bunch of people you don't know . . ."

"Are you kidding?" Reba told him. "A week away from here, out in the woods—sure."

They gave her a list of what she had to bring, and for the next few days Hank helped her pack her bags while Luke puttered around the house and grumbled. Rain jacket, rain pants, wool socks, two sweaters, hat, gloves— "It's cold up there," Reba said—water bottle, wool pants, sleeping bag, flashlight, shirts, plastic bags. And then she was gone. She left at four one morning—Hank drove her to the university and watched her pile with the others into a yellow van pulling a trailer with six canoes arranged on a rack like long gray fish.

When she came back she was very quiet. "It rained six of the days," she told him. "But the people were interesting. Luke's mad at me because I went."

"How come?" Hank said. "Did he ask you not to go?"

"Not really," Reba said. "But I think he thinks he did."

Hank had printed Reba's programs up while she was away, and he gave them to her that afternoon. A few nights later, as he was walking past on the dark road, he spied her and Luke arguing. The light was on in their kitchen, and he could see Reba fixing supper while Luke paced back and forth, yelling about something. Yelling at Reba, Hank could see. *He hates the way you yell at me,* he remembered Reba saying the night, years ago, when she'd kicked him out. *I never yell at you,* Luke had said then, but he was yelling now. Hank meant to turn away, but when Reba spun from the stove and started shouting back at Luke, Hank stared at the open circle of her mouth and then crept into Reba's yard. Thinking—he wasn't sure what he was thinking, except that he wanted to be there in case she needed him. Their windows were open, and their voices carried clearly.

"You think I don't know?" Luke said. "You think I don't know what you're doing? You vanish for nine days and then come home and won't talk to me, won't touch me, tell me you're distracted because of this damn recital . . . you think I'm *blind*? And then hanging those recital programs all over town, without even telling me . . ."

"I want a full house," Reba said stubbornly. "I pinned some up at work, and in my practice room at school, and at the Red & White, and at Rad's . . ."

"Great," Luke said.

"I have to do something," Reba said. "Especially now.

I need some money of my own, and this is a good way to advertise lessons."

"Yeah?" Luke said. "Want to tell me what you need the money for?"

"Because I *need* it," Reba said. "*We* need it. You could get a normal job, and sell that stupid land, and wake *up*, but you won't. And I'm tired of living like this."

Hank had never heard her talk like that. As he watched, Luke sighed and then knocked his head softly against the cupboards. "You're *always* tired of living like this," he said. "Always have been. You think I don't know? And it's not like I'm not doing the best I can. I just bought a whole new load of wood."

"Sure," Reba said. "So you can work on those stupid drums. Who do you think's going to buy them?"

"You got a better idea?" Luke said. "That's what you want, isn't it? For me to make some money. Grow up. Act responsible. And if you think I'm going to watch you make a fool of yourself, you're dreaming. I have to *work* that day —you didn't even check with me about the date."

His voice crept higher, and Hank stole away before he could hear any more. He hadn't known, until that night, that they fought at all. Although he'd often wondered what it would be like to be Luke, alone in that house and waiting for Reba.

"You got money troubles?" Hank asked Reba the next day.

She shrugged. "Just the usual. I owe Mrs. Koerami for six weeks of lessons, and we owe on some wood Luke bought and for the transmission Rad put in the Cutlass, and—you know—stuff for the house . . ."

"Why didn't you ask me?" Hank said. "I could help."

She sighed. "Since when have you had any money?"

"I could find it," he said, his mind leaping toward

banks, cash registers, payroll checks, jars of pennies in children's closets.

"It's all right," Reba said. "I sold some stuff on my way home from work. You know that junk shop on Westfall?"

Hank nodded.

"The guy there took the stuff I scraped together—the silver teaspoons Luke's grandfather left us, and Great-aunt Alice's onyx pin with the pearls, and that hair ring that was Dad's grandmother's. He offered me a hundred and fifty bucks for the lot, and I said no. Then he started checking out my wedding ring."

Hank looked down at her bare left hand, remembering the glitter of sapphire and white that Mag had given Luke to give to Reba, the ring that had once belonged to Lily. He didn't want to imagine what Lily would say when she discovered it was gone.

"Gave me four hundred bucks," Reba said.

"Pretty cheap for all that."

Reba spread her bare hand before her, twisting it this way and that. "Luke and I had a big fight the other night," she said. "About money, and about the recital, and the camping trip. I just wanted to get some money without making a big deal of it."

"You've been pretty distracted since you got back," Hank said. "Maybe you scared him."

"Maybe," she said. "But you know what scared him more? That I asked him to sell that land of his. He talks all the time about going up there to live, just the two of us, never seeing anyone else. All the time saying that this, what we're doing now, is just getting ready for our real lives. And when I tell him our lives are what we're *living*, he doesn't hear me. He had this burst of energy when we first came back here and started fixing up the house, and now he's lost it all. You know what he's been doing these last few months? Laying a cabin foundation up there in Conway. It's like he doesn't understand we have to finish this house and pay back the money we borrowed. And it was his idea to borrow it."

"He'll settle down," Hank said, wondering why he was pleading Luke's case. "Give him a break. You love him, and everything . . ."

"Do I?" Reba said quietly. "Is that what this is?"

So there was that to get Hank going, that little crack he thought he'd seen between Luke and Reba, and into that crack, over the next few days, slipped Louis Gottschalk. Reba started talking about him each time Hank saw her, and she dropped facts about Gottschalk's life in a way that seemed meant to reproach Hank. Gottschalk, Reba said. A man with soul, who left New Orleans for Paris when he was just a little boy, who studied and played all over Europe before returning to America as famous as a rock star. He'd headed for the tropics at twenty-five, zipped through the West Indies and the Spanish Antilles and Cuba and Brazil, leaving a trail of broken hearts and dashing music behind. By forty he was dead in Rio, and Reba made even that last point sound glamorous.

Hank had turned twenty-six the week Reba told him this, and he couldn't help being embarrassed by his lack of adventure. Here was this man, Reba seemed to be saying, who'd traveled the world before he was Hank's age and played to screaming crowds—and here was him, Hank, in the town that he was born in, with a nonexistent social life and a stupid job. *What are you going to do?* Reba seemed to be asking him.

He didn't know. He hadn't told Reba about the job he'd been offered—several weeks ago, a biologist from the university had brought in some lecture notes to be printed up and had gotten to talking with Hank about his research

project. "Owls," he'd said. "Breeding habits, communica-
tion, feeding behavior, nesting—I'm watching a popula-
tion down at the Quabbin Reservoir."

"You get to stay outside all day and watch birds?"
Hank had said. "They pay you for this?"

"Sure," the man said, laughing easily. "I could pay *you*
to do it, if you were interested. I need an assistant, somebody big and strong who's used to being out in bad
weather, and at night. All you'd have to do is watch the
birds and take notes. You spend much time outside?"

"Plenty," Hank said. "And that sounds great. I can't
right now, but maybe some other time. . . ."

"Call me," the man said. He'd left Hank his name and
phone number.

It was that easy. One call and he could be out of
Rockledge, out of the print shop, off on his own doing
something interesting. All he had to do was leave Reba
behind. He looked at Gottschalk's picture on the sheet
music Reba had given him, hoping to find a clue as to
where his life was headed. But all he saw was a thin man
with a large head and enormous eyes and hollow temples,
with a drooping moustache and Reba's bat-skinned hands.
A man meant to break hearts gazing out at him, who
hadn't broken anyone's heart in ten years. He begged
Reba to play him the song, but she couldn't and he
couldn't read the music. During the days before her recital she played parts of all her other pieces for him, but
she withheld the Gottschalk until he found himself thinking about it all the time, trying to imagine what it might
sound like and humming notes to himself, as if he somehow might discover the tune.

Hank couldn't get Gottschalk and his music out of his
mind. About then, he decided to make Reba a present for
her recital. He thought about printing some fancy little

poem for her, but this didn't seem to say what he meant. What he did, instead, while he was in the print shop running off wedding announcements for Bonnie Percival, was to carve a woodblock picture of Reba's hands. He carved the block in relief because he meant to print it: left hand and right hand side by side, thumbs nearly touching, fingers splayed; fine bones and tendons showing as lines and the webs hinted at by soft swirls. He carved the hands so they'd fit next to each other in a repeating pattern, and as he did he thought of Gottschalk. This thin guy with eyes like eggs, holding Reba and dancing under the moon on one of those islands Hank had never seen and knew he'd probably never see. One of those places where maybe his father had ended up, where they grow hibiscus big as platters and hand out pineapple drinks. Bowen's latest postcard had come from the Everglades and had hinted that he might leap off the continent altogether; now Hank pictured Bowen in a white suit with wide lapels, all the tight misery gone from his face and his scarred hands miraculously smooth again. Leading a choir of dark-skinned women in white robes with voices rich as silk, and smiling, smiling, as he never had at home.

Hank made a couple of test prints and fine-tuned the right hand, and then when he knew it was good he printed a hundred pairs of Reba's hands strutting down a roll of creamy paper. Each pair at a slight angle, tilted first right and then left to make a dancing pattern like leaves, a pattern a hundred feet long and eighteen inches wide. He printed the last pair and then caught his breath, because there it was: She had their father's hands, and always had.

On the Sunday of Reba's recital, two-thirty came and went and left only seven people in the Wyatts' house: Reba, Tonia, Mag, Hank, and three old women—Lily and her friends, Aurora Swensen and Lenore Pryor. Luke was in Conway with his friends Champoux and Scarpatowski, setting sills into the cabin foundation. Mrs. Koerami had the flu. Nelson and Lorrie and the others Reba worked with had all made their excuses, and Hank hadn't been able to convince his friends to come. Even Lily had come only reluctantly, under pressure from Hank; she brought her two friends in a battered car and she sniffed at the unfinished house, muttering under her breath when Reba didn't start the recital on time. She and Lenore and Aurora sat impatiently on three of the sixty folding chairs Reba had rented, chatting among themselves and stroking the long folds that creased their cheeks in front of their ears. Tonia and Mag sat together near Hank, Mag browsing through a Chilton's Manual and Tonia reading softly to Hank from her laboratory notebook. Her hair rose above her head in a crest held by two pink combs. "You remember Lawrenz," Tonia said to Hank, and then she read:

> "King Lawrenz gathers
> all his band together.
> Whistles made from nuts
> they play, and drum,
> the steel bars. Wave a
> wand, bars open! Like
> a song. Play three
> tunes and march
> around, why not
> make a happiness?
> Cats are in a
> nother room."

"They escaped?" Hank said. "Your rats?"
"*Yes,*" Tonia said, and then looked around quickly. No

one else was listening. Three o'clock, and still no Reba; Hank wanted to ask Tonia if the rats had escaped for real or only in her head but he went into the kitchen instead, hoping to coax Reba out. She was sitting at the table, crying and drinking wine, and although she said he couldn't know how she felt, he thought he did. She felt the way their father had, trapped with the chickens in the barn; the way everyone felt each time the world narrowed down a notch.

"Come on," he said, trying to cheer her up. "Men wear hats." Sometimes, when nothing made sense to them, they played games with phrases from Bowen's strange notes.

"Big water," Reba replied, trying to play along.

"The Gauley," Hank said, in an oily, radio-announcer's voice. "King of Dams."

"Plants in the Everglades look like hair. Air-boats like blowdryers," Reba said, but then she kicked at the table legs and said, "Oh, *fuck.*"

Hank patted Reba's shoulder and said, "This isn't the end of the world," and when she kept crying he said, "Wait —I have something for you." He ran across to the print shop and got the roll of hands he'd meant to give her later. He tripped on the doorsill on his way back into the kitchen, and the hands unrolled across the floor to her. In the sun they looked spectacular—all these colors, ame- thyst and ruby and sapphire and jet, jade and turquoise and topaz and lapis, hands printed every jewel color he'd been able to find. *Your heart in your fingertips,* he thought, remembering something she'd told him about Mrs. Koerami.

"*My* hands?" Reba said, wiping her eyes and bending for a closer look.

"Yours," Hank said.

Reba waited expectantly, and Hank realized this was the moment he was supposed to tell her what to do. The hum of voices beyond the door rose and then broke into laughter, and he found he couldn't say anything. Reba took the roll of paper and unwound it the rest of the way, stretching it across countertops and tables and chairs, back across the floor, over the stove, around the refrigerator. She was quiet for a few minutes, and Hank heard Lily's voice rising above the others. Finally Reba said, "Thank you. It's beautiful."

"I'm not sure where it's meant to go," Hank said. "It's so big."

"I'll roll it onto two dowels," Reba said. "One at either end, so I can look at it like a scroll."

She walked into the living room, touched Tonia's head, and then launched into the first movement of the Beethoven. Lily and Lenore and Aurora closed their eyes and tapped their knees gently, each apparently hearing a different beat. Hank listened as best as he could, using everything Reba had taught him. He knew she was playing well. Spectacularly, in fact, and he was smiling by the time she got to the second movement, which was rollicking and gay. Tonia rose quietly and walked to the open window, smiling down at something Hank couldn't see. He followed her and looked down—there in a row, with their feet threaded between the shrubs, were the youngest of the neighborhood children. Ricky Wilkins, Sally Robb, Flora O'Keefe, and Jamie McMahon, all about the age Reba's own twins might have been and hanging on to each other as if their parents had already abandoned them. Their hands rested on the windowsill, and their heads were tilted up to catch the music. Tonia was smiling down at them, conducting with a pudgy finger. Sally Robb jumped when she saw Hank, but relaxed when he smiled at her.

"Want to come in?" he whispered.

They shook their heads no.

"Like the music?"

They shook their heads yes.

I want a daughter, Hank thought, with a piercing suddenness. *Someone of my own.* He left Tonia watching over them. Reba played the Beethoven straight through, pausing for only a minute before she began her Schubert Impromptu. When she finished, Hank clapped until his hands stung and so did everyone else, even the children hidden outside.

Reba stood up, bowed, and left the room without playing the other pieces on her program. After a few minutes, Hank realized she wasn't coming back. He looked at Mag; Mag shook her head, gathered up Tonia, and left. He looked at Lily; Lily said, "That's it?" When Hank nodded, Lily said, "Well, that was very nice, I'm sure," and then she put on her ruffled hat and took her friends home. The children outside drifted away, leaving only Hank in the living room with the folding chairs stretched before him in silent rows. He conjured up the audience that should have been: the children he and Reba had played with, in starched dresses and too short pants; Bowen and his brothers, dead and alive; Luke and Roger and Chuck and Jimmy, and possibly their parents; Jamie Rondine with his red wagon; Lily's cats in matching collars; Mrs. Koerami and Reba's other friends. Did Reba have friends?

Reba joined him in the empty room. "No Gottschalk?" Hank asked, almost pleading. "I waited all this time."

She smiled tiredly. "I'm not in the mood."

"Please?" he said. "For me?"

He sat down on the window ledge and folded his arms, prepared to wait all afternoon. The sun had vanished behind a cloud; the folding chairs were vacant. Reba looked down at her hands and spread her fingers, stretching the skin between them. And then slowly, liltingly, she began a song that had the saddest, gayest, strangest syncopation to it, a song Hank knew he shouldn't have made her play and shouldn't have listened to. She closed her eyes and swayed above the piano until the tempo picked up, changed, slowed down again, until it seemed to Hank that everyone in this cold dark town of theirs, doctors and teachers and store clerks and builders, mothers and children and cats and dogs, pigeons and mice, spiders and ants, must be dancing to this compelling beat.

Behind his closed eyes, Hank saw a picture—him and Reba, the kids from the village, Luke and the others from the outlying farms, all gathered down at Rockledge Gorge, where they splashed in the stream and drank beer on the stony cliffs. There, when he was fifteen, he'd fallen in love with Cybil Staudemeyer and she, scorning him completely because he wouldn't run away with her, lit out for Springfield with pale, hollow-eyed Paul DiRiccio, who was twenty years old. There he'd failed to notice what Reba was doing, where she was headed; there, Reba had escaped.

The music made him remember this, and it also reminded him that, although he could go back to the Gorge anytime and remember Cybil, it was never going to do him any good. "What could be worse?" Reba had once said to him, when he'd been trying to get her to recall some childhood scene. "What could be worse than being a child again? Trapped, held prisoner, always being pushed and pulled and dragged, can't take care of yourself or change things or live on your own, with all the smarts you'll ever have and none of the stuff you need to use it, seeing everything but can't understand the half of it—why would you want to remember that?"

He opened his eyes and danced his way across to Reba, ready to propose an immediate move to the islands —him, her, Lily and Max, Tonia, the piano, whatever she wanted, all in some place where tropical breezes blew or waves crashed or whatever it was she needed. Anyplace. It was time for them to leave. He smiled at Reba, ready to tell her this, but she kept her eyes closed until she finished the song. Then she handed the music to him, tucked the roll of dancing hands beneath her arm, and walked out toward her car.

"Wait," Hank called after her. "I want to tell you something."

"I'm going for a ride," Reba said softly. "Just to cool off."

She drove away, leaving behind the house she and Luke had partly put together, the lilacs she'd planted along the road, and the used piano Luke had managed to buy. She left Hank, already dreaming of owls, and a handful of odd remains: in the arborvitae behind her backyard, a gap that would take some years to close; in the print shop, a carved woodblock propped over the door; in Hank's hand, the sheet music for an obscure song. She left Hank humming a melody that already he was beginning to forget.

LIVES OF
THE COMPOSERS

The camping trip, Reba thought, as she sat in her dark kitchen making lists and waiting for the night to pass. Black spruce. White spruce. Balsam fir, jack pine, quaking aspen. Bearberry, trillium, bunchberry, starflower—*that was where it started.* The trees and plants surrounding the lakes had been different from those in the swamp, and she hadn't paid attention.

There had been six cold lakes in a row, framed by forest and edged by stony beach. And six canoes, as gray as the water, bearing twelve passengers two by two: two women who knew each other and two who didn't; four young men split into pairs; two older men who always trailed the others; and two people paired by accident, Reba and the trip leader, Martin. Stretched in a line across a lake, the canoes resembled the fins of a giant fish slicing through a silver mirror. In the distance paper birch bent their slim trunks, crowded by endless spruce and pine.

Reba had paddled with Martin for seven days, hoping each morning that someone else would choose her for a partner. No one did. Martin was short and boring, obsessed by rules—hold the paddle so, pitch the tent this way. Smug in his position, snug in his dry clothes, he pored over his compass and map and ignored the constant rain. When night fell, the group cooked dried foods over a round fire and then crept into three tents, each of which held four bodies on a damp nylon floor. The four women who paddled together slept in one, giggling and telling stories into the night. The four young men slept in another. And the two odd men out, the older men, slept with Reba and Martin. Ambrose, the electrician, wrapped himself in a smoky red shirt and slept against one outside wall. Martin, in a blue watch cap, slept against the other. Sandwiched in between were Reba and Dory Poole.

That was how she met him—Theodore Poole, Jr., always called Dory, never called Ted, who was fair-haired and exceedingly tall and forty-nine. Long before she slept with him she slept beside him, curled a warming inch from his back while she listened to the steady rain. Loneliness, not lust, had turned her toward him at first—the rest of the group had fused instantly, excluding only the inhabitants of her tent. The trip was nothing like what she wished for, her companions nothing like the friends with whom she'd shared the swamp at home.

At night, in the dark Maine woods, she'd leave the others singing and drinking whiskey by the campfire, and she'd huddle on a flat rock some distance down the shore, listening to the loons and the owls and the prowling raccoons. A whisper of needles in place of the rustle of leaves, loons and swallows instead of sparrows, nighthawks buzzing and diving in search of bugs and an occasional heavy cracking that hinted of bear or moose or lynx—she realized, to her surprise, that she'd never been alone outside at night. Her tent was silent; the three men she shared it with often retired hours before the others, and by the time Reba joined them they'd all be breathing softly and twitching with their dreams. She never expected to see Dory Poole glide from the shadows late one night, long after he should have been asleep. For a minute, she thought he was a bear.

"Sorry," he'd said smoothly. "Didn't mean to sneak up. Mind if I join you?"

She let out her breath and nodded. This was before her recital, and so she was playing her Gottschalk in her head, drumming her fingers on the rock beside her and thinking about the performance she meant to give. When Dory spread his poncho out and asked what she was doing, she told him the truth.

"A musician?" he said, and she didn't contradict him. "I should have guessed. I've been trying to figure you out all week." He held a lighter to his pipe and examined her in the amber glow as if he'd never seen her before. "And terrific-looking, too," he added.

Reba shrugged. "What about you?" she asked. "What do you do?"

"You mean for work?" Dory smoothed a layer of pine needles into a neat cone. "I teach in the English department—I'm a poet, primarily."

"That's right," Reba said. "I remember now." She knew who he was, although it hadn't clicked before— she'd seen the jacket photo, minus hat, blue anorak, gloves, on his one slim book of poetry, and she'd printed some of his Czechoslovakian translations from his last trip abroad in the alumni magazine.

"I'm flattered," he said, and he made a mock bow in her direction. Then he sighed and said, "It's so pretty here —how come I want to go home?"

Reba laughed. "Because it's cold!" she said. "And wet, and lonely . . ."

"You too?" Dory said.

That first night they talked about music, and when Reba asked how he knew so much he said, "I sang fairly seriously when I was young—baritone. Didn't do much for years, but then I got into classical Hindu music through a student of mine. About five years ago, I guess. I sing every day now." Then he surprised her by crossing his legs beneath him, throwing his shoulders back, and softly singing a raga in a voice that was nasal and pure at the same time, hypnotic and repetitive. The scale on which the music was based was one she'd never heard before—she wasn't even sure it could be called a scale. The pitches slid like fish, scooping from low to high and shooting back down.

"That's . . . *remarkable,*" Reba said when he was done. The clouds had lifted just enough to expose the moon, and in that kind light Dory reminded her of Luke. Same straight nose, fine hair, small chin. Luke's voice, before it changed, had once had a similar pure coolness.

"It's all in the breathing," Dory said modestly. "There are ragas for every time of day, for every mood—*raga* comes from the Sanskrit for color. Shades, you know. Infinite nuances. I have a ton of records at home. Maybe you'd like to borrow some?"

"I would," she said, and that night, after he fell asleep, she let herself touch his back.

Only his back, only for a touch of comfort so she could sleep, but he was what propelled her from Rockledge for good after her recital. It wasn't the lack of an audience, or Hank's gift, or Luke's absence that drove her away, although all those things had counted. It was her recognition, halfway through the Gottschalk piece, that she was ruining it, along with her clear sense that the palace of daydreams she'd built around Dory was why.

You think I don't know? Luke had said when she'd returned from her trip. *You think I don't know what you're doing?* She hadn't known then, but it had come clear the day of her recital. As she played she'd seen that she'd sleep with Dory, that she was only a breath from that, and without hardly knowing him she knew that he'd be trouble. *Our lives are what we're living,* she'd said to Hank, but what she was living was no life at all. The smallest hint of interest, even from someone like Dory, was enough to send her spinning into space. And she was tired of drifting like an asteroid. *Tamaracks are turning yellow,* her father had written, and she envied him that easy vision.

After her recital she closed the lid of her piano and promised herself she wouldn't make music until she could do it right. She left Luke to his cabin in Conway and went back to working full-time and taking music theory courses at night. And then she fell into Dory anyway, because there wasn't a scrap of romance left in her life. Singing was romantic but she'd lost her voice with the twins; playing the piano was romantic the way she did it, and that was what was wrong with her technique. Mrs. Koerami had gently refused to give her any more lessons, and Reba thought she knew why. It wasn't because she had only a small talent—she'd always known that. It was because something in her kept distorting it, pushed her into making music with the depth of greeting card verse and the passion of bad opera.

Dory, true to his word, brought some records by her office a week after she left Rockledge. "Try singing along with these," he said. "You don't have to understand what the singer's doing—just let your voice go."

She took the records to her friend Lorrie's place, where she was staying, and at night she sat cross-legged before Lorrie's stereo, breathing deeply and trying to imitate the haunting voice that twined between the sitar and the tabla. Hopeless, but she liked listening anyway and let the ragas soothe her to sleep. A few harmless records, which had to be exchanged for a few others and talked about over lunch and then over drinks after work—that was how Dory courted her, and she'd been seeing him for only a few weeks when he asked her to get a place of her own.

They couldn't go to Dory's house in Leverett because of his wife, couldn't go to motel rooms because Dory swore that people recognized him everywhere. Reba, who'd been planning to share a house with some students from her music class, said, "I can't afford a whole apartment." But Dory said, "Get someplace little," and in his words she read a promise that they'd spend more time together if she did. This despite the way he talked about his wife; despite the way he stroked the shirt Reba once complimented and said, "My wife orders these specially—I have to have pure cotton next to my skin." When she went back to her sofa at Lorrie's place and thought about the end of herself and Luke and how she'd given up music altogether, been reduced to a listener, she couldn't find a reason not to do what Dory asked.

The dark, bleak studio she found in Northampton was the best she could afford. She had roaches, and mice behind the walls, and bars across her windows; a hallway littered with gum and hair and a twenty-year-old refrigerator painted navy blue. She had windows propped open with blocks of wood and neighbors right on top of her: three old women living on their social security checks; two young men of indeterminate occupation about whom nothing could be easily guessed; an old man whose English was heavily laced with Finnish and who kept a forbidden Chihuahua; and seven young women besides herself. They were separated only by cheap hollow doors, thin ceilings and floors and walls, and she could hear the old man clearing his throat at night, working and working at some density he couldn't get up. Cupboards banged, doors creaked, water ran and dripped and splashed, the Chihuahua yelped, someone's finches peeped, voices rose and fell and TVs hummed well into the night and woke Reba again at dawn.

She decorated with scraps of home. Hank's roll of hands stretched from the doorway around the corner and behind the couch, where she kept the remaining eighty feet scrolled as tightly as cabbage leaves. Above the table she pinned three stanzas of the Lawrenz Rat story, which Tonia had copied out especially for her. In the space above her bed she had a picture of Lily surrounded by her cats, and another, which Rad had taken, of Mag on a dolly beneath a rusty Pontiac. And one more picture, a childhood picture, which she'd managed to save from her parents' chaotic home years ago—her, Hank, and Tonia, hardly more than infants, side by side in a white tub filled with bubbles. Their soapy hair had been pulled and piled into ridiculous shapes—horns for Hank, a topknot for Tonia, a pixie's pointed fairy-locks for herself.

Lorrie gave her the name of a lawyer who promised a cheap divorce, and Reba started the dry rustle of papers that would set her free. She took Zozie back and turned a cold ear to Luke's pleas, which finally turned to anger and released her.

"You're making a mistake," Luke said to her, the night they met at Flo's Diner to settle things. "You'll end up with someone just like me, only worse."

"The hell I will," Reba said, pushing Dory from her mind.

"Watch," Luke said bitterly, setting his coffee cup down so loudly that two men at the counter turned and stared. "Just watch. I know you better than you think. You,

your whole family, so crazy you can't even think straight
. . . *I'd* have to be crazy to take any more of this." He'd
marched out the door, twisting a plastic straw into a stran-
gled knot.

Luke sold the house and went to stay with his father in
Gardner; she got a check for a hundred dollars from him.
After all their work, all they'd done to the house, that was
what remained when they paid off the loans. Nothing was
left of their life together but documents, shooting back
and forth in the mail.

Sometimes, when she lay alone in a bed as narrow as
the one she'd dreamed for Mrs. Koerami, she had to bite
her hands to keep from calling Luke. She wrote to him in
the sphinx code they'd used as children—long, gentle,
explaining notes that resembled music on the page, a
flurry of triplets and barlines and rests. *Remember,* she
wrote in their secret code. *Remember the chickens? Remember the swamp? Remember the times we hid in the
Gorge?* She went to the clinic to see if she could get some
sleeping pills, and the pictures the young doctor kept on
the wall behind him tore at her heart. Four children, as
sunny as Nelson's, as lovely as Robbie's—that night she
filled three sheets of music paper, trying to explain to
Luke why those pictures had touched her so. *Those men
look like trees,* she wrote in her code. *Trees in the swamp
with their sheltering branches, those children like deer
and rabbits and ferns gentling up to the trunks.*

"You don't need pills," the doctor had said, his hands
warm and dry on her back. "Stop drinking coffee. Relax."

For a minute she wanted to marry him; for another
she wished she were one of his children. *Remember when
we were friends?* she wrote to Luke, and she woke the next
morning startled at the litter of paper on the floor around
her. She folded the sheets into tidy thirds and stuffed them

into envelopes. She addressed the envelopes to Luke in Gardner and then tore them up, knowing just enough to realize it wasn't her husband she wanted back. She wanted the Luke of her childhood, the friend of her heart.

Two small lines carved themselves on either side of Reba's nose, making her look permanently strained, and she noticed that the other young women she passed in the halls wore this look as well. Like her, they rushed out each morning with their fingers still fumbling at buttons and zippers and returned each night with stingy bags of groceries. Anita, Brenda, Laurel, Kathy, Hetty, Tina, Diane— Reba knew their names from the mailboxes, although she failed at first to attach them to the right faces. Once a week or so she'd spot a good dress and a blush and a smile on one of those women, and then the groceries she saw would be altogether different—cream, a bottle of wine, the shy tips of asparagus poking above the bag. *Visitors,* Reba would think then, and she'd smile at her lucky neighbor and try not to feel envious. Later, she'd hear moans and thrashings from one of the apartments, and she'd have to put her head under her pillow to sleep.

There were few secrets in that building, and yet Reba told no one about Dory—to her family, to her neighbors, most of all to herself, she steadfastly maintained the fiction that she was finally on her own. Dory visited once a week, no more, and she tried to tell herself that he hardly counted. An amusement, an anesthetic; someone to take the edge off her loneliness and give her a break from the awful business of shedding Luke. She looked at the men she glimpsed in the halls, those visitors with their ducked heads and averted eyes, and she thought that what went on between herself and Dory was no different than the lives her neighbors and their visitors led. The lives of married men; the lives of the women of married men. Lives that happened in the late afternoons and early nights, truncated in time to tuck children into bed.

Dory had no children, but she didn't think to wonder when he, lying on her bed in the twilight before he returned to his house, would stare at the frieze of hands, at the rat poems, at the childhood pictures, and say, "Tell me about your family," in the same words Nelson had once used. She never suspected that he was different, never guessed until later that he picked through her tales like a magpie, pulling out the gaudiest baubles with an unerring instinct for what she'd least like revealed and bending what had caught his eye into awful poems.

But the poems came later. Before the poems came Philadelphia, where Dory was to spend three days in mid-December giving a series of lectures. He asked Reba to come along and Reba agreed; she hated the Christmas season still and she welcomed the distraction. She packed in a dither, not considering where she was going to stay or what she'd do while Dory's hosts entertained him.

At his suggestion, she and Dory took separate seats on the plane and emerged into the Philadelphia airport without exchanging a word, all to foil discovery by some imaginary stranger who might recognize Dory from the jacket picture of a book that had sold six hundred copies. Gold and blue flames from the refineries near the airport flared all around them. They shared a cab into Rittenhouse Square; at the hotel, Dory suggested they take separate rooms. "In case someone drops by," he said. "You know— to see me or something. Or in case my wife calls. Get one on the same floor as mine."

The hotel lobby was draped with red and green tinsel; in a corner stood an artificial silver tree. Reba had to pull

Dory aside and tell him she didn't have a credit card or enough money to pay for her room.

"Oh?" he said, and then, "Of course." He reached into his wallet and paid for her room in cash, folding the receipt for his own room into a neat square he tucked into his wallet. "Business trip," he explained, and then he walked away and left Reba to follow. The rest of the night ran into a painful blur—the lecture Dory gave on contemporary Czech poets, which Reba almost missed because she got lost walking over alone; the moment when, applauding from the doorway, she moved toward Dory only to watch his colleagues bear him away; the long walk back to the hotel by herself, in a cold persistent drizzle that would have been snow at home.

What am I doing here? she wondered. In her purse was the book Mrs. Koerami had given her more than a year ago, which she'd seldom looked at but had grabbed just before she left and packed as a sort of talisman. Now she hunched by the window and read at random. *Lives of the Composers*—Berg, she read, had died from an insect bite that gave him blood poisoning. Mahler had lived on water and spinach and fruit. Schumann's syphilis gave him aural hallucinations and plagued him with angels and demons; Elgar passed his early years conducting the staff of an insane asylum in concerts meant to calm the patients. Her eyes fell on the entry for Verdi, whose operas Jessie had loved; then on Donizetti, Bellini, Rossini. Crazy, all of them. Crazy with love.

She closed the book and went to the mirror and painted dark lines around her eyes, the way she and Jessie used to when they'd listened to Bowen's old operas and struck extravagant poses. *Jessie,* she thought. *Lost to the man with the long white hands.* You could always lose a woman to a man. She hummed an aria from *La Traviata* and tried to convince herself that this trip with Dory was like one of her outings with Jessie, an exploration of the dark. She ordered a bottle of bourbon and killed a third of it before Dory returned, and still she couldn't get herself in the proper mood.

Dory reappeared at eleven and made Reba a half apology. "Let's get you something to eat," he said—the closest he came to admitting he'd abandoned her for dinner with his friends. "You must be starved."

Reba fluffed her hair and tried to smile. Dory took her to a cheap restaurant on South Street, where he picked at a salad and where most of a cheese-steak sandwich found its way, as if magnetized, onto her new silk blouse. He was full of chatter about his evening, and when they finished eating he walked Reba for miles around the waterfront. Names, names, as if any of them would matter to her. This poet, that poet, another one's wife. She wanted the Starlight Motel if she wanted this at all; a starched pink shirt and her blue shoes swept away. A kid riding an old black Harley screeched around a corner and spattered mud on Reba's skirt, but Dory hardly noticed. Girls with blue hair, boys with none, paraded by; Dory paused before a shop window filled with studded leather bracelets to stare at a girl in a skintight vinyl dress.

Finally they entered a bookstore, where Dory scanned the poetry section for his book and scowled when he couldn't find it. Reba waited for him with her back to a bulletin board and her skirt spread before a radiator, trying to drive the dampness away. A dirty white cat slept on a pile of old comic books. On the bulletin board, in with the housing notices and the concert ads and the lost-dog signs, was a poster that caught Dory's eye.

"Alethea," he whispered over Reba's head, so that she craned her neck to see what he meant. "Damn." He touched the spot at the back of his head where his hair was thinning, patting the loose strands into place.

Reba looked at the poster, a black-and-white print of a strong-boned woman with soulful eyes. "Reading," the caption said. "St. Bartholomew's Church. 8 P.M." The date was a week past, but the damage was done; Dory looked at her so expectantly that she was forced to say, "Someone you knew?" And of course it was. While the cat on the comic books yawned and turned over, Dory told Reba in exasperating detail about his affair with Alethea. On the way back to the hotel he told her about the first woman he'd slept with after he got married; in the hotel he told her about a handful more, as if she'd somehow pulled a plug in his brain. *What I did to Hank,* Reba thought then, recognizing herself in Dory's voice but quickly pushing that thought away.

They slept in her room that night. In Dory's room, where they stopped to pick up a shirt, his rinsed-out Jockey shorts hung neatly on hangers over the tub. A cautious man, Reba thought. And yet remarkably indiscreet. Dory went on and on, describing women tall or short, with blue eyes or gray, and as she listened Reba remembered all the men who'd passed through her hands during her time with Jessie. Poets or dancers, Dory went on. Singers or scholars, all of them younger than him— Reba had never thought she was Dory's first affair, but she'd hoped she was one of a small, select group. Instead, she was forced to see herself as part of a habit, necessary as nicotine.

She'd dreamed of something different—of the place, perhaps, where Gottschalk lived, the place she and Jessie, and probably all the young women in her building back home, had read about when they were girls. The scenes of those fat historical romances, sneaked from the library's top shelves; the place where the bold swirl of passion lived, where the steamy vortex had its source. No panty hose there, to be tugged off one leg at a time. No old underwear or creased skin or stuck buttons or snaps, no flesh suddenly inadequate or sore. She knew this place—it was where Dory lived in her mind and perhaps where she lived in his. Dory liked her to dress to approximate his fantasies, and so for the past three months she'd slithered about the office uncomfortably on the days they planned to meet, minus underwear, sweaters, socks. She wore wrap dresses held in place with one complex bow, and she let Dory stud her apartment with fat candles in shallow bowls. For a while that had been enough; now it no longer was.

That first night in Philadelphia, Dory tried and failed to make love to her. After they'd struggled for a while, he rolled over and said, "Tell me about your lovers" in the same way he'd once asked her to tell him about her family. Bowen and Mag, Lily and Max, Tonia and Hank had all come before—now, having nothing else to offer, she started with Jessie and radiated backward and forward from there. *Berg died of an insect bite,* she wanted to say. Instead she placed pictures in Dory's head, hoping these would satisfy him.

He closed his eyes and touched himself as he listened, and when she stopped speaking and turned to him he grunted and said, "Keep going. Tell me what you did." In the room's harsh light his body looked different than it had in her candle-lit apartment—slack, pale, as if the skin was gradually freeing itself from the bone and muscle below. Small wrinkles above his knee, a loose fold where groin met thigh; where his upper arm crossed over his chest a groove appeared, and a small mound, as it would on a young girl pressing her arms together to create the illusion of breasts. For the first time, Reba wondered if Dory's candles had been meant to be kind to him rather than her. The more Reba spoke, the more excited Dory became. He wanted details; he wanted specifics. He wanted her to speak in Jessie's voice and pretend he was the man with the long white hands; he wanted her to be Alethea or one of the others or all of them at once. The bed was full of people, none of them Dory, none of them Reba, all their dreams fighting for elbowroom. Reba's own shadow flew up to the corner and perched on the ceiling molding there, watching her body, distant and cold, next to a Dory who squealed and groaned and refused to open his eyes. *The animal symphony,* Reba thought. *In the basement of the VA.*

She folded her wings against the walls and let what had to happen happen, knowing Dory wasn't touching any real part of her and thinking how dreadful it was to know so much about someone you didn't love. The curiosity that had always made her play a scene out to the end was at work in her, and so was a need to please Dory and a pride that couldn't stand to let him think she knew less than his other women. *No center to him,* her shadow thought. No center at all—a dense ball of surface, like a ball of twine. Unraveled there was only another pose, another attitude, another idea of himself demanding another idea of her. Her body did what he wanted but had to fake liking it, and afterwards, when Dory fell asleep, Reba's shadow flew back to her side and tried to sort out what was happening. She thought she saw a certain logic —from telling her about his wife, Dory had progressed through his other women and had finally taken hold of a handful of dreams disguised as her.

She woke with a bruise on her thigh and a sour heart, and when Dory left to give that day's lecture she called

221

the airport and arranged to fly home alone. But she didn't leave—she walked around the city instead, from Rittenhouse Square to South Street and back, and by the time she had, she'd convinced herself that what she'd felt the night before was wrong. She looked into the calm faces moving past her, peering easily into shop windows and picking up cats, and she thought perhaps she'd read something evil into what was only meant to be a game. This was Dory, after all, with his cotton shirts and his gentle songs and his sentimental poems. The man who, clothed, everyone loved.

When he returned that night she lied about how she'd spent her day and, wanting to make amends for her thoughts, she gave him Mrs. Koerami's book.

"This is great," Dory said, touching the worn red cover. "Where'd you find it?"

"In a bookstore on Sansom Street," she told him, lying again. As soon as he touched the book she knew she'd made a mistake. The book was the last remnant of her other life; her other life was all she hadn't given Dory.

"I love this stuff," Dory said, flipping through the pages. "Chopin and George Sand, Liszt and Marie d'Agoult, Wagner and Liszt's daughter—poets have nothing on musicians."

He took her to bed again, and for the next two nights she listened to more of Dory's tales and played more games and grew more and more depressed, lying awake until morning and wondering if the women in her building lived like this. She could imagine the shadows of all of them hovering over the building at night like a flock of starlings, swooping and dipping in search of a place to rest. She could join them; she could ask them what this meant. But if she opened her mouth she might say the wrong thing, and then they'd all turn to gape at her.

Or she could ask Dory what he meant—Dory, the man who knew everything. But she sensed that as soon as she asked, he'd leave her and start whatever this process was on someone who couldn't yet frame the questions. *Innocent,* he'd said to her once. *I like that.* And he did. His wife was his friend, his friends were his lovers, his lovers were his students and the wives of his friends, his friends' wives had lovers of their own and all of them assumed the identities of each other and of strangers as well. And meanwhile she wanted a corner to call her own. Wife, mistress, friend; one thing or another, an apple or a beet.

Those three nights they spent in Philadelphia turned out to be the only three nights they'd ever spend together. Back in Northampton, distressed by Dory's stories and games, depressed because Dory was angry with her because she was distressed, Reba saw dark shapes flutter around her building and found the courage to dump him. She got sick after they split up—not queasy-sick, or sniffly-sick, or even run-down, but sick between her ears, as if someone had vacuumed her brain away and filled the space with demons.

Fool, she thought as she stood over her kitchen sink trying to wrest the paper-wrapped package of giblets from a half-thawed, store-bought chicken. That's what she'd been, with no more sense than the white turkeys who used to drown in Luke's backyard after the rain. She and Luke would float boards in the puddles so the birds would have something to cling to; often, even that wouldn't be enough. The package of giblets tore, leaving half embedded inside, and she threw the pale carcass away and wept. Dory had been a board spiked with nails and she was drowning anyway, and the water she was drowning in was Luke. Nelson, Robbie, Dory—not one of them had kept her afloat, and she'd wasted all this time on them.

They'd left her with no more direction than kohlrabi, no more energy than dirt, and although she knew Dory had brought her down and didn't deserve the credit, still she couldn't pick herself up. She'd wake alone in her apartment and hear the other tenants waking lonely too, scuffling around their kitchenettes in terry robes. And she'd talk to herself then, a low murmur meant to convince herself she was still alive. There was a life somewhere she was meant to live, and she tried to read its future in her tea leaves and coffee grounds. She was ripe for signs, for omens and odd predictions, for any hint as to how she'd pissed her life away and where she might find another to replace it.

For two months she haunted her apartment like a zombie, months that made her time getting over Robbie seem like a pale rehearsal. She threw away the records Dory had given her, tossed out the candles and burned her old sheets. And then she went on a sort of anti-health-food diet, designed to purge herself of Dory and his vain ways. No sprouts, no tofu, no salads, grains, juice—none of the things Dory had nibbled so fastidiously in an attempt to retain his youth. She swept away the brown bottles of kelp extract and yeast pills and obscure minerals Dory had foisted on her, and she ate cooked, dead things instead. Fried eggs. Pot roast. Hamburgers. She threw away the clothes Dory had liked and went to work in baggy pants. She and Lorrie designed a brochure for the Annual Fund and went right over Nelson's head; she astonished everyone with the fugue she wrote for her theory class. She wrote a six-part suite and bought a new pen, and she was able to laugh, finally, when she told Lorrie about her trip to Philadelphia.

But she didn't shed Dory completely until the May afternoon when she discovered his poems, which were bound in creamy pamphlets piled by the dozen inside the university bookstore. She'd gone there looking for a field guide that Hank had recommended—his way of cheering her up was to try to get her interested in the outdoors. But instead of a harmless book, all bright color plates and dry descriptions, she found this stack of pamphlets titled *Lives of the Composers.* She found Mozart and Chopin and Liszt and all their lovers and diseases, but she also found Jessie, and Hank and Luke, and Mag and Lily chanting Hungarian spells while Tonia fed rats. All of them cast as pajama-clad primitives, setting fires in the woods and bound in a dark web; herself cast as dreamy and dim as Emma Bovary, her lost children trailing her like cats. That was her, humming Italian music while she chased a bubble of romance through the sordid gray farms. Her, dreaming manufactured dreams in the basement of the VA. In the title poem, Dory had woven together Donizetti composing *Lucia di Lammermoor* while Bellini died in Naples, and her and Jessie, a century and a half later, weeping over the mad scene while wearing backless swansdown slippers.

Her tongue swelled as she read. Dory had changed the names and places and added exotic details he'd culled from Mrs. Koerami's book, but this was her absolutely, her family and her life, and as she read she saw why Dory had questioned her so closely. He was an only child, with no children of his own and no sense of a family except what he'd been able to steal from her. He'd taken the fine, everyday web of history that linked her to everyone in her life, and he'd distorted it to draw connections so obvious, she'd never thought to put them into words. When she could catch her breath she slid the pamphlet into her purse and then stormed across campus to Dory's office, meaning to rip off his head.

All around her, bulbs bloomed in great colored masses. Tulips, daffodils, hyacinths, anemones, pale narcissus; the air was thick and sweet and made Reba feel tired. By the time she reached Dory's office, all she wanted to do was sleep, but she threw open his door instead and stood there yawning. Dory looked up as if he'd seen her only yesterday.

"Reba," he said mildly. He was sitting behind his desk, pale in a light cotton shirt. On his nose were brown-framed glasses, which he quickly removed. "What brings you here?"

On his desk a huge flower bloomed in a pot, crowning a thick green stem. *Amaryllis,* Reba thought, remembering the scaly bulbs Luke used to bring Tonia from Maglione's. Ugly things, uglier still when they sent up their thick foliage, but typical of Dory. One overblown spot of color on his smooth teak desk, where heaps of papers were carefully arranged to look haphazard. On a corner, in a ray of sun, a glass half filled with water cradled an avocado pit, suspended from toothpicks as it sent out wormlike roots. Sent in by Dory's wife, no doubt, a touch of home. A raga droned from a cassette player set in a bookshelf.

"Reba?" Dory said. "You want to sit down?"

Reba reached into her purse and held the pamphlet she'd stolen out to Dory, still unable to say anything. She saw herself frozen, leaning out her window night after night and scanning the streets for him, wasting time. And she wondered, then, why she hadn't bound herself to the seven other women in her stony nest. They might have had advice—avoid dark seeds, don't perch on wet branches, beware of cats. Something like that, species wisdom. They might have told her something if she'd been able to ask. Over the winter several of them had invited her out and she'd gone once, reluctantly, to one of their parties. A woman named Tina had stood, she remembered, near a laden table, patting her full lower lip thoughtfully and gazing at the desserts as if the most important decision she had to make was whether to try Anita's double-fudge cake or Brenda's macaroons. All seven of them laughing like they'd figured out their lives, and still she hadn't had the sense to let herself become part of them. She'd thought she could fix this on her own.

Dory rose and moved toward her, one hand smoothing his shirt and the other fussing with his hair. "You like the poems?" he said. "They were for you. Especially the title poem. . . ."

On his desk sat the butane lighter he used for his pipe, the one with the long blue flame. Reba snatched the lighter, flicked the catch, and held the flame to the pamphlet. She meant it to smoke, to smolder, to curl blackly at the edges—*There,* she thought. *There.* A gesture, nothing more; hundreds of copies still sat in the bookstore. But the cover was made of some fancy rice paper embedded with long brown stems, and it caught like tissue and flared in Reba's hands. In her panic, she flung the pamphlet away and it flew toward Dory, who put up an arm to defend himself. The pages opened and settled around his forearm and his shirt started smoldering, which set him dancing about the room and shaking his arm furiously. Reba screamed and hurled herself at him, and their knees collided. She seized the glass of water on Dory's desk and flung it, avocado pit and all, at him. In a second, the fire was out. *Water for burns,* she could hear Hank telling Luke, years ago. The pit bounced and rolled under the chair, its roots like spider legs.

Dory lifted his head and stared at her, one hand

plucking at his scorched wet shirt. "I'm all right," he said quietly. "Shit, Reba—what the hell? I'm all right."

Reba turned her head away and tried to compose her face. Melted eyes, fried flesh, vanished hair—were those what she had meant? She felt as if she'd burned her own face. *He's like me,* she thought, watching his fingers play with his shirt. He wasn't like Robbie, like Nelson, as she'd thought all winter. He was like her. They were related, or they would be if she didn't do something soon—both of them embryo Hitlers, annexing more and more territory and never having enough. Germany, Austria were not sufficient; Russia was barely big enough for dessert. Their childhoods were lost and they had this instead, this endless, repetitive search for love, this way of casting their own visions like dark cocoons over the faces of those around them.

She could imagine Dory as a boy, appropriating other families and other lives the way she'd done with Adele Bonfrere and Jessie and Luke, with Nelson and even with Robbie. The way Luke had done with her. She'd lost Luke by doing exactly what she'd accused him of, living in a dream instead of in reality. She'd spent her life on a series of men no more fruitful than Luke's land in Gardner, where a concrete pad sat buried in dank weeds. *Luke,* she thought, remembering his stricken face the night she'd introduced him to Jessie and allowed Jessie to make fun of him. She'd started that far back, and now he was gone forever.

"Reba," Dory said quietly. "What do you want?"

He was nothing to her. She turned to face him and said, "I want you to say you're sorry."

He shrugged. "What's to be sorry for?"

He held out a hand to her, but she backed away.

"Don't touch me," she said. The flames had left him as unmarked as if he were the devil himself.

He smiled as if she'd complimented him. "Come here," he said, his voice as low and luring as an owl's. "Let's go outside. We need to talk."

"Fuck off," she said. Nelson had once asked her to walk through the woods, and he hadn't meant it either. In that instant she thought she saw another life, arching before her like a tree.

"So coy," Dory said. "Charming." He rested his long fingers on her arm as she backed toward the door. "Look at you," Dory said. "You're shaking like a leaf. You don't set fire to someone you don't care about."

She turned and ran from the building, through the heavy sun, and when she got to her office she sat down and wrote a note to Luke. Not in their sphinx code but in English, on normal paper. "I'm sorry," she wrote. "For everything. You don't set fire to someone you don't care about." Then she stuffed the note in an envelope and mailed it away.

THE MUSIC
OF GHOSTS

REBA and Hank and Tonia returned to the swamp that August, marking the anniversary of Reba's final departure from Rockledge. They entered at the cut where the creek slipped in and then marched in single file down the deer path—Hank with a tape recorder in his hands, Tonia with her notebook in a knapsack on her back, Reba with the picnic basket. Some boys were down by a flooded pool, trapping minnows and laughing shrilly, and a pair of ducks sailed by with their fluffy brood. As the Dwyers crossed over the creek on a bridge of fallen trees, a dark spot below a boulder turned into a frog and leapt away.

The swamp was noisy that day, full of wind and birds and the burbling creek, the leaves' silky whispers, the squirrels' sly conversations. A branch beat against a trunk in three-four time, and Reba remembered her father chanting *ONE-and-TWO-and-THREE* as she and Jessie sang. In the shadows Reba saw him, his eyes fogged, pulled from his music to adjust the heat in the brooder where the day-old chicks had huddled for warmth. Six weeks until they grew feathers and could fend for themselves, and him cursing them every day of that, angry that they hadn't been born complete. *A life could be ruined,* he'd said then, and Reba hadn't known whether he'd meant hers or the chicks or his own. *Things could be broken so badly they couldn't be fixed.* Something had nudged her father over the edge between one life and another, and all their lives had followed his.

Unusual people, he'd written once, and they were, all of them. He'd sent her a birthday card in June, from someplace on St. Croix where palm trees waved and the water broke over coral reefs. A few weeks later he'd sent Mag a small check. *I don't need this,* Mag had said, but she'd bought into Rad's service station that week. Reba's birthday card had been oversized and embossed with pansies, its message printed in ornate black script. But the inside was blank—no sign that Bowen missed them or that he was coming back; no indication of how he'd gotten from here through the rivers to there, how one state had yielded to another. That bunch of chicks had died of coccidiosis and he'd waved his arms over them and said, *This is what happens. This.*

Reba hummed a few notes to herself, unaware that Bowen, on his island, heard them as if he were tied to the swamp by a vibrating string. He had a room in Christiansted, down by the docks and above a bar that was popular with the tourists. His room was small but had a balcony; each morning he took his coffee out there and watched the chameleons flash over the stones as the tiny yellow bananaquits sipped from dishes of sugar water. He'd found work on one of the battered catamarans that shuttled tourists from the harbor to Buck Island and back, and five days a week he held out his steadying hand to the pale, overweight passengers climbing aboard. He sorted snorkels and flippers and masks, served weak rum punch from a red cooler, smiled at the captain's wry, West Indian patter as if he'd never heard it before. On the lee side of Buck Island he dropped the anchor, lowered the ladder, and taught his charges how to snorkel through the shallow warm water.

"We don't have sharks here," he told the worried women. "The barracuda won't bite." They believed his reassurances as easily as Mag once had, and they nodded seriously when he steered them away from the sea urchins and from the small green fruits, resembling apples, of the poisonous manchineel trees on the shore. On the windward side of the island, he led them on underwater trails that snaked through the coral reef. He answered questions about the fish: the wedge-shaped ones were copper sweepers, the blue-and-yellow-striped ones French grunts, the darting iridescent ones dancing in schools were Creole wrasses. Parrot fish came in blue and red and made a noise scraping coral with their jaws. Blue tangs had pouting mouths and were bright yellow when young. His most serious passengers, always women, carried waterproof books and scanned the pages while they were submerged, wiggling with excitement when they matched a fish to its colored photograph.

He felt a hundred years old. Everywhere he went he saw the faces of his children, frozen at the ages they'd been when he left. He'd seen them in the rivers, the gorges, the woods; he saw them even here. Underwater, the shadows made by elkhorn coral suggested Hank's hands, brain coral looked like Tonia's hair, the long and delicate trumpetfish reminded him of Reba. He'd meant to live alone, like that hermit whose house he'd glimpsed in the swamp; he'd meant to live like Lily, but now he was haunted instead. He didn't know Lily shared her house with Max. He didn't know Reba and Luke were divorced; he didn't know they'd been married. He didn't know about Tonia's job or the Lawrenz Rat stories or Hank's new occupation, and so he imagined his children helpless still, stuck in the snow he'd escaped. *God, I hate the snow,* his brother had said, and he'd replied, *I do too,* thinking how the snow silenced everything. In the still white glare of the tropical days he could hear at last, but what he heard most often was his past.

Bowen? he heard. Mag calling him.

Daddy? That was Tonia and Hank.

On Sundays, when he played the organ at Lord God of Sabaoth Lutheran Church, he often thought he heard Reba's voice, rising above the others as she sang the alto line. A handful of whistles, an odd letter, had sent him off; a vision of Lily alone in her cabin and Ginger floating below the ice, *tok, tok, tok.* What had he done? What had he meant? On this particular Sunday he closed his eyes and knew he heard Reba, and he saw her in the swamp with Hank and Tonia as clearly as if they'd been hiding only a few feet away.

But he saw them young. He played three notes especially for Reba, and in the swamp Reba heard the wind moaning through the trees, a low nasal song that made her see her father and the whistles he'd once carved, along with her lost twins, the fairground, the brown rumpled hills of the Holyoke range glimpsed from a small blue plane. *Got you,* her father had said the night the car burned down. He'd laughed and punched Luke's arm and said, *Got you—only kidding,* and she and Luke had waited to get him back. What had he meant when he'd said, *This is what happens?* That love brought death, disappointment, decay? Surely he'd meant them to understand more than that.

Reba turned to Hank, a question on her lips, but just then Hank turned sharply left and she asked him instead where he was going.

"A little bit further," he said. He was thinking about

Bowen too, and about Lily and Luke and Mag and Max, but mostly he was thinking about his owls. He was working as an assistant to the field biologist he'd met in the print shop, and he'd moved into a cabin by the edge of Quabbin Reservoir, where he spent his days tromping around with binoculars and a tape recorder and a notebook of his own. Owls—he felt like he'd been waiting for them all his life. He, and not Reba, had led the three of them into the swamp this time—he'd taped a series of calls at the reservoir and he wanted to show his sisters what would happen when he played them. *Birds,* he thought, as they marched into the center of the swamp. The trees they lived in, the creatures they ate and the songs they sang; the way their wings grew like magic from single feathers lapped side by side. Above his cabin at the reservoir, raptors glided stiff-winged through the sky. Sometimes, three, or six, or eight —raptors lived alone but appeared together, associated in the most delicate of ways. He was connected to Reba in a way no one could understand, free to live apart from her now that she'd stumbled to her feet, and yet bound the way a pair of sharp-shinned hawks above a cliff were bound by an invisible updraft of common air.

He set his tape recorder on a stump and prepared to astonish his sisters, but before he could start Tonia interrupted him. She set down her knapsack, loosened her hair, and proceeded to dance a brief swamp dance—the soft rushes flickering before the wind, the silver maples turning gently to each other. She included the creek, the birds, the salamanders, the rocks and dragonflies, the moths and moss and lichens and ferns, and then she added the men upstairs in the hospital, the pale men in soft slippers that whispered as they walked. When she had Reba and Hank's full attention, she stopped.

"Now I will read," she announced, looking around

happily. "Before we eat." It had become her habit to read before meals and other family occasions, somewhat in the fashion of a blessing. Reba set her basket down and Hank folded his arms. Tonia took her notebook from her pack and softly, she read this:

> "King Lawrenz, King of Rats,
> creeps upstairs with his
> wand. Paper he finds,
> everywhere. All grown men
> in white sheets, write
> with white heads. Light
> hums. Men write a poem,
> very nice, for Reba Queen.
> Come back! it say.
> Why not say,
> I love you? Little one,
> so angel beautiful, why not
> hear the secret harmonies, count
> birds, fish, ferns, and trees. Count
> stars, sand, grass, and snow; divide
> by God, the answer shows. All
> music comes from these. Hear
> the secret harmonies."

Behind them, the reeds rustled as if someone were slipping through. *Lawrenz Rat, ate a cat, wore a hat, had a bat, couldn't sat, he was so fat* . . . that's what Tonia had said, the night she and Reba had held their race in the basement of the VA. Now Tonia had a desk in her room and three notebooks of Lawrenz Rat stories.

"That's . . . *lovely,*" Reba said to her sister, startled by a forgotten memory. When she'd first returned to Rockledge from music school, Mag had told her how

Bowen had gotten a strange letter a few weeks before he took off. Some sort of chain letter, Mag had said, with an odd poem stuck in it. Mag hadn't saved it, but she remembered a version of the poem and she'd repeated it to Reba, something about birds and fish and trees, something like this. Tonia had been sitting with them that night, but Reba hadn't thought she was listening.

"You made that up?" Reba said carefully.

"I found it," Tonia whispered, not sure she should tell Reba how she spent part of each working night at the VA wandering through J Wing and befriending the patients who couldn't sleep. One man, with a shaved head and hollow eyes, had led her to the common room and showed her a drift of papers stuffed beneath the table there like snow. All the papers had borne the same message. "We copy them," her friend had said gravely. "Over and over and over again, have to mail away someday, no stamps, no envelopes. . . ." Tonia had said, "I could have one?" and her friend had said, "Take these," pressing a bundle into her hands. "Give to friends," he'd said. "To strangers." She'd mailed all but one to the people she found in the phone book under the letter *K*; from the one she'd kept she'd lifted the pretty part for Lawrenz to say, nothing more than she'd always done.

"You like it?" she asked Reba shyly. "Makes a present, for you."

"I love it," Reba said. Stars, sand, grass, and snow. In the house in Rockledge had been Mag, Bowen, Tonia, Hank, and her. On a winter's day she could still remember, Hank had wrestled with Ginger, their golden retriever, while Mag fed Tonia strained peas. Reba had knelt on a chair, turning the pages of a picture book that Lily had given her. The book was old and might have once belonged to Mag; in it a large family moved happily about a farm painted in clear, bright colors. A tidy white house, rolling green pastures, fat spotted cows, gold chicks; some city person's dream of rural life, complete with a father broad and strong in blue overalls. A picture as false as the one she'd had of her life with Luke. Reba had looked up from the book at her own father, who was trying to fix the toy piano that had been her Christmas present. Cheaply made of plywood painted red and green, its eighteen keys gave out tinny, tinkling notes. Three of the notes were so flat that they drove Bowen crazy, and after a long day of drinking he'd disemboweled the piano in a fit of sudden anger. He was trying to take out the small metal plates that substituted for strings, and when Mag, in her dry voice, said, *Leave it till after supper,* Bowen had dashed the toy to the ground.

Reba could never remember where she and Hank had ended up that afternoon. Down at the creek, perhaps, or out in the woods; maybe over in the Wyatts' toolshed with Luke and his brothers. *So let's use the code in the book,* Luke had said, when they'd been grounded. *Let's make our own,* she had told him. Luke was gone now, but back then they'd floated from one place to another, from one family to the next, always together until Reba had met Jessie. After that Reba had hidden at Jessie's, and Reba could see herself and Jessie at fifteen, tumbling back through Jessie's bedroom window after a long night down at the Gorge with two blankets, two boys, and a bottle of Southern Comfort. They'd sprawled on Jessie's twin ruffled beds, laughing hysterically, safe again, and Jessie had said, *Fuckin' outlaws, aren't we? What a pair.*

Reba remembered thinking then how there was no one like them. They both had perfect pitch and harmonized easily by ear; they'd made a bond, a pact, setting themselves off from what they'd hated by doing what no one else did. And so proud of that, not seeing for years that what they'd come to early was only what everyone else came to later. They had suffered only from love, or from the dream of love, a bump in the road that had altered their lives forever.

His parents were home, Jessie had said.

There was dancing.

They had meatballs.

Nothing had been the same for Reba after that. She saw a misty clearing, a double row of tree stumps set squarely in the middle. Circling around were all her family, all her friends, playing a game that resembled musical chairs. Musical ghosts—because the people were shadows the stumps never filled and there was room for everyone. No one had to be left out. When the wind blew, a squirrel called A-flat and a bullfrog answered D, one of those secret harmonies that bound all the parts of Reba's life into one peculiar pattern. *He said I was good,* Jessie had told Reba proudly. *He said I was a natural.* Reba was hearing music in her head, voices bubbling in her ears and connecting, adding, amplifying, flowing like double-counterpoint, like a braid.

Your eyes, Nelson had said. *They're somethin'. Tell me about your family.*

Everything was easy then, Robbie had said. *Get up, get high, get laid, get paid, get some sleep.*

It's all in the breathing, Dory had said.

She would never tell the story of her life again in words, not after Springfield, Nelson, Dory; she'd given up trying to draw it after Robbie. But these days she heard the lives and voices of the people around her as a song. The shadow in her that was always dreaming, watching, plotting an escape in the arms of one man or another had finally dropped away and cleared her ears. When a chickadee peeped the pitch her radiator in Sunderland had hummed when the heat came on, Reba saw Luke in the basement apartment there, making a desk she'd never use. Luke had remarried Sally and adopted Pearl and moved them all to Gardner, but part of him was there in the swamp with Reba and Reba felt his presence as a sound. *Tap-TAP, tap-TAP,* his hammer driving nails home in a rhythm like a mambo, like a heart. Once he'd bent over her stomach and listened to their twins tapping out the same faint dance.

Take the coat hanger, so, Luke had said the night he set the kitchen curtains on fire. *Wad of cotton on the end, lighter fluid on the cotton . . . Presto!*

There was some small bit of magic to him still. In Gardner, Luke was high on a rooftop overlooking the furniture mills and the smooth brown river. His father and uncle were hidden from him behind a gable, but their hammer blows echoed his steady pace. While his hands worked, strong and steady and proud of the roofing business the three of them had started, he thought of Sally across the city in their small apartment, cooking the big family dinner they always shared on Sunday nights. Pearl would be drawing faces on hard-boiled eggs and performing absentminded arabesques, and the slim white kitten they'd adopted would be shredding paper. Sally was pregnant, her neat body unchanged except for her smooth hard belly, and Luke thought he'd never seen anything so lovely as her swaybacked silhouette and radiant face.

Not like Reba, Luke thought as he tore open a new package of asphalt shingles. Reba had swollen and sickened when she'd been carrying the twins, but he didn't think that had been her fault. The twins were never meant to be; that night at his and Hank's apartment was never meant to happen. *I hate this,* Reba had sobbed on

Rad's shoulder. *I have to be alone.* Luke started a new row of shingles and let his life with Reba wash over him. No disloyalty to Sally—Sally seemed to understand that his time with Reba had been like a fever, like holding his hands in a fire and thinking he could grasp it unharmed. *Let her go,* Lily had said, and Lily had been right. What bound him to Reba was a childhood shared on their farms, their mouths open round in a fright that had come out as song until he lost his voice. *Just sing the melody,* Reba had said. *I'll pick up the harmony.*

But he couldn't sing. He could see Reba creeping through the rushes, calling him in a whistle meant to imitate a cardinal. *What-cheer, cheer, cheer.* What cheer. She'd called, he'd answered; he could see her now. Three times in the past year she'd sent him notes—once to apologize, once to tell him she was all right, once to congratulate him on Sally's pregnancy, which she'd heard about from Hank. So far he hadn't written her back, but he was beginning to think he might, beginning to imagine all of them meeting someday at Lily's house as part of some hybrid family.

Reba thought she saw Luke's face in an arrangement of lichens and mosses, but the shadow vanished quickly and she blinked her eyes. *I never should have kissed you,* he'd once said to her over the phone. *I never should have kissed you at the fair.* That had been last September, when she was staying at Lorrie's place; she hadn't known what to say then but she did now, and she sent a silent message back to Gardner. *I never should have kissed you back.*

A mosquito hummed a mellow E and Reba thought how the radiator in her Northampton apartment hummed that pitch, how she left her door open now so her neighbors could move freely in and out while she bent over her music books and drew notes on dark-ruled staves. *Modulate!* Mrs. Barinov had once shrieked at her. *Make like bell, like bird!* She thought how her life might make music— real music, not words encoded as notes. She heard the wind's high A-minor chords, the birds, the bugs, the crickets and frogs, the chickens' squawks and the soft hiss of air escaping their slit throats, Gottschalk and Bach, the lives of her family, the lives of the composers. There was a world out there, dense with life and connections, and she thought she might make music from that. *Don't do it,* Lily had whispered at Reba's wedding. She'd been right then; but earlier, when she'd said, *That's what you need, missy. A man who can name the important things in your life without thinking twice,* she had been wrong.

Hank fiddled with the tape recorder and then said, "Stand back a little." He pressed a button and stood back himself. Low, strange sounds flew into the air, silencing the swamp so quickly, so completely, that Reba thought the silence itself was a sound.

"What *is* that?" she whispered, almost to herself. *Would you do it if you weren't pregnant?* Hank had asked. Perhaps she wouldn't have after all.

"That's the birds going quiet," Hank whispered back. "They hear the owls making hungry sounds, and they all hide." He was thinking of the woman he'd met at the reservoir, a pale-haired student who had the same effect on him that the owls had on the swamp. *Wait,* Lily had said to him. *You'll know when it's right.* He had waited and now he knew he was right. Last week he'd left a bundle of wildflowers in the cabin where the woman slept, and a few days later they'd crossed paths when he was taping his owl calls. She'd smiled at him; next week he might speak to her. He could see his daughters hiding in her hips.

There was a great rustle as of angels' wings, and then a

pop of air pushed aside. Purring and trilling, a screech owl pounced on the tape recorder and reared back at the touch of the plastic case. A great horned owl stormed the stump next, hooting lowly, and was followed by a tiny, red-eyed saw-whet owl, chasing the shrill whistle of his mate on Hank's tape. On Whittaker Lake, Lily and Max set a bird feeder into the window. Mag fixed a carburetor at Rad's garage, Bowen played the last hymn of the service on St. Croix and gathered his music together, Luke hammered another shingle into place on his rooftop in Gardner. Sally cooked; Pearl danced; Robbie and Nelson played with their children; Dory flattered a young woman and prayed she wouldn't laugh. Somewhere Jessie, bent on her own course, rounded a corner and vanished into the night.

"I called them!" Tonia said triumphantly, looking at the ring of birds hovering around them. And she might have, or they might have been responding to the voices Hank had recorded. In the owls' polyphonic cries, Reba heard a four-note motive that might be the basis for a melody. Four notes that might stand for Luke or love or loss or all three—it would take her years to learn all she needed to write the music she meant. *Sing!* Bowen had screamed at her and Jessie. *From the diaphragm!* Perhaps that was all he'd meant them to understand.

The tape clicked, screeched, grunted, and howled, and a barn owl zoomed down with his eyes crossed in his snow-white, heart-shaped face.